THE OMEGA CORPS I

Into the Breach

Keith Huntsman

TREATY OAK PUBLISHERS

PUBLISHER'S NOTE

This is a work of fiction. None of the characters or events is based on actual people, living or dead, or their lives or circumstances. Any similarities are a coincidence and purely unintentional.

**Printed and published in
the United States of America**

TREATY OAK PUBLISHERS

ISBN 978-1-943658-38-1

THE OMEGA CORPS I

Into the Breach

CHAPTER 1

He was so absorbed in his book that he flinched when the doorbell rang. Under the double incentive of sound and movement his tortoise-shell cat launched herself out of his lap, leaving the tingle of feline skid marks across his thigh. He winced, more in irritation than in pain, set the book open face down on the side table and levered himself out of his battered recliner. The hardwood under the worn area rug creaked as he made his way to the heavy front door of the old rental house and pulled it open.

The vision waiting on the porch wiped the impatience from his face in an instant. She stood poised a few feet back from the door, tall and ash-blonde and splendidly proportioned, with wide-set hazel eyes glowing with obvious intelligence from an oval face of creamy perfection.

She smiled, a warm languid expression that dimpled her high-boned cheeks and lit her eyes like the dawn. "Jackson Alexander Steele?" Her voice held a natural lilt of purest music.

He pursed his lips into a smile and nodded. "That's more of my name than I've heard in years. What can

I do for you?"

"I'd like to speak with you, if you have the time." With a flicker of lashes she looked beyond his shoulder into the house, and he stole the moment to absorb her with his eyes. Even in little makeup, or perhaps because of it, she was entrancingly gorgeous. "May I come in for a few minutes?"

He smiled in return, captivated in spite of his normal wariness. "I don't see why not." He stepped back and she glided past him, leaving a whiff of delicate fragrance in her wake.

He bowed her to the couch with a sweeping wave. She swayed over and settled into the aging cushions, her knee-length powder blue dress swirling around her silky legs like a waterfall.

He resumed his own chair, eyes never leaving her. "Call me Jander," he offered. "Life is too short for the rest of it. I suppose you're here to recruit me?"

"Ah – um, no... I mean, yes... well, sort of," she chuckled. "How did you guess?"

He popped the recliner back and crossed his ankles over its footrest. "You're good," he said, "really good. One of the best they've thrown at me yet. But you're about the twentieth world-class hottie I've had aimed at me since I got close to my doctorate." Her expression did not change, but he saw a sharp flash of offended intelligence blink into her eyes. He went on without pause, "Though how anybody expects it to work, I'll never know. Anyone bright enough to be worth hiring would be too smart to fall for it."

"I suppose so," she said. Her eyes suppressed the

momentary affront, but their twinkling warmth was retouched with something that was not quite humor. "Consider it a test. If you could fall for it, I'd think a lot less of you. Actually, I'm kind of glad I don't affect you."

He gave her the regulation long, slow look, deliberately tickling the nerve he knew he'd struck. "Obviously, you're not reading my mind."

She looked startled, then burst into good, honest laughter, a rich and genuine tone. Somehow he knew she was not the giggling type, yet her reaction to his lame comment seemed rather out of proportion.

"No," she subsided into chuckles, "as a matter of fact, I'm not." She sent her penetrating gaze around the room, acting out an exaggerated search of the spare furnishings. A tall antique hutch with shelves dotted with academic awards among vintage leather hardcovers was the only thing that appeared to catch her interest. "Where's the library? And the lab? And where's Cinnamon – Cindy, right? Where's that tortoise-shell cat of yours?" Smiling still, she uncrossed and recrossed her elegant legs.

He refused to be distracted. "Game over." He hit the lever on his recliner and dropped his feet to the floor with a thump. "Just how much do you know about me?"

She caught his tight scowl and sobered, leaning backward into the couch with a much more solemn expression. "Jackson Alexander Steele. Jander for short, never anything shorter. Age, twenty-five, one of the youngest doctoral candidates in your field, which is behavioral and quantum physics." She ticked off her list with delicate flicks of her fingers. "Almost four point oh straight through graduate school, could have finished sooner but took some extra courses to broaden your mind. IQ never measured but clearly in the high genius, a more than perfect student with a habit of arguing successfully with your professors. You recently completed your dissertation in magneto-gravitic wave propagation or some such thing I can't begin to comprehend. No emotional attachments except for one female cat, which I hope isn't the same thing..."

His guarded expression did not change. "You've done your homework."

She seemed to take that as an invitation. "Parents killed by a drunk running a red light four years ago, one older sister with husband and child. The rent money comes from inherited investments. Six foot two, two hundred pounds or thereabouts – pretty darned good-looking, I might add – like to read, fence, play tennis or mess around in your own private lab in your spare time. Brown belt member of a martial arts slash exercise gym downtown, and a fair hand with a dueling saber. A girl by the name of Kathy broke your left – "

"That's enough." His voice remained even, but such was the natural grit of command that she stopped short. "You're way past the point of casual introduction. You've proven you know more about me than you could have found out easily. Now it's your turn. Who are you, and whom do you represent?"

She met his gaze, erg for steady erg, the flippancy gone. "Fine, but before we begin, we have to reach an understanding. I've come here at great risk and in secret. What I'm about to tell you would put me and my friends in serious jeopardy if it got out."

She leaned forward, her eyes boring unblinking into his. "If any part of this conversation leaves this room it could mean the ruin of us all, including, or especially, you. I checked your background so thoroughly because I've got to have trust in your utmost integrity. I'm satisfied." She leaned back. "So, it's up to you, Jander. Do you think I can trust you?"

He kept his stare for a moment, then looked away, left hand reaching back to massage his neck. "You're not the first to ask me that. As I told you, a lot of people have tried to recruit me for their organizations, many of them classified and not all of them savory. So far, I've kept them confidential when they asked me to, but then again, none of them have obviously broken the law or gone against what I think are my noble instincts."

He met her gaze again. "My one caveat is that if there is anything illegal, or against common human interest, I won't be a party to it – threat or no threat. Whether or not it leaves this room depends on the severity of it, so you have to decide how far you want to go."

She stared back with narrowed eyes, then pursed her lips and looked away. "Fair enough. Like I said,

I wouldn't be here if I didn't think I knew your character, and what you say follows that. So, here goes."

She took a deep breath and rolled her shoulders to shrug away the last of her hesitation. When she spoke again, her stare was direct and her voice was strong, calm and earnest.

"My name is Victoria Lee Cunningham – Vickie to most. I'm a psychologist, and a telepath."

Except for a quick slackening of his face his expression did not change, but his muscles tensed as his automatic defenses clicked up yet another notch. Whatever amusement the verbal sparring may have engendered was no longer there. He would sooner have expected her to claim she was a man – and would have believed it just as readily.

"A what?" The iron in his voice was unmistakable.

She gave him a slow nod. "A telepath. I can perceive the thoughts of others – most others, not all."

He took a deep breath and exhaled slowly, his narrowed eyes never leaving hers. "Proof."

She shrugged, with both shoulders and eyelashes. It was a smooth, calming motion, clearly designed to disarm him. "Impossible, at the moment. I can't read your mind at all; that's why I'm here. But I can prove the possibility."

She looked around the room and spotted the book he had been reading, resting open face down on the table beside his chair. Her eyes narrowed.

The book stirred and lifted, floated effortlessly

up to his eye level without the slightest wobble or drift, and stopped at a comfortable reading distance in front of him. A page turned with a smooth rustle, of its own accord.

He was so stunned he automatically started reading. He caught himself with a blink, feeling his jaw gaping open. Teeth and eyes both slammed shut and he gave his head one hard shake, then he pried his eyes open and looked again. The book was still there, bobbing up and down as if waiting for something to happen.

His hand trembled a bit as he reached out. The book settled between his fingers with no sense of transition. He stared at it for seconds, then closed it and set it back down on the table.

"I... see," he said at last.

"Um-hum." Her melodic voice held a hint of amused compassion. "Telekinesis. I can't prove my telepathy because yours is one of the few brains in the world I can't tap. That's why I laughed – I really wasn't reading your mind, though I was trying with everything I've got."

She waited until he regained some measure of composure, then leaned forward on the arm of the sofa and caught his eyes. "Jander, we have pretty much determined that a normal person's mind is an open book. Only the genetically variant have natural mind shields that prevent unwanted intrusion – and you, Jander, have the strongest such block I've ever perceived." She held her gaze, studying his reaction with clinical intensity.

"You mean, I'm..." Still dazed, he shook his head, then again with more emphasis. "No way. No way I can do that." He pointed at the book. "I can't do that." She gave him a breathy laugh of sympathy. "Not yet, no. Maybe not ever." She lounged back, the long, sleek curves of her body well complimented by the soft fabric of her gossamer dress. Having captured his full attention, she went on.

"So far, we've activated seven variants besides myself − two other telepaths, one more telekinetic, and each of the others has a different ability. And we have one guy who hasn't been able to do anything special yet. Probably, he hasn't thought the right thoughts to activate that special part of his nervous system. I'm the only one so far with more than one... power." She flicked her hand in apology. "Superpower sounds kind of ridiculous, but I guess that's what you have to call it."

"How did you... how..." He held up one hand as if to stop time, closed his eyes for a moment, then tried again. "You say, 'activated'. Activated how? And who discovered this... process, if that's what it is?" He took a deep breath, his mind clearing as his thoughts cooled into the analytical mode that was his stock in trade. "Can you... do it with anyone?"

"We haven't tried it with just anyone, Jander. That would be terribly irresponsible."

"Good answer, but not exactly informative." He leaned back in his chair, still wary, but more receptive. "Why don't you start from the top?"

Vickie nodded, then rose to her feet in a motion too smooth to be by muscle alone and wandered about the room, fingers twining in front of her. "I grew up in a small town in Montana, you know, a gas station and feed store in the same building sort of place. My boyfriend at the time – this was eight years ago – his name is Jacob Anson. He's an old-fashioned ham radio bug, and a country boy at heart.

"One day back in high school, he hiked into the hills about ten miles out of town and pitched his tent in a stretch of virgin forest. He was hunting around for firewood when he found a tree uprooted by its age, with something shiny under the roots. He dug a little but decided it was too big for what he had with him, so he went back to town and brought back some clearing tools and his younger brother Arden. After digging around the edges for a while, they uncovered a door."

She sat down on the couch, her eyes focused on the memories. "Imagine the thrills. What they found was the control room of a small spaceship built for a body shape different from ours, so old that any organics inside were nothing but dust. Still, there was a little bit of power lingering from somewhere, or maybe awakened by the sunlight – we still don't know for sure. Jake tinkered with part of a console and somehow got it working, heaven knows how. It made anything he'd ever imagined look like an erector set."

She raised her eyes to his, and he nodded. "There are plenty of concepts that have to be universal, regardless of the application. Juice is juice."

"Okay." She took a deep breath. "Attached to that machine was a thing like a mesh beanie with some wires attached. On the kind of impulse you'd expect from someone that young, he put it on his head and punched a button next to where it was plugged into the console."

Her lips twitched. "Of course, he got zapped. Vicious pain, believe me, sizzling through the entire body and popping the brain like a kernel of corn. But when it abated he didn't feel any the worse for wear, so he figured he got away with it."

She rose and strolled to the front window, leaned a hand on the sill and gazed out into the oak-shaded street. "Until they got back to town. Then he discovered he could read anyone's mind, except his brother's and mine." She paused, immersed in her thoughts.

He thought he knew what was bothering her. "That's a lot of power to carry around. I'll bet he did a lot of soul-searching."

"Oh, you don't know the half of it," she sighed, and returned to perch on the arm of the couch. "It was hard enough for those of us who came after. To be the first and only with such power was almost mind-breaking. Besides, before he learned to control it, he was under fire from every mind in town. In a big city he would have gone mad." She slid back down to the cushions of the sofa and squeezed her eyes shut.

He nodded. "So, where do you come in?"

"Third." She took a deep breath and reopened her eyes, and traced the pattern on the arm of the couch with a fingernail. "Arden was the only one who knew what was wrong, so partly out of compassion and partly out of curiosity he went back to the spaceship and took the zap himself. Same pain, but when he got back to town he couldn't read any minds. So, he decided to go home." She flipped her wrist. "Zing, he was home."

She answered his raised eyebrow. "That's how we discover our talents. Somewhere in our junk DNA are combinations that just need some kind of stimulation, and the zapper supplies it. Once activated, we only need to think of something we want to do, and depending on our latent talents, our minds can do it for us. I didn't know I was telekinetic until I reached for something and it came to me instead. Oh, Arden is a teleporter. He can travel in an instant by visualizing his destination and willing himself there."

"I'm sure the physics is a bit more complicated."

She waved it away. "That's your department. Anyway, Jake and Arden compared notes. They figured out that besides being brothers, they had one other thing in common: it took a lot of effort to communicate with each other mind to mind. So, they called in the only other mind in town that Jake couldn't read, which was me. You know what I can do."

Jander nodded emphatically. "Too well. So you've

been looking for others ever since?"

"Not really," she said. "For one thing we're hard to find, since unactivated variants are so hard to detect telepathically. Those we have run into, we've investigated thoroughly before we approached them. Any hint of questionable character and we give them a pass."

She turned her high-powered hazel eyes on Jander. "Which brings us to you. I've been all over this town checking you out. You'll be happy to know that except for the usual jealous geeks I couldn't find anybody who has a bad thing to say about you. You're fair-minded, supportive, generous, and even when you argue you're level-headed. The only people you can't tolerate are aggressive types that are too dumb to realize how stupid they are. Everything I've read tells me you qualify as one of the good guys, without the flighty quirks a genius usually has.

"So." She leaned toward him and took a deep breath. "Would you be willing to take the zap? You know, see what you've really got in that big brain of yours?"

"Whoa." Jander had a quick mind, but even he had his limits. He froze for a moment, his customary ordered thinking a jumble of free association. It was his turn to get up and pace.

As it always did, the effort of wearing ruts in the hardwood cleared and stimulated his mind. Vickie had presented her argument in the way that would most intrigue him. She had emphasized the most negative and challenging aspects first, with little hint of reward. And she was very right in doing so. The power she was describing was tremendous, frightening, inconceivable – and quite possibly fatal. What would the fierce and paranoid human race do to a proven telepath? They could face persecution, capture, aggressive interrogation, psychoanalysis, experimentation... a slow death by any account.

But the possibilities inherent in using such power in a constructive way were just as captivating. In the past few months he had been inundated by job offers and opportunities, some of them lucrative, many of them self-governing, but none of them very compelling to his way of thinking. He found himself loath to take a job in a lab or a boardroom at his young age, with his urge for adventure unfulfilled. He wanted something more, something to satisfy his sense of wonder along with his will to make a difference. He wanted what Vickie offered.

That, of course, was assuming he was all she seemed to think he was. He turned back to her, still sitting on the couch with as neutral an expression as she could manage. "Are you sure I'm a mutant?"

She winced. "We don't use that word. It implies something might be randomly wrong with us. We call ourselves variants, a term that could just as easily describe skin color or lack of wisdom teeth. We're still Homo sapiens, maybe on the cusp of change, but with no more or less in our genome than anyone else. We just got our latent potential activated by an artificial means. And yes, you've got a strong potential. I can't read you mind, and as far as we know an unconscious mind shield is the best indicator. It's certainly not because you have a thick skull." She grinned soberly.

He snorted. "You have no idea." He resumed his pacing. "How did you find me, then?"

"I was on campus checking the university as a possibility for post-grad work. I practically bumped into you a few weeks ago. Usually, I can get something even from a variant if I try hard enough, but I couldn't even get an empathic hint from you. So, I followed you."

He stopped his pacing and frowned at her. She chuckled – he was right, no giggle – and said reprovingly, "You had to be the only man on the street who didn't notice me. I was a little put out by it. But you were headed for a visit with a dean, so I can let it pass this time."

He smiled. "I'm sure I had to be pretty distracted. Let me guess – you read the dean's mind."

"And a bunch of others – dozens," she nodded. "I learned all I could about you, then dolled myself up – I admit it – and came here." She dimpled mischievously and flicked her skirt. "Got in the door, didn't I? Oh, by the way, your dissertation has been accepted. As a matter of fact, everyone's in total awe over it – and all I could understand was 'therefore' and 'however'. You'll be notified in a day or two."

She bit her lip coquettishly, long lashes waving. "So what do I get for taking you out of your misery?"

He chuckled and shook his head, surrendering to her allure with no further resistance. Still, her proposal was a sobering one. He dropped back into his chair, his smile fading as he thought in dark abstraction, his eyes fixed on her now solemn face.

Cinnamon the cat padded in from a back room, paused to glare at the stranger in her tortified house, then popped into Jander's lap to claim him and to contribute her purr to his thought process. He stroked her soft fur without taking his eyes from Vickie's sincere gaze.

The woman had reached out to him at just the right time in his life, when his formal education was complete and his future wide open. He had to admit that although the other avenues presented to him were vast, none had captivated him like this one. What Vickie had to offer was a chance to pioneer new ground, to truly make a difference. And more than anything, it promised to be the adventure of a lifetime.

At long last he stirred, and answered her question. "You get dinner. And a trip to Montana."

She threw back her head with a deep sigh of relief.

CHAPTER 2

Eight days later Jackson Alexander Steele, Ph.D., and his lovely companion boarded a smallish plane for Missoula, Montana. They had spent very little time together in the preceding week, with Jander making the congratulatory rounds, packing his sparse possessions for storage, and laying strategic smokescreens by continuing to entertain job offers while telling anyone who asked that he'd be taking a wilderness vacation first.

Vickie kept her distance, maintaining the illusion that they had no point of contact. Nonetheless the pair still managed to find times and places to get better acquainted. Now, seated together within the rumbling jet, they could speak in private of variant things.

"Jake and Arden's parents moved to Florida years ago," Vickie continued the conversation, "and they've kind of grown apart. Jake sold the old place in town and bought himself a goodsized chunk of ranchland in the foothills of the Cabinet Mountains. He's made it something of a refuge for us. In that kind of isolation, we can practice our skills without anyone being the wiser."

"So, who is 'we'? You, Jake, Arden, who else?"

Her eyes took on a vacant look as she used her

telepathic gift to scan the nearby passengers for anyone who might be listening, then continued in a low voice. "Jake married a telekinetic redhead named Brenda, a homey type with an archaeology degree. She makes it her job to ride herd on all of us. Then we have Thelma Grant in New York, a very well-respected model. She uses her telepathy as an informer for the police and the DEA, acting in secret under the code name Minerva. She's raising havoc in the drug trade, something near and dear to her. She lost a brother and a cousin to it."

She paused as a flight attendant came and went, giving Jander a moment to absorb Thelma's story. The model's course of action struck a chord deep within him, a spirit of purpose that harmonized with his own character. He looked forward to meeting her.

When they were alone again, Vickie resumed. "Another is someone whose name you might recognize – Wade Gayland."

"The impressionist?"

"Sure, how do you think he got so good? He's a personal transmutator, a multimorph. He can alter his larynx to approximate that of the person he's imitating. The thing is, he can do it with his whole body. He morphed himself to look like me once and Jeff almost fainted. It was perfect."

Jander looked at her from the corner of his eye. "I hope he doesn't go in for practical jokes."

The passenger across the aisle took off his earphones, inched his seat back and made it his business to stare sideways at Vickie. She turned her face away to gaze out the window, depriving the ogler of his view but also ending their conversation. Jander pretty much had to accept it as part of their cover story.

He was rather surprised at her complete lack of concern for security when opening up to him. She must have investigated him more than thoroughly to be so certain of him. In contrast, it seemed that as a group they possessed remarkable self-restraint, as well as considerable intelligence. Other than Gayland, none of them appeared to be using their variant ability for personal gain, and even the entertainer's approach fit into the normal world with no one the wiser. Jander's respect for them, and the psychologist-recruiter at his side, was growing exponentially.

THEY PICKED UP VICKIE'S SUV at the airport in Missoula and Jander drove them north in comfortable silence. The abundant twists and turns in the hours-long drive through landscape formed by tectonics and glaciers kept his attention sharp.

Around them, in the hollows and tree shadows, the last of the winter snows were surrendering slowly to the late spring sun. Vickie lounged half asleep in the seat next to Jander, his green-eyed tortie snuggled in her pleasant lap. Cinnamon still refused to associate with her titular master, as his punishment for making her suffer the indignity of a cargo ride.

Jander found himself enjoying the opportunity to drive the nearly deserted two-lane highway through the rolling hills beyond Flathead Lake, past ranches and occasional small towns interspersed through long swathes of untouched forest covering the ridges. He had his window cracked open to the scented air and the kind of silence never found in the city.

Vickie turned to gaze languidly at him as he relaxed at the wheel. "What are you thinking?" she asked.

He glanced at her and chuckled. "It must drive you crazy to be with someone you can't read."

"As a matter of fact, it doesn't." She turned back to watch the scenery.

He waited a bit, then prodded, "What are you thinking?"

She cocked an eyebrow with a wry smile. "Oh, how things are, and how they might change." She turned away again.

He said nothing, burning with curiosity but not wanting to intrude on her. It was clear that something itched in her mind, but he knew not to push.

Miles passed before she shook her head and shifted to face him. "I'll be honest, I like not being able to read your mind. People ought to be able to keep secrets from each other. That's the reason Jake and I broke up after we zapped – there was no mystery in it. Funny as it may sound, I like being with a man I'm not sure about. I wonder what you think of me – and I don't want to know." She reached across the console to touch his arm. "Is that too frank?"

He smiled soberly. "No, I can understand how a telepath would have to be frank. Being able to tell truth from lies – it's bound to have an effect on your personality. So, I'll be truthful, too. I hope you never can read my mind. It's been a nice eight days."

Vickie absorbed that for a moment and liked the taste. And so, womanlike, she segued the subject. "Jake doesn't seem to mind. Put your miracle brain to work on that."

Jander gave it serious thought, ignoring the wisecrack. "What does Thelma think?"

"She feels the same way I do. Of course, being an African American from Newark and drop-dead gorgeous, she knows what's on any man's mind from the get-go. But Jake's a telepath, too, and he doesn't seem to care. In fact, he likes being in rapport with Brenda – or rather, it's a state they're both comfortable with."

"They're in love. That helps. Nothing is more mind-expanding than unconditional love – or so I've heard." He shot her a fleeting grin. "But generally, men are naturally more aggressive, and knowing what's on someone else's mind is a definite advantage. As for myself, as a scientist, I like mysteries I can solve. I'll let you analyze the woman's view – I have my sensitive side, but I'm happy to say I don't have the perspective you'd have."

"Glad to hear it. But telepathy is so... well, involving that it's a real burden to go beyond surface conversation. I never go after more than I need."

He nodded. "I'd be hesitant to probe too deep into someone's mind, too — there's so little privacy in the world as it is. But I'd be okay with just touching the surface — that's just communication, the word and deed of human interaction. It doesn't resonate so much on the emotional level. Looking deeper would be an intrusion, though. I'd have to be pretty comfortable with someone to share that kind of intimacy."

"Mmm. I guess that's what opens me up, too. One thing everyone needs, man or woman, is a sanctuary, a comfort zone, a secure place where there's nothing to fear or guard against. Maybe that's the difference — maybe what I'm looking for, what I know you can't establish by just talking to someone or reading a mind, is... trust."

He glanced at her, eyes clouded in thought. After a while, he said, "Thank you. I think you've hit on the thing I've always had trouble with. I've always been on the outside looking in, years ahead of my age group, bigger and brighter. I got a lot of attention, but never any camaraderie. A pedestal can be a hard seat."

She returned a breathy laugh. "We do have that in common — brains and beauty. As I was growing up I sometimes just wanted to scream at people, let me be real! I never asked to be special. That's why I keep looking for people like you — people like us — and rejecting those who can't see past the first impression. I've only found a few who can, and I cherish them like life itself. It's like I'm an only child adopted into a big family, and there's no place I'd rather be." Her eyes misted.

He grinned crookedly, touched by her passion. And so, manlike, he changed the subject. "So, since we don't have any perverts listening in, tell me about your organization."

She responded with her soft chuckle and returned her gaze to the road ahead, stroking the purring cat. "We don't have one, to be honest. Jake has the ranch he bought from stock profits. Nobody can inside trade like a telepath, though he stopped that when his conscience started keeping him awake nights. But thanks to him, none of us is hurting for money.

"Anyway, we get together at the ranch fairly often, but other than that we don't do much as a group. We're pretty much pursuing our own goals. I'm finishing a master's degree in psychology. Everyone else has at least a bachelor's except Thelma, who's been modeling since her tweens. Arden will get his master's next fall. He's got a degree in aerospace engineering and already has a couple of patents. Funny, how our interests somehow match our variant gifts."

"I've noticed that. Maybe I'll be a transmutator or some such."

"We have one, thank you – Terry Kirkland, who by the way has a wardrobe you wouldn't believe. She's an intern in trauma surgery. Her two passions – sewing clothes and people. Anyway, Jake has a doctorate in electronics, which touches on communications but has nothing to do with the mind. Brenda has a master's in archaeology and brings in some income as a freelance graphic artist. She and Jake met when he serviced some sensor equipment at a dig she was illustrating."

"Tell me about Denny."

She frowned, lips curled in perplexity. "Poor ol' Denver Connors. Doctorate in mechanical engineering, and from telepathic contact seems to be a strong variant. But nothing has shown up yet. Of course, he hasn't been activated that long, just a few months.

"There's another thing: the rest of us are as good specimens physically as we are mentally –"

"No argument, either way."

She dimpled briefly, "– but Denny's an exception. Something over seven feet tall, but skinny as a rail. Strong for his weight, though. How do you figure it?"

"I can't if you can't. Telekinesis? Levitation?"

"Not a nudge. Nothing, anywhere. He's awfully bugged about it."

"Can't blame him."

"Neither can I, considering the fun the rest of us have. Turn left up here."

He made the turn and drove onto an indifferently kept blacktop that wound upward toward the Cabinet mountain range. "That's everybody, then. Funny you've only found eight in eight years, nine, counting me. And mostly by accidental meetings at colleges. Are we that hard to spot?"

"Pretty much. It takes the efforts of both minds to establish a good telepathic contact between variants, and of course an unactivated variant can't help. Besides, we haven't exactly been looking for recruits. We're leading pretty normal lives. I've wanted to use my abilities to help people, and pursuing a career in psychology is a part of that, but I haven't gotten up the nerve to come out in the open."

"That would be a very bad idea, my friend. Exploitation is the least you could expect – though I can't see anyone doing anything to you that you didn't like. But envy and persecution are pretty much a given. When you compare what you've got to the petty differences that set some people off, you'd be dodging bullets the day after you opened your pretty mouth."

She ignored the sport. "I've thought about having a secret identity and that whole shtick, but with the money-making problems and all it could never work out in real life. Thelma's approach is risky enough – even as careful as she is, she's still on the wet edge of the knife. And we can't all be high-priced models setting our own hours. So what do you do?"

"Maybe drop out of sight entirely." He bit his lip and glanced at her, then back to the twisting road. Something in what she said made him uneasy, enough to make him want to squeeze a little. He chose his words with caution. "Let me think about this. I may have some ideas on how we can use this stuff profitably. But I don't want to mention anything until I know what I've got."

She was silent for a troubled moment. "Okay, I'll go along with that. I don't see how you could make it work, money and all, but you do have the most capable mind I've run across yet. But..."

Her telekinetic "foot" touched the brake and they rolled to a stop on the gravel shoulder. She faced him squarely. "But, like you said when we first met, if you try anything against common human interest, I swear I'll fight you with everything I've got. And I have the second most capable mind I've ever run across."

"No argument here." He started to make light of it, then looked again at her expression. He played it straight. "Seriously. And I don't doubt you'll do as you say. I learned a while back how honest you can be."

She almost flinched, but held her ground with narrowed eyes. His respect for her looped higher, and he hated himself for throwing her own honesty back in her face.

"I apologize for that. As you said to me once, call it a test. I believe you, and believe it or not I thank you for questioning me. If we do come out of this with a purpose, there's no one I'd rather have with me than you. I really do believe I can trust you." He turned his head back to the road. "Though it may have been a rough way to find out."

He shifted and pulled the car back onto the road. Vickie stared straight ahead in silence for miles before she spoke.

"It's all right, Jander. I spent almost two weeks studying your character, so I guess I can let you test me once." Cindy, sensing the change in mood, rose up and butted her chin. She smiled down at the cat and relaxed back in her seat.

It took a while for the conversation to ease back into normal, but soon they were chatting comfortably about little things from their childhoods, education and experiences. Jander, the academic genius, was a little awkward with small talk, but Vickie's practiced and penetrating style opened him up. The future, however, was not part of the discussion.

After hours of driving, they passed through a small crossroads town not far south of the border with British Columbia. A few miles later Vickie directed him to a wide exit between two tall, rectangular monoliths of bedrock, bridged twelve feet in the air by a wider but thinner slab. Mailboxes were sunk into the left column beneath a carved wooden plaque lettered, ANSON'S KEEP. Jander drove through and onto a well-kept gravel road that curved back and forth through a mixed forest of lodgepole and ponderosa pines and junipers, a barrier better than any wall to conceal what lay beyond.

A mile or so later the forest opened onto a huge rolling meadow divided by sturdy wooden fences. Their arrival was keenly observed by a trio of well-groomed horses in a pasture next to the road. A white three-story house with a forest green roof and trim was centered in a manicured lawn shaded by hawthorns and tall junipers. Behind it was a sizeable bare patch waiting for the springtime plow.

Beyond the house was a long mudroom that attached it to a huge red gambrel barn with a metal roof that boasted banks of solar panels, suggesting that the property was completely off the grid. Two corrals and a busy chicken coop were nearby.

Across the circular drive from the front porch was a long, open-faced vehicle garage sparsely occupied by two SUVs, a double-cab pickup and a mid-sized tractor with accessories. In the grass center of the circle drive was a wood sculpture resembling a cross between a jungle gym and a loose beaver dam, squatting between two tall poles flying the U.S. and Montana flags.

Scattered about the fields and pastures surrounding the compound were several outbuildings in various states of repair, along with a few milk cows and a dozen or so beef cattle to complete the definition of a hobby ranch.

The big house was the focal point of what must have been hundreds of acres. Jander had to believe that it would take every member of the variant club to maintain the place.

At Vickie's direction he pulled the car into the circular drive and eased to a stop by the front steps. He smiled over at her, popped the door and started to get out.

"Jander." He turned back to her, and for a long

moment they held each other's eyes. At length she said, "I meant everything I said – everything. I could and would… stop you, if I had to."

He studied her sober face, then nodded once, his own expression softening into a reassuring smile. Again, he turned and dropped his foot onto the driveway.

She stretched for his hand on the wheel and held him back. "But it has been a nice eight days."

His smiled broadened as he squeezed her hand.

CHAPTER 3

Side by side, they climbed the broad plank steps and onto the covered porch that stretched the full width of the house. The door chimed with the sleigh bells it brushed as Vickie turned the antique brass knob to let them in.

Brenda Anson met them in the granite-tiled foyer. She was quite a bit shorter than Vickie's five foot eight but just as well proportioned, with glittering green eyes, a magnificent mop of vivid copper-flecked red hair and one of the most pervasive freckle fields Jander had ever seen. She welcomed Steele with a firm handshake and a serene smile and nod, and immediately appropriated his cat from Vickie, cooing with delight. The diversity of moods told him of a temperament as changeable as the glistening high-lights in her fiery hair.

"Jake's in the radio room. He's discovered something that'll knock your teeth out, Vickie. He can listen to radios!"

"He what?"

Steele caught it on the bounce. "You mean, he's picking radio waves out of the air?"

"Hey, you're okay. Yeah. He's up here!" She dashed

through a door and out of sight, a wide-eyed and squirming Cinnamon latched on with all grapples.

Jander looked at Vickie. "I hope you know your way around this palace."

The house was a rambling maze that suggested extensive additions that had to have taken place over many decades. He followed Vickie out of the foyer and through a sitting room into a spacious living room, then up a broad staircase to a parlor with bedrooms in all directions. A second set of stairs led to a finished attic running the length of the house, with walls slanted inward to accommodate the broad-beamed ceiling.

Six large dormers, three each overlooking the front and back of the house, were furnished as offices. Their windows, along with two at each end, dimpled the space with diffused sunlight. One end of the open floor held an array of exercise gear on a reinforced platform; the other was crammed to the roof with radio equipment.

Jacob Anson was a strong-looking man of medium height, with Ivy League cut brunet hair and piercing dark blue eyes. He was sitting in rapt attention in front of a vintage tube-based shortwave radio flanked by a huge but silent set of speakers. Brenda shifted the clinging cat to free a hand and reached out to nudge his shoulder, making him jump and spin in his chair.

"Oh, hi, Vickie." He brought his mind back from wherever it had been and rose to greet Steele. "And you must be Jander. Vickie's told us all about you. In fact," he grinned at her, "she's singing your praises right now."

"Jacob —" The man whipped heels over head and hung with his worn moccasins an inch from the vaulted ceiling. Still clutching the cat, Brenda went to his rescue, and the two telekinetics had a tug-of-war with the man's head two feet off the floor. Jake shouted and pleaded and begged forgiveness for a good thirty seconds before Vickie handed command over to his wife. "If you must read my mind, you slob, keep it to yourself!"

Jake, beet-red and dizzy, shot her a conciliatory glance and said, "Now, you'll give our guest the wrong impression doing things like that." He brushed back his disheveled hair and extended the other hand to the staring Jander. "Proud to meet you."

Steele shook his hand absently, looking at each of the three in turn. "Uhm…"

Jake laughed and clapped him on the arm. "You'll get used to us. We like to practice as much as possible in case we ever think of something to do with ourselves. But you want to take the zap. Come on."

"Wait — wait a minute." Jander stayed rooted to the spot. "I thought I was ready for this, but let me catch my breath."

"Of course, Jake," Vickie came to his rescue. "Give him a chance to get organized. He's only human — so far, at any rate. Besides, we're hungry."

"Oh, sure. Come on, folks, let's get some grub." He headed for the stairs.

Brenda neck-rubbed the discomfited Cindy as she stepped in his way. "You'll have to wait, guy. You got so hung up about your radio I let supper go. I'll have to whip up something quick." The bouncy redhead preceded them by floating herself down the stairs, Cinnamon still attached.

Vickie spoke to Jake as they made their way down to the ground floor living room. "That's right, what's this about you being able to read – intercept? – radio waves?"

"It's something I just found out – or rather, Brenda did. She walked into the radio room and there I was, listening to a speaker that wasn't even turned on. That was a few days ago, and I've been up there changing mental stations almost ever since. I guess that makes me a radiopath, right?"

"And finally, you've got a link to your professional interest," Vickie agreed. "I wonder how often you've done it in the past and didn't even realize it? And do you have to be near a radio?"

"I don't know yet. I don't see why – we don't need to be near a mind to read it."

Steele broke in, "What is your mental range?"

Jake grinned. "I don't know exactly, but I can tell you this: when I said Vickie told us about you, I didn't mean by phone. But she has the stronger mind; she may have put more into it than I did." He turned to Vickie. "We should experiment for distance. Right now, all we know is that we reach, or we don't."

"I would," Jander said. "Like you say, you never know when you'll have to use this stuff. Hi, sweetie." Cindy, freed at last but with lashing tail carried low in this madhouse of flying people, greeted him with a low-toned plurp and tucked herself behind his legs. "Too many changes for her, too." He noticed a large yellow tom staring at her from the top of a bookcase, and envisioned the tangle that would ensue when the two alphas met.

"Sorry about that." His host swept an arm at the variety of seating and added, "We're expecting Arden and Terry to show up a little later. Arden said he was going to stop in L.A. and pick her up." He flopped on the sofa and looked intense for a moment, then said, "I can't reach him. Anyway, you can meet them and get acquainted before you zap."

Vickie was also thinking hard. "I've got Denny. He's well outside Helena, and says he'll be here in a couple of hours."

Jander took a moment to pick up Cindy before selecting a comfortable chair and settling her down in his lap. "Pardon me, but I thought you said it was hard to read variant minds." Cindy gave his knuckles a tentative chin rub but kept her head on a swivel.

"Oh, it is, in a way," Jake explained. "With normal people we can read clear down into the unconscious. With untreated variants, maybe some surface thoughts." He stared at Jander, who realized the telepath was trying to tap his mind.

"Don't bother," Vickie told him. "He's harder than a diamond wall." She took up the explanation. "With activated variants, the telepath instigates the contact with an all-purpose jab. The target either accepts contact and opens his mind or not, his choice. It can't be forced and it's never unnoticed — like answering the telephone. Mine was off the hook when Jake caught me upstairs — wide open."

Jander frowned in thought. "So, it does take a telepath to create the contact." Both nodded. "So maybe the non-telepath conjoins the ability of the telepath, sharing the power by sharing the contact."

He leaned sideways on the arm of his chair. "What I'm getting at is this: From a practical standpoint, a nerve synapse is a unit of energy like any other. Two power sources linked together will always be stronger than one. The closer they are to each other, the stronger the link."

The two variants stared at each other, and Jander could almost hear the conversation. After a moment Jake turned to him and said, "Vickie wasn't kidding — you're going to turn us upside down. You may be right. It occurs to me that Arden will be picking up Terry later, meaning he'll take her hand and teleport the two of them right into our humble living room. Sharing contact, sharing power."

"What does that do to his range?"

He shrugged, "Cuts it, of course. He's carrying that much dead weight. But it's nowhere close to half, come to think of it. Terry must be contributing something."

Jander stared at him, his mind racing. "Try reaching your brother again."

Jake concentrated, then shook his head. "Nothing." He looked to Vickie, who also tried. "I can't reach him either."

"Now, think a minute," Jander said, shifting to the edge of his chair. Feeling squeezed, Cindy relocated to the cushion beside him. "What happens if the two of you link power? You're both telepaths, so you'd both be carrying your own weight. Not only would you not drain each other, but you could actually augment each other – like batteries operating in tandem."

They blinked at him, then at each other. Without a word, Vickie moved to join Jake on the couch. They touched hands and concentrated together. Shocked amazement appeared on both their faces. A few seconds of hard thinking, then they turned to stare at Jander. He closed his eyes and tried to help, concentrating his already prodigious mind in an effort to unlock a door without a key.

The telepaths slumped back with a sigh. Jander took a deep breath of his own and sent them an enquiring look.

"We reached Arden, yes; he thought we were right next door," Vickie told him. "But we still couldn't reach you. Maybe with Thelma..." She shook her head, but she was smiling. Jander remembered that she honestly did not want to read his mind.

Jake added, "We got as much zero together as we did alone. You've got some kind of brain."

Brenda had returned and had been watching their efforts in silence. "Well, if you super-people are done thinking yourselves to death, supper's almost ready." She turned and left, with the wise and opportunistic Cindy at her heels. The yellow tomcat thumped down from his high perch in cautious stages and trailed after them.

They rose to follow. "Don't let her fool you," Jake said. "She's just as impressed as we are. You gave us as much progress in half an hour as we've had in eight years!"

CHAPTER 4

"Thelma sends her regrets," Jake said, and the cluttered cellar sent the words echoing to seven pairs of ears. "She's trailing a pusher to his supplier. He's a new kid, and she thinks she might be able to scare him clean with a little nudge. I tell you, if the rest of us had her guts, we could really do some good.

"By the way," he gave a respectful nod to Jander, "we've never been able to contact her directly before. But with the two of us linked at this end and Thelma helping from the other, we made solid contact."

"I don't feel right taking the credit," Jander said. "You had it all along. I don't know how you overlooked it."

"That's easy," Terry Kirkland smiled. She was a slender brunette with penetrating brown eyes filled with quiet intensity. "We've never had a leader before. It takes a special gift to coordinate the efforts of many."

"Hail to the chief!" Denver Connors raised a stick-like arm and bumped his bony elbow on a beam – he was that tall. His voice was a deep and reverberating bass. "Maybe you can think of something for me to do." He rubbed a broad but thin hand over his sand-colored crew cut as if he was used to massaging scalp bruises.

"I'm flattered, people, but don't you think we should find out what I'd be leading with? I might turn out to be the world's greatest potato peeler or something." Steele would remember those words later. He was absolutely right.

"I agree." Wade Gayland was a surprise visitor. He had been in Los Angeles and had dropped in on Terry, and hitched a ride with her on Arden's brain. "We should zap him before we swell his head bigger than mine." His face seemed to melt and flow, and in seconds he was a perfect copy of one Jackson Alexander Steele – but with an exaggerated cranium. "My fellow weirdoes, we are gathered here tonight –"

"Wade, stop," Vickie said through chuckles. "He's jittery enough as it is." Wade grinned with a slight bow and returned to his own fade cut curly hair and light brown eyes.

Jander shared in the laughter somewhat weakly. It was indeed an intimidating demonstration. "Let's do this, before I lose my nerve."

"This way." Jake gestured toward what looked like a solid wall lined with shelves of Brenda's preserves, and his wife stepped forward and stared at it. A catch concealed on the other side was slipped and a large section of concrete rumbled upward and inward like a garage door.

Arden Anson was already inside the hidden room, having teleported ahead to prepare the machine. Watching him vanish had given Jander another queasy shock.

"Terry helped us make this secret room," Jake explained. "She loosened the rock by cutting it into blocks – dissolving sections in long planes – and the other girls carted them away. Remember those pillars at the road entrance?"

Jander remembered. They were made of blocks three feet cubed. The weight must have been tremendous. "Another clue – didn't you two work together to move all that? It's the same principle."

"I suppose so," Vickie said. "We were in rapport to coordinate our lifting the blocks, but we didn't blend our efforts – we were on either side like two people using their muscles. We should have seen that we could combine our telekinesis to envelop the rock. You've shown us that two people thinking the same thoughts can in fact augment each other. We just didn't make that intuitive leap." She turned and looked deeper into the hidden room.

"It's checked out and ready." The blond Arden's voice was a high tenor, belying the fact that he was a much larger man than his elder brother. He moved aside to reveal the machine. Jander stepped in to examine it.

It was apparent that the mechanism once had been part of a larger console. The raw ends were now framed in pine, in contrast to the blue-gray metal of the machine's surface. The original metal showed no blemishes other than the transmuted edges left when it was wrested from its ancient seating, but the square keyboard appeared to be of a plastic composition that obviously had seen the passage of millennia. It was clearly useless. But next to the keyboard was a larger square button of the same metal as the console, its red plastic plating eroded almost to nothing. Just above it, a depression in the metal held what looked like a thin ski cap.

The mesh helmet was of the same blue-gray metal as the console. Jander guessed that it was non-conductive, since a pattern of what looked like fiber optic line encased in the same metal was woven through it. The wires linked seven gold-colored disks to a larger cable that connected the meshcap to the console. "What powers it?" he asked.

Jake said, "We think the original power source was solar, but I've got it rigged to take electricity. It took a while to work out the amperage, but I was young then." His smile was meant to reassure him.

Denny moved past him, soft-footed despite his size, and double-checked the amperage gauges with the critical eye of an engineer. Jander noticed the outline of an antique plierench jammed jaws first into the back pocket of his jeans. The slot screwdriver at the tip of one protruding handle was shiny from frequent use.

Jander had been told the routine. He shrugged his shoulders to ease his tension and moved to the recliner set next to the machine. He settled himself into the chair and Arden draped the helmet over his head, shifting it so that two of the disks were at his temples, one above each ear, and one each at the forehead, top and base of his skull. The sides draped over his ears and the back stretched down to his shoulders, giving him the impression that the cap had been designed for a skull somewhat different from a human's. The cable dangled down the right side of his neck as he popped the chair and reclined full length.

Jake flipped the human-made power switch built into the pine border of the console. Jander discerned no sound or visible sign that the machine was on, but he felt the cold weight of the mesh contract to fit his head, pinching the top of his ears to his scalp.

He took a deep breath and released it slowly, willing himself to relax. "Ready."

Jake reached for the console, but Vickie caught his hand and, staring at the supine Jander, pushed the button herself.

PAIN!!

Howling, screaming, blinding pain, killing pain. Every bone shattered, every nerve fried, every cell sundered. He was caught in the exact center of a nuclear reaction, feeling his body, his mind, his very being shattered atom by atom and scattered up and around in a mushroom cloud of excruciating agony. He was dead and unborn and recreated, experiencing all the force of all the cataclysms that ever were and ever would be. He was burning and withering on desert sands; drowning in ice and in lava; falling through airless space and into the hellish heat and crushing gravity of all the mightiest stars in the galaxy. Pain as he had never imagined, agony no Icarus or Persephone or Tantalus could ever know.

It lasted no more than the tiniest instant. He jerked convulsively, every muscle knotted in agony, and blacked out, down and dead into the deepest pit of oblivion.

HE AWOKE TO SCREAMING. The chair was gone. He was lying flat on a contoured surface that made his back tingle with savage intensity. They were all shouting their alarm, yelling their concern, and Vickie was screaming and screaming and screaming, all of them blending in a mad cacophony of deafening uproar.

"Shut up! *Shut up! SHUT UP!*" The clamor ceased, leaving an almost equally deafening silence. Through the ringing in his ears, he began to hear their voices, hushed whispers that he did not unscramble until hours later.

"*What was he hearing?*"

"*I have no idea. Nobody ever had that strong a reaction. It looked like it was tearing him apart.*"

"*Hey, I can't touch him anymore. He's in a shell of some sort – look, my hands stop half an inch away from him.*"

"*My god, what have we….*"

"*Maybe we should leave him alone, let him come*

out of it on his own."
  "Someone should stay with him."
  "I'm the doctor..."
  "No. I'll stay. I owe him that much."
  "Take it easy, Vickie. He'll pull out of it."
  "Everybody get out. I'm staying. Out!"
  Silence.

HIS NEXT AWAKENING was tranquil and dream-like. He was floating in a gentle mist of warm, harmonious colors, wafted by gentle breezes through a sweet and quiet air, content and serene in the closeness of... her... man...

He pushed the thoughts out of his mind. Vickie's thoughts. She was lying on the bed close beside him, her arm thrown around him the only part of her in his field of vision. He reached out by instinct to taste her dreams again. He did not want to leave their warmth.

He remembered the voices of hours before. He remembered the shield. Carefully, as gently as his shock-fogged mind would allow, he willed a similar shell around himself, lifting Vickie's arm off his body. He rotated himself within it until he was facing her, then let the shell sink back into his skin. With the fragrance of her hair and the colors of her mind swirling within him, he fell into a deep and dream-saturated sleep.

CHAPTER 5

He opened his eyes and stared straight up at the darkened ceiling. The splashes of color were still there, as they had been there behind his eyelids... not just colors, but waves, spinners, helices and whorls of every conceivable spectrum, from the most profound subsonic bass to the most dazzling streamers of radiation. Far, far too many for the finite mind to sort out.

But then again, his mind was no longer finite, as he may have understood the term. He knew what he was looking at, knew their origins, knew the physics and mathematics and quantum mechanics of each and all of them. Every scrap of knowledge that had ever come to his senses was available to him, from his first awareness of motion a few months prior to birth to the awesome sensory blast of the activator. He felt that he could count every breath he had ever taken, select one of them, and detail its ambient heat, humidity, chemical content and duration. He had never imagined himself so powerful, so intelligent, so aware, so completely, utterly... confused.

"Help..." His voice was a whisper, but it reverberated through his body, the bed, the room, jarring him to the core.

He felt his arm flex, sensed the surge of energy,

knew the caloric cost of the motion. Vickie stirred beside him, and he sensed her thoughts, as colors, as warmth, as reason, emotion, as part of her fundamental life force. She sighed softly, a warm, sibilant, humid stirring of the air, scented with the tang of beef and broccoli from supper, given soft-firm physicality by the expanding and contracting press of her breast against his ribs.

"Help…"

She came awake with a swirl of thought, as her own superb mind absorbed the situation and its cause in an instant. He could see her anxiety as she raised herself on one elbow and took in his staring eyes. He quickly closed them to spare her their depth.

"Jander, can you let me in?" Her hand slid across his chest and up his neck to the jaw, sending a tactile blast through his heightened nerves that threatened to unhinge him. It seemed so automatic to construct and deploy the rigid molecular shield to lift her touch from him. She gasped and flinched away.

"I-I'm sorry," he whispered. "It's t-too much…"

"Let me in, darling. I can help."

He tried to shy away from her emotion, but did not know how. "That's just it, Vickie. I can… read you to the soul, but I still can't let you in. I want to, but I can't. My mind… won't let me."

"Let me touch you, then. Personal contact strengthens the bond. You showed us that. If you really can read me, look for the techniques I use to make contact, and try to help from your side."

"Focus on it, then. I've got too much else going on right now..." He willed himself to relax, willed the physical shield to dissolve.

"Okay, then, let's start with focus. Don't try to open up to me just yet. We need to get you organized first." She shifted enough to get both hands on him, skin to skin. "Over the years I've had to develop concentration skills to block out whatever I don't want intruding. I'm going to put them at the top of my mind. Your job is to see how I do it, and copy the technique."

"I'll... try..."

"Wrong, bucko. You're a damned sight brighter than I am. If I can do it, so can you. So, let's get started..."

CHAPTER 6

The subdued after-breakfast conversation ceased abruptly as they strode hand in hand into the dining room. The other variants had spent the night in sleepless vigil, having had no word from Vickie on the fate of Jander since the two of them had been left alone the night before.

The silence was broken in a rush. "What happened?" "How do you feel?" "What have you got?"

Vickie shoved her palm at them like a traffic cop. "Cool down, everybody! Give the man some breathing room. He was hit harder because he had so much more to hit. As for what he's got, I'm not sure even he knows yet."

"I'd be a lot less sure without her help," Jander told them, squeezing Vickie's hand. "This is one alpha prime psychologist we have here." The glance they exchanged suggested that they had shared a lot more than mental exercise.

They found seats at the huge table, and as Brenda dashed to the kitchen for their breakfast. Jander was introduced to Thelma Grant, a slender six-footer with her hair in a straight side bob that accented her deep brown skin and artfully sloe eyes. Arden had fetched the charming model from New York earlier in the morning.

Denny lost patience with the small talk. "Well, chief, spill it!"

Jander perceived the unconscious pun as he mentally lifted a mug of coffee from Brenda's tray. The very concept of such an act would have sent icicles up his spine yesterday. Now mental transport was quite natural and well within reason.

He took a moment to savor all the myriad sensations of a steaming mug of coffee; then, as Vickie had taught him, he put those sensations aside. "First of all, I can read your minds at will, all of you, completely and without interference. Question: do you know of any normal people around?"

"In town, about twenty miles away," Jake told him.

"Can you read them?"

"Sure can," "Easily," "No sweat," the three telepaths responded.

He studied their mental processes and tried to duplicate them, then shook his head. "Well, I can't. I can read only your minds – variant minds. And if you have blocks, I can't feel them."

The three linked hands over the table and gave him that penetrating stare. He saw their minds meld into one overwhelming force, so strong that the sensitive Dr. Kirkland frowned in the backlash. Vickie grasped Jander's hand to try to extend the bond to him.

Jake broke the contact first. "We can't read you. Your block's as strong as ever, maybe stronger. Even with three of us, we couldn't get a thing." He gave Vickie a sideways look.

"I was trying," she protested. "I've been trying for hours. I don't want to read him, but if I can I want to know now."

"I know." Jake looked contrite.

Jander squeezed her hand. "So do I, and believe me when I say I was trying to reach the three of you. I could read you clear to the unconscious, and none of you noticed."

"Just like we can read normals." Thelma eyed him from under stylishly arched eyebrows. "I bet if we're one step up the ladder, you're two – or three."

"I can't agree," Wade spoke for the first time. "I'm a multimorph, Arden's a teleporter, and so forth – we all have talents different from each other in one way or another. Even the telepaths have their differences. I'd guess Jander just has a new kind of mental screen."

"And not only mental," Terry supplied. "I tried to check your vitals last night, and you had a shell I couldn't breach even with my transmutation." She grimaced. "I can imagine what would have happened if my hand had been touching you when the shield went on."

"You'd grow another one," Arden quipped. "How about it, Jander? Some kind of telekinesis?"

"Let me show you." Jander concentrated on an empty coffee mug in front of Denny. It sailed into the air and stopped in front of Thelma. "Pick it up – by the handle."

Thelma gingerly reached out and grasped the handle of the mug. She lifted it with no effort. "So?"

"Put it back in the same place."

She half-closed one eye and lowered the cup, then let it go. It teetered precariously, then toppled sideways. Thelma drew back with a little yip of surprise.

Brenda caught the mug with her own power. "What happened?"

"She missed the spot. It isn't telekinesis. I used a forcefield, a saucer made of a plane of cohesive molecules. Maybe I can make it visible." He concentrated again.

In the air before him appeared a shimmering red disk of energy. Ignoring the murmurs of the others, he picked up the beleaguered mug and brought its lip into contact with the edge of the disk. It appeared to travel through the field without incident. But when he shook the mug slightly, the top half centimeter dislodged and dropped to shatter on the table.

"Summ... buck," Denny breathed.

"Virtually two dimensional," Jander mused, "the edge so minute it can't be measured." The plane buckled into itself and became a sphere. "Now three dimensional, or at least contoured, like the one I grew last night. I know what it's made of, though only Arden might have the math to understand it, and I can alter it to be opaque to light, air, even gravity." The sphere shot away at a tangent, and disappeared as he disincorporated it. "West by southwest.

Following, or rather ignoring, the spin of the planet. Complete negation of gravitic force."

Vickie broke the ensuing silence. "There's your profession, Dr. Steele. Physicist, knowledgeable in the workings of all natural forces. A forcefield projector."

"And analyzer, too, assuming you can sense them enough to manipulate them," Denny rumbled.

"And one other thing," Jander added. "That gravity equation was one I barely understood before, and never remembered clearly. Now I know it, and a bazillion others, like I know my name. My memory is perfect – total comprehension, total recall. Eidetic."

Thelma hissed a breath through her perfect teeth. "Step aside, world," she murmured.

"Anything else, before we run and hide?" Jake put in.

"Like I said before, hail to the chief!" Denny sent a bony grin from the end of the table. "Which reminds me. I know it's your moment and all, but put your humongous brain to work on me, okay? What the hell am I?"

Jander, feeling a bit embarrassed, hid for a moment in the huge country breakfast Brenda placed in front of him. "I'm not the one with that answer," he said around a bite. "Terry's the one to ask."

"Me? What do you mean?"

"Think about it a minute. How do you transmute, or duplicate something?"

"I visualize its atomic structure and repeat it,

setting off a chain reaction that continues until it runs out of raw material, or it encounters something incompatible, or I stop it myself." She ticked off the points with quick nods of her head. "I don't do anything nature doesn't do, just tremendously faster."

"You can look without acting, can't you?"

"Of course. It's like microscopic vision."

Jander nodded. "Take a look at Denny, then, and tell me what you see."

Terry closed her eyes and took a deep breath. "I can see his atomic structure. I don't see anything I haven't seen before."

"Don't mess with me, por favor," Denny shifted a bit.

"Wouldn't dream of it," Jander grinned, and turned back to the doctor. "Let's try something different. Can you expand your sight to see molecular structure, not just atomic?"

"Of course. I do it all the time."

"How about groupings of molecules?"

"Sure, but only so much before it gets too big to grasp."

Jander leaned forward, his own mental probe following her shifting thoughts. "I want you to look... bigger. Try to climb up another notch, to his cellular structure, the chemical balance of a single cell."

Terry squeezed her eyes even more tightly shut. The room held breathless silence for long moments as she struggled to expand her point of view, until she slumped in resignation. "I'm sorry, I can't."

"But you're close, I'm sure of it." Jander closed his eyes in thought, then went on. "Vickie. Remember that exercise you taught me this morning, on how to shut all those doors in my mind? I'd like you to try to open a couple for Terry."

Vibrant hazel eyes met sincere eyes of brown, and both women nodded. They linked hands and minds across the long and narrow maple table, and Vickie went hunting.

Jander stayed in their minds, following their journey through Terry's consciousness and into the subconscious. The others watched in rapt attention as he muttered directions to them, guiding them with his far more complete picture of what was in the doctor's mind. He spotted the obstacles in their path and directed the psychologist to them. Vickie in turn eased Terry around or through them. At last they encountered the true barrier: the doctor's instinctive deference to the sanctity of life, her reticence to intrude upon the body at such a personal level.

Jander withdrew to let Vickie work her magic, mindful of his own reluctance to open up to just anyone. He looked around to clear his mind and noticed Cindy sprawled on the dining room hutch, looking her usual regal self except for a bright red scratch showing through the mottled fur coloring her left ear. The yellow tom was nowhere to be seen. Score one for the tortie queen.

By the time he finished eating, Vickie and Terry

were smiling through moist eyes, their own battle just as decisively won.

Brenda used her telekinesis to usher around fresh coffee as Terry pulled herself together. After a few sips of the invigorating brew, she looked to the tall engineer and said, "I'm ready to try again, if you are."

Denny cleared his throat. "After seeing that, I'm game for anything."

Jander smiled and nodded agreement. A small part of him was still astonished that anyone, much less himself, could have orchestrated such a breakthrough as they had just witnessed. His hand slid under the table and found Vickie's; she squeezed back with a passion equal to his own.

"Okay, then." He met the doctor's eyes. "I want you to decrease your magnification. Pull out a bit, like the lens of a microscope, and examine Denny again."

This time she looked directly at her subject, eyes hooded but no longer closed as she focused her inner sight. Then: "I've found it! I see his DNA — More! I see the structure of his cells! What a break for my career!"

Jander laughed as the rest of the variants at the table spontaneously broke into applause. "Congratulations. It's a break for Denny, too, if I'm right. Do you have a good mental picture of his structure?"

"Do I!" She stared fascinated, enthralled as only a scientist making a major discovery could ever be.

"Great. Now look at mine, or your own, or anyone's. See if you detect a difference."

She tore her mind away and shifted her inner gaze to others in the party. "There is a difference," she said. "Denny's cells are smaller, more compact than ours. More per cubic millimeter, by far."

"I suspected as much." Jander poked a finger at the baffled engineer. "I got a clue from last night. For someone with so little apparent muscle, you have a tremendous grip. How much do you weigh?"

"Around two eighty. Why?"

"You look like two twenty or less. Your real weight is about what would be right for a normal-appearing body of your height. And there's your answer." He sat back with a grin and spread his hands.

After a few seconds of perplexed silence, several competing side conversations echoed through the room, arousing Cindy from her slumber on the hutch. Jander grinned and tapped his head, turning their demands for enlightenment into a contest.

It was Brenda who howled, "I've got it! I've got it!" She went on in the abrupt silence. "It was right under our noses all the time. All our gifts came to us nearly full-blown, like we were born with them. But Denny's will have to be developed – pure strength!"

"A rose for the lady," Jander applauded. "Our friend Denver has the potential to be the strongest man on Earth. Some meat on him, a good body-building program... When he reaches the correct-looking covering for his bones he'll have three or four times the strength, and two or three times the weight, than he appears to have. More cells per measure of muscle and bone, more weight per cell and more strength per pound. Terry?"

The doctor considered, staring hard at her patient, then grinned. "You're absolutely right."

Denny let out a howl that might have been heard in Idaho. He leaped up, dropped to his knees beside Jander and caught him in a jubilant bear hug. "I'm your slave!"

"Hey, take it easy!" Jander laughed as he disengaged himself by building a wall of energy. "When you get some weight you could kill somebody." He was rescued by the others, who gathered around the fledgling titan to share his joy.

"Order! Order!" Jake got their attention by banging a spoon against that much-abused coffee mug. The others interrupted their backslapping and returned to their places at the table, turning their attention to their host.

"Ladies and gentlemen, a week ago none of us knew this man. Yesterday he was only an exceptionally smart man, who may well have gone on to become one of the world's greatest scientists. Now he's about two steps short of godhood, and I for one am willing to put my fate in his hands. I hereby pledge myself in the service of Jackson Alexander Steele, Lord of the...."

"Omega Corps," his wife furnished for him.

"Lord of the Omega Corps. You have already

proven to us the advantages of combining our talents for the common good, you have proven yourself sharper than the rest of us combined, and you have most definitely proven yourself capable of wise and able leadership. Whatever you want me to do, I'll do. We can make this world a paradise, all of us together, under your direction. What say you all?" Instant and emphatic agreement came from around the table, even from those who would be giving up lucrative careers. "So say we all." Jake sat down.

Jander swallowed hard, and again. It took him a while to find his voice. "I can see in your minds that you mean it, and I'm... overwhelmed. I'll be honest with you. I had visions of some sort of organization when I came up here, but all my preconceptions seem so childish now. I'll have to do some heavy thinking.

"But I can tell you this much. Thelma has the right idea, secret and underground operations, no limelight, no honors, no publicity. It will be tough and dangerous, and discovery may well lead to persecution to the point of genocide. So I want all of you to think, too, really think, about what we're about to start here – because once we start, there's no turning back. It's a life sentence. And I'll need you a lot more than you'll need me."

He stared into the eyes of each of them in turn. Each stared back in their own personal way, their souls exposed for him to see. Some were eager for adventure, some were dedicated to an ideal, some were just glad not to be alone. But for all their differences, they had one thing in common: an unshakable bond, a steady, unwavering resolve, the look of true champions.

Without another word, he rose and walked almost blindly from the room, leaving the eight variants to exchange that same look with each other.

It was Wade who broke the long silence. "I'm glad he's on our side – wherever that is."

CHAPTER 7

Jander returned to the guest room they had carried him to the night before and stretched out on the bed he had shared with Vickie. He allowed his spinning mind to dwell on that for a moment. He had kept out of her mind during their lovemaking – he preferred to keep some mysteries, after all – but had crept in during the aftermath and had seen the same warm colors on wafting breezes he had seen the night before. He smiled and closed his eyes.

The door opened and closed, and Vickie lay down beside him. "Can I help you think?"

He slid an arm around her and pulled her close. "You can help me do a lot of things."

She chuckled. "I haven't even had breakfast yet." Cindy had slipped in with her and hopped up onto the foot of the bed, purring from the proximity.

"I didn't mean that – not at the moment, anyway," he grinned and squeezed her shoulder. "I mean I have visions of you being my... first officer? Second in command? Chief of Staff? How about first mate?"

She groaned and nipped at his shoulder, her concerns about his tactile sensitivity long gone. "If you make jokes like that you can work alone. Besides, what do you need with a second in command

– especially me?"

"You're fishing. You told me yourself that you have the second strongest mind around, and I agree – very humbly, of course." She poked him in the ribs. "And I can think of plenty of other reasons. Most of the things I don't have, you do. There will be times I have to deal with normals. You read their minds, I read yours, and we're both fully informed. As for the team, you'll be my liaison since I can't communicate mind to mind. And I wasn't kidding when I called you our alpha psychologist. It's you, as much as I, who has sparked the breakthroughs of the last couple of days."

He paused in thought, pressing his newfound analytical powers to their fledgling limits. "I don't think you've reached your own full potential, Vickie. There is something in your brain that I haven't figured out yet. It has to do with telepathy, but of a different order, and immensely powerful. That gives you something that, say, Jake, even with his binary talents, doesn't have, and it might well come in handy when you figure it out."

"Any idea what it is?"

"I'm afraid not; I only know it's there. Maybe when I see you in action, I'll be able analyze it." He rubbed his thumb over that special spot he'd found beneath her ear. "The way I see it, my first task is to find out what I have, and what I can do with it. Second, I should search for other variants. If I can read unactivated variants as well as activated ones

I'd be much better suited to locating them than you or Jake or Thelma are."

"True," she mused, "complete reads with no interference. And I have no doubt there are more of us around. Three of us growing up in the same tiny town stretches the law of averages way out of shape. And it's also true that if you're going to turn us into an operational unit, we'll need more members. It's a big world."

"That's going to take more thought. I had visions of such trimmings as masked uniforms and secret identities and the whole ball of wax, but that's downright silly in the real world. All that would do is call attention to us – and that would be very bad, believe me. For every person who admires and envies us there will be ten more who hate and envy us. You and I, and Brenda, can defend ourselves, and Arden can jump out of trouble, but the rest would be sitting ducks."

"So what, then?"

"So, like Thelma is doing – anonymous. Only we'd be doing a lot of the dirty work ourselves, not just informing. The trick would be to divert attention toward the 'what' of our activities while doing whatever we can to distract from the 'who' and 'how'. Our goal must be nothing more than results that bring justice."

Her finger traced a meaningless pattern on his shirt. "Not the least thankless of jobs."

"Certainly not. We can't take the risk of looking

for thanks. We may reach to shake a hand and grab a bullet instead. And we can't allow ourselves to become an ally or tool of the police, or any government entity. We are the ultimate weapon, and our very existence, whether we're branded as an American organization or someone else's, could cause a war."

Vickie pondered that troublesome thought in silence. After a while Steele continued, "One of the first things we'll have to do is skip over to Europe and dig up a few variants from other countries. With that, if our existence is suspected we can parade a few folks with genuine non-American accents. The more international our base, the better."

"You're talking money, friend. Globe-hopping adventurers are traditionally filthy rich. I, for one, don't have a dime that Jake's stock trading hasn't earned me."

"So we steal some from the filthy rich." He felt her stiffen, and went on hastily, "And I do mean filthy. Later we can make more from investments and such, but for working capital we can pluck the dirty birds we'll be hunting. Call it money laundering for the good guys."

"Now, that's a thought," she reflected, and the light grew in her eyes. "That's really a thought. We finance our operations and weaken the baddies at the same time. I like that idea."

"But that's thinking ahead," he said. "The Omega Corps as an effective force is a long way off."

"The Omega Corps... the ultimate human agency

with the ultimate human agents. Brenda nailed it. That field work she did in Greece paid off."

"How is she content to be a housefrau, with all her talents?"

She chose not to point out that he, not she, was the one who could read Brenda's mind unnoticed. Telepathic ability took some getting used to. "Archaeology isn't what you'd call a lucrative trade. And home is where your trowel is, which doesn't suit her style. She got into it for the forensic art. Besides, you don't know Jake that well yet. He's one heck of a catch – though not as heck as you are." She grabbed his shirtfront and tugged.

"How could you know? You don't even know what I'm thinking." He rolled toward her and ran his hand up and down her back.

She chuckled through reaching lips, "Oh, I think I can figure it out…"

CHAPTER 8

Jander repeated the repeatable parts of the conversation over lunch. "So, the first thing I'm going to do is go out into your fields and start practicing. I don't want to do it in the house – if I take off like that red sphere did you could wind up with a rather large hole in the wall."

"I wish I could stay and watch," Wade said, "but I've got a gig tonight. Give me a lift, Arden?"

"Sure. I have to get back to school, anyway."

"Take me, too," Terry said. "I go on duty at three. And we have a cancer patient I might be able to save, thanks to you." Her eyes were glittering with emotion.

"Go easy on the miracle cures," Jander warned her. "We have to be quiet about this."

"No worry. You see, this little boy goes in for biopsy today. If the cancer is malignant, I can alter its genetic composition to make it benign – save his life with no one the wiser." Her eyes misted a bit.

"Now, that's what I'm talking about, folks." Jander jabbed two fingers at her for emphasis. "You know your business, and you know ours. As long as they're compatible I'll go with you one hundred percent." He grinned. "As a matter of fact, I'll provide you with the sharpest scalpel you could ever hope to see."

"No thanks, guy – I can see it taking off in the middle of the operation." She saw that Denny had almost finished his steak. With a wave of her hand she motioned him away from his plate, then narrowed her eyes and concentrated.

Jander could sense a stirring of the air as Terry began to manipulate its fundamental elements. Cleaned bones from other plates dissolved into a pinkish gray protein mist and wafted toward Denny's plate, carried to its destination by stimulation of the gaseous molecules surrounding it. Slowly at first, then with increasing momentum, a fresh slab of medium rare beef grew from the bone. After a long, silent minute, the doctor sighed and indicated that her work was done. Another half pound of grilled T-bone was ready to eat. The other plates were clean even of juices.

"Hey," Denny rumbled, "is this real?"

"Absolutely real, and germ-free. The only difference is that it used to be another part of the cow."

The giant took a tentative bite, then plunged into the new steak with gusto.

"I'd sure like to keep you around, Doc," Brenda chuckled. "Feeding this guy from now on is going to be a full-time job."

Denny grinned around a mouthful. "Have to keep up my weight, you know."

"You have to put it in the right place, too," Jander said with mock sternness. He stood and planted his hands on the table. "We'll set up an exercise yard in a pasture, maybe a gym in the barn to supplement what's here in the house. And the rest of you, try to stretch your limitations. Telepaths, try to find your range and stretch it. You, too, Arden. Wade, try turning yourself into an animal." The mimic raised one eyebrow, then pursed his lips, intrigued.

"What about me?" Terry asked. "Suggestions?"

"Well, it appears that you have some kind of clairvoyance, microvoyance, you might call it. Keep trying to expand on what you can see – how large and how small. Jake, high and low radio range." Jake gave him a brief nod, already thinking about it.

"Well, I'm off to the back forty." He took a last swallow of Brenda's marvelous homemade raspberry punch and rose from the table. "Vickie, I'd like you to stick with me if you're agreeable."

"Believe it!" She jumped to her feet.

"Mind if I come, too?" Denny wolfed down the last bite of his steak and pushed himself away from the table.

Thelma looked beseechingly at Brenda. "Go ahead," the redhead grinned. "I can use the practice." One by one the dishes lifted off and skimmed into the kitchen. Brenda followed, genie-like, on a cushion of air.

"I thought I was the mind reader." Thelma preceded Jander out the door, past the yellow tom who gave them an accusing look from the porch rail, and the four headed for the fields beyond the barn. "I take it we'll be using this place for a headquarters, right, boss?"

"For the time being. My plans aren't even close to being set yet."

"I was thinking," the model continued, "Arden can't spend all his time as minister of transportation, and I for one have commitments quite a ways away. We ought to find someplace more accessible. We're in the sticks here, Jackson."

"Jander," he corrected her. "Just Jander. We can't be too centralized, Thelma. Ours will be a big operation. We're going to need plenty of elbow room."

"There's all kinds of room in the Big A. It just doesn't look it."

"Could've fooled me. My last trip to Manhattan, I couldn't find air to breathe. Let me think about it, though. Keep in mind that once my plans gel there might not be any reason for any of us to make an honest living."

"Well, I'm not crazy about my job except for the paychecks, but it's a great cover for what I do. I won't abandon my peeps."

"Nor would I ask you to. But I'd also like you to teach your methods to whatever new recruits we get. Your experience on the street is a huge asset."

Her coffee skin pinked a bit. "Why thank you, Jander. If that's your vision, I'll go for it in a heartbeat." She gave Vickie a wide-eyed look and got a knowing smile in return.

They arrived in a rolling field about half a mile from the ranch house. "This spot will do," he said, and faced the distant pines. "Stand behind me in case I lose control of something." Denny looked to the sky for the position of the sun, and moved back toward what he knew was east. Vickie and Thelma joined him.

Jander sat down in the fresh-smelling spring stubble that would soon be hay and marshaled his thoughts, reviewing the things he had managed to do and extrapolating how he could undertake other tricks. During his mental exercise with Vickie he had analyzed the form-fitting defensive shield he had built around himself right after he was activated, an invisible sheath that had proven impenetrable. He created a similar barrier now, but in a more manageable spherical form.

As it grew around him he rose in the air, suspended in a bubble of... how does one describe material nothing? Vickie probed with a telekinetic field and found herself unable to penetrate it; the gravitic force she wielded slipped around the frictionless sphere like wet fingers on an ice cube.

Inside, Jander began to test his limits, pulling data related to longitudinal and transverse waves and molecular motion from his crystal-clear mind. First, he altered the globe to refuse sound waves. All outside noise faded to silence as the sphere refracted the audible range of wave vibration. Then he thought his way up the electromagnetic spectrum to block all light, from ultraviolet through the visible to infrared. He found himself engulfed in a blackness so intense that it dizzied him. He released the shield and thumped hard to the ground.

"What was that?" Denny thundered. "You disappeared completely!"

Jander looked at each of them as he recovered his senses, then probed their minds. "Ah, I see what happened. When I cut off all visible light..." He contemplated the experience, abstruse equations whipping through his mind in purposeful confusion. "Maybe it goes something like this: When light ceased to exist as far as the sphere was concerned, the sphere ceased to exist as far as light was concerned. That's the best I can explain it without math. Could you see the woods beyond me? Oh, yes, I can see that you did. Perfect refraction. Hmm..." He concentrated again and made himself disappear. "Can you see me now?" Remembering, he altered the sphere to allow sound waves. "Can you see me now?"

Thelma jumped. "I gotta lay off the grapes."

"No, we can't," Vickie told him, pacing to her right as she spoke. "And I can't detect any reflection, or any distortion of the horizon. You're flat-out invisible."

"Good, I can make the effect one-way, then. I can see you perfectly." He reappeared, standing with his crosstrainers half a foot off the ground. "I am now building," he continued, his voice clouded by concentration, "a personal shield of molecular cohesion such as the first one I made, as a defensive reaction when I first woke up. It conforms to the contours of my body, invisible to you, but impervious. It allows light and sound waves, but nothing larger than air molecules as far as matter is concerned. Vickie, try to lift me."

She reached for him with her telekinesis, and he could see the strain of unreserved effort reflected in her face. "I can't do it," she said. "You're rooted solid."

Denny ambled over, placed his hands half a centimeter from Jander's chest and pushed with his already prodigious strength. "I can't budge it."

Thelma circled around him, slapping and poking at the screen. Almost playfully, Jander allowed his screen to absorb the sound, eliciting a breathless chuckle from the model. "Outrageous. Outrageous."

Jander grinned. "This does take a little effort, since I'd just zip away if I didn't compensate for the spin of the Earth. Now I'll try to expand on that. Stand back, everybody." His eyes clouded again, and the others ducked away to the east to watch what was next on his mind.

At last his eyes flickered open and he rose higher into the air, a grin slowly spreading across his face. He looked skyward, weaving back and forth as he tested his control, then put on a burst of speed. He darted straight up and arrowed toward the west, curved in a long, graceful roll and dove straight back at the three spectators. They ducked away in alarm as he flashed over their heads with a banshee whoop, skimmed the fluttering grass and looped into the sky.

He buzzed the house in a whistling dive, terrified the horses in the pasture next to the barn, then spun a spectacular series of wild barrel rolls, loops, spirals and Immelmanns, faster and faster as he mastered his mental controls. After several minutes he whipped back to his astonished gallery and settled to a perfect two-point landing in front of them.

"Free!" he howled, throwing his arms wide in pure joy. "That's more fun than I've had in a thousand years. Free!"

"You'll never live to see thirty if you keep that up," Vickie admonished with a huge grin.

"C'mon, let's go for a ride!"

"Not on your life!" She dodged out of his reach.

Jander laughed almost hysterically and hurled himself into the air, climbing higher and ever higher, soaring like a hawk over the countryside, whipping through the scattered clouds that billowed at his passing; higher, until the ranch and its outbuildings and fields were lost to sight, until the distant mountains were far below.

Above him, the sky began to darken despite the early afternoon sun, and as the atmosphere became rarefied he changed his sheath into a spherical shield and learned how to alter his screen to attract and concentrate oxygen. He stared upward in awe as the stars became visible above him, the constellations blazing forth without the twinkle effect of a blanket of air.

High enough to see the soft curvature of the Earth, he turned his back to the planet and floated unencumbered through the troposphere, with nothing but the newfound power of his variant mind to shield him from the radiations of outer space. Only when the effort to attract scattered atoms to convert to oxygen became prohibitive did he allow gravity to reassert itself.

He plummeted in controlled free fall nearly the full distance, almost casually deflecting the heat of reentry, and used a telescopic screen to relocate the ranch far to the north of his position. Soon afterward he spiraled in and alighted before his applauding friends, not the least bit winded and only slightly fatigued.

· "Oh, the glory of it!" he marveled. "You'll never begin to understand how it makes me feel."

"No," Denny said with a sober smile. "I know exactly how you feel. It's just how I felt when you showed me what my power really was. It's a sense of... completeness, like you've at long last found your true self. I know exactly how you feel."

Jander sighed and sprawled full length on the grass. "I could see the stars! I could see the constellation Orion, in broad daylight. There he was, hanging in the sky like the immortal guardian of my dreams, almost within arm's reach. That's what you have given me." He stared upward with moist eyes.

Vickie sat down beside him. "Any fatigue? Were you nervous up there? Did the air, or lack of it, bother you? How complete was your control?"

Her pointed questions brought Jander's mind back down to earth with his body. "Fatigue? A little mental fatigue, nothing physical – and a lot of the mental is probably due to excitement. I'll have to see what my endurance is. Control was easy. I only had to think of where I wanted to go and the shield obeyed me at the speed of thought, as automatic as shifting your eyes. No problem with air speed – I tightened and contoured the shield in front of me to deflect the current. I also shielded myself from ozone, ultraviolet and cosmic radiations so I didn't toast. The air did become kind of tenuous, but I can fix that by creating a separate bubble and compressing it like a scuba tank. Whether that would work in water or airless space depends on how strong the shield is. I'd have to determine that by experiment." He relaxed his analytical look and smiled up at her. "Thanks, I got a little carried away – so to speak."

She chuckled and stretched out beside him. "I don't blame you. I might join you up there after all."

"Whoops." Thelma woke up to their changing mood. "Time for us to ease back to the den, brother Denny."

"Time for my after-lunch snack, anyway." He followed her toward the house, leaving Jander and Vickie in comfortable silence.

They lay together for a long time before Vickie raised herself to one elbow and rubbed his muscular chest. "What are you thinking?"

He smiled. "What am I thinking?" His eyes took on a faraway look, as if surveying his new domain.

"Denny hit it right on the head – this is what I was born for, and what I could never be complete without.

I was *at home* up there." He took her hand and kissed its palm, his mind again in the clouds. "I've reached the edge of space all by myself. What couldn't we all do, all of us together?"

She dreamed with him for a few moments, then chuckled in her rich melodic tone. "I'm tempted to ask you for a star – and scared to death that you'd deliver."

He just smiled and pulled her closer.

CHAPTER 9

Over the following weeks the Omega Corps began to take shape. Steele took a second-floor bedroom next to Vickie's as his own, and moved his library, lab and other personal property to the ranch. To cover his tracks, he spent hours on his tablet politely turning down all his employment offers and declaring a sabbatical to everyone, including his sister, saying he would be out of touch for a while.

In anticipation of expanding their roster Jake decided to add on to the already enormous ranch house, and all of them contributed their special talents to the effort. Jander felled trees and shaped lumber with his super-sharp planes of force; Terry cured the wood to aged perfection, the telekinetics wafted the boarding into place; and Denny, already stronger than any two of them and gaining, pounded in nails with one blow of his framing hammer.

The foundation of the new wing came from the bedrock removed from far beneath the house, where further development was hidden from view. More of the rock had been pulverized and mixed with loam from the nearby forests to expand the truck garden behind the house. Brenda and Wade, who both had a love of making things grow, together planted enough crops to feed the household with plenty to spare for Mother Nature's inevitable claim.

And two new members joined the Omega Corps.

Jander took a trip to New York with Thelma to test the extent of his telepathic powers. In no time he discovered a young African American and a petite Puerto Rican with strong minds he could read, within blocks of Thelma's stylish apartment in Queens.

Richard Ford was a high school dropout who had managed to stay clean growing up in the civilized climate of Springfield Gardens, and made his living as a taxi driver to pay the medical bills incurred during his single mother's lost battle with cancer. Wary but adventurous, he succumbed enough to Thelma's charm from the back seat of his company cab to meet with Jander.

Steele was so impressed with the young man's intelligence and integrity that he offered him the zap despite his lack of academic skills. Under Arden's coaching he developed into a wide-ranging teleporter.

To recover him from years of sitting behind a wheel, Steele put him on a physical training regimen to build muscle and increase his stamina. Brenda took it upon herself to tutor him in the schooling he had been forced by necessity to miss. He proved to be a quick and eager student for all of it.

Carmen Rodrigues, systems analyst, hailed from the tough Harding Park neighborhood of the Bronx and had waitressed her way through Queens College with keen and stubborn determination. Diminutive in size and scrappy in temperament, the energetic Puerto Rican took the activation and proved to have an eidetic memory to go with her insatiable curiosity and drive. Jake and Thelma took her under their wings and put her to work researching organized crime.

Thus it was that a New York office safe was burgled, yet the owner declared less than ten percent of the loss to the police. Even so, the NYPD was not too sympathetic; thanks to their ace informant, the mysterious Minerva, they had a good idea where the money had come from. They were much more puzzled as to how the thief had entered a guarded and alarm-protected room and cracked a time locked safe.

Thus financed, Jander and Vickie traveled to Europe to recruit their first contingent of international variants, leaving Jake in charge of operations. They had decided to bring back six Europeans as a starting point.

Chelsea Winschell, a pocket-sized blonde, they found working far beneath her intellectual station in a London pub. Jander's first approach was rebuffed with practiced ease, but the little Brit was caught by Vickie in a small café and after a telekinetic juggling act was talked into a vacation out of the city.

The up-and-coming artist Lorraine Ardelle hailed from Nice and plied her craft in Paris, but faced the frustrations of her competitive trade with high-strung exasperation. Vickie had reservations about her delicate nerves, but Jander saw the high potential of her artistic vision and made the offer.

The two Germans, programmer Maximilian Elser and pet store operator Walter Rosenberg, were picked up in Hamburg. The deeply analytical Max was stuck in a low-profile job in the telecom business and was eager for a more stimulating challenge. Walter, the small and quiet grandchild of a Holocaust survivor, loved his job working with animals but missed the country living he had grown up with; the relative wilds of Montana called to him.

Fifth was a small diversion from policy: Virginia Carter, a honey-blonde beauty from Macon, Georgia, was found taking in the sights of Paris and proved to be too strong to pass up. She and Vickie, both insanely gorgeous, hit it off in an instant and came back from their meeting with a double load of shopping and Ginger's enthusiastic acceptance of a chance for greater substance in her life.

Last, but not least by far, they stumbled upon Pavel Kalanev, former Soviet agent, expatriate Ukrainian, and current international courier operating out of Switzerland. The aging undercover man was by far the hardest to approach, but Jander so valued his experience in clandestine operations that he threw all his own considerable cunning, along with Vickie's psychological coaching, into the effort to win the man over.

After a great deal of cautious stalking and talking, and a demonstration of power by the two Americans, he was sold enough at least to try the zap. Jander took note of the older man's reservations and vowed to keep a sharp eye on him.

Kalanev slipped out of Zurich alone and flew to London to rendezvous with his new colleagues. It was late at night, and the Ukrainian was wary of his exposure. Some of his former adversaries had long memories.

He found the seven others crowded into Chelsea's Norwood flat. He looked them over with professional care, struck by their diversity. To his practiced eye, their nationalities were stamped on their faces and clothing like neon signs. "Well, this is a happy group."

Jander gave him an iron stare, well aware that his leadership had to be affirmed immediately. "You are partly right. We intend this to be a team, all of us together. I make no promises about trusting you yet, but you'll get a fair test like the others."

The Ukrainian appeared unimpressed. "I do not doubt the truth of what you have told me. As for what you have not —"

He jerked erect, ice-gray eyes snapping, and spun to face the door. Just as Vickie shouted a warning it crashed open and two men rushed in, crouched and trained their guns on the group.

Kalanev flashed a hand for his own weapon, but the two were taking no chances. A short, sharp pop echoed from a silenced weapon, and Kalanev spun sideways and down, his Beretta clattering to the floor.

Jander and Vickie were a split second too late for him, but not for the others. Jander threw a protective screen between the door and the six recruits, read which man Vickie was taking, and took the other. A baseball-sized reddish sphere materialized in front of him and came alive, smashing into the gunman's hand and then cracking into his temple before he could complete his double tap on Kalanev.

Vickie telekinetically tore the pistol from the other's hand and hurled him against the doorjamb. The two collapsed side by side, battered senseless.

Steele leaped to help the fallen Ukrainian. He was struggling to remain conscious, gasping and bleeding from a leaking tear in his upper chest. "Not good," Jander growled. "Where the hell were you, girl?"

Vickie started to protest, then closed her mouth with an audible snap, telekinetically pushed the broken door shut and bent to read the two men.

"Russian heavies." Her voice had lost all of its musical quality. "Muscle sent by a black marketer to take him out, but they don't know why. Probably crossed their boss sometime in the past. Bad people."

She rose and stared at them, deep worry in her eyes. "They'll talk, Jander."

He nodded as he blocked the blood flow from Kalanev's wound with a forcefield. "We have to get out of here." Jander was grim; he was seeing for the first time the worst side of his chosen vocation.

He checked the others in the room. Ginger was backed wide-eyed against a wall with a hand covering her mouth. Walter was in a half crouch in front of her, frightened but protective, while Lorraine had found refuge in Max's arms with her face turned away from the scene. Only the worldly Chelsea was in motion, backing toward a door at the rear of the flat that led to the kitchen. Jander read in her mind that her concern was for the wounded man, so he let her go.

Kalanev was more conscious now, grimacing with pain. "What now, American? I suppose I am now a liability?"

Chelsea came back with a folded towel and handed it to Jander, who pressed it against the wound and held it tight with a forcefield as he sought the bullet with an immaterial probe. He glanced from Pavel to the fallen thugs. "You have put us in something of a bind. But we'll all get out of it."

"How?" Vickie asked, distress filling her voice. As rattled as she was, she still had the presence of mind to scan the surrounding flats to see if any of the occupants were curious enough to investigate. The neighborhood was rough enough that none chose to show themselves, but one older woman was heading for her phone.

Vickie telekinetically disconnected it to give them some time. "What's going to happen when they tell what we did to them?"

"What do you think —" He bit it off, struggling to control his quivering nerves. "Vickie, get the others out of here, fast. Get to Heathrow and take the first flight you can find heading west. I'll take care of things here."

The girl took a long look at him and, telepathic block or not, she understood. "All of you, grab your luggage and come on. We have a van outside." They obeyed, and she herded the grim and frightened five out the door. Chelsea, with no time to pack, took a last look around the home she never expected to see again and tugged the damaged door closed behind her.

"What now, American?" Kalanev repeated, watching him with an expectant sneer. "This is what I believe you call the moment of truth. Let us see how committed you are." Gritting his teeth against the pain, he sank back.

Jander pulled in a shuddering breath, then rose, part of his multi-capable mind still tending the wound. He stood over one of the thugs, who was beginning to regain his senses. It had to be now.

He built a sphere a quarter inch in diameter and, lips set but with no further hesitation, drove it into the brain of the man before him.

He repeated the heart-rending task with the other man. Turning back to the Ukrainian he grated, "In this case there was no other way – we were taken by surprise. But I'll tell you this: with you to teach us, we will never be this sloppy again."

Kalanev studied him with new respect. "You are a realist, after all. I believe you now, and I will accept your offer." He grimaced and groaned in pain. "If I live, of course. How bad is this?"

"Hold still." Jander used forcefields to cut away the jacket and shirt and narrowed his eyes in concentration.

The Ukrainian's eyes screwed shut and he wheezed in pain as his shoulder quivered from the inside. In seconds, shreds of cloth exited from the wound and floated into Kalanev's coat pocket, then the bullet pulled free with a soft smack. The Ukrainian let his breath go with a sigh of pure relief. Steele took the slug in his own hand and examined the misshapen lump with distaste.

"The silencer kept it from being a through and through, but at least it's a clean hit. Dangerously close to the subclavian artery, but if we keep movement to a minimum my forcefields should keep the wound clean and closed. I'm going to take you back to Montana."

"How can you do both that and keep me still?"

"Watch and see." He went to the window facing the alley beside the third-floor flat and opened it, then turned to the Ukrainian and concentrated.

Kalanev gasped as he rose in the air, and Jander altered the invisible pallet to make it a milky opaque for his peace of mind. The Baretta floated back into its holster and Kalanev's briefcase snuggled next to his undamaged side.

Jander set the pallet in silent motion and floated it through the billowing curtains and out into the humid night. Using more fields of force, he piled the two bodies into a stack with their weapons on top, lifted them out of the room and attached them to the underside of the pallet.

Another forcefield scraped the spilled blood off the hardwood floor into a small ball, then Jander formed his personal sheath and followed his collection outside. Fingers of molecular cohesion closed and locked the window as soon as he cleared it.

As they rose between the neighboring tower blocks he built a sphere of invisibility around them, elevated it above the flat roofs and started them soaring toward the west.

"I'm afraid I won't be very good company for a while," he said. "This is taking a hell of a lot out of me."

Kalanev watched in grim fascination as the city gave way to countryside far below, and swallowed tightly. "I certainly hope you have enough to last."

"So do I. I have yet to try to walk on water."

He settled cross-legged at the feet the wounded man and tried to relax his body, but felt the tension in his jaw anyway. Faster and faster the sphere sped, Belfast and its lough speeding past below as he settled himself into the most economical orthodrome flight path to Montana.

As soon as they were well out of sight of land he eviscerated the two corpses so they would sink, released them along with the bubble of blood, and watched them fall into the North Atlantic. Relieved of their bulk, Jander lay face down beside his passenger, reconfigured his sphere into an aerodynamic bullet and drilled it westward. Higher, then, faster, to the speed of sound and far beyond they flew, and the tip of Greenland curved into view on their right.

Faster, Pavel unconscious now, Jander's brow beaded with cold sweat and his fists clenched with the effort of keeping his concentration on his many tasks: the polar magnetic path captured by an analytical screen and sketched in his mind, Pavel's wound dressing, the shaped pallet and its bullet sheath, a breathable air supply, and their mach two-plus speed.

They caught up with the sun off the coast of Baffin Island and Jander corrected his course the merest shade south.

Slower now, as the miles took their toll; lower, weaving in their flight, they passed to the north of Helena and into territory Jander recognized. At long last he spotted the ranch ahead and a bit to the right, almost spot on after a free flight of over forty-five hundred miles.

Despite the accomplishment it never broke into his straining mind to congratulate himself as he slowed and brought his many constructs toward the house. Shakily, almost bouncing, he disincorporated the bullet-shaped shield and set the pallet and its raggedly breathing passenger down in front of Jake and Dr. Kirkland. The forcefield bed deflated like an air mattress and lowered the Ukrainian onto the porch.

"Take care of him," he said hoarsely, and collapsed.

SO ADEPT WAS TERRY WITH her expanded variant power that Kalanev's wound was healed within an hour. The shock and nerve damage, of course, would take a lot longer. As for Jander, only sleep could help him. They put his exhausted frame in bed still clothed, rather than risk waking him or invoking his personal shield.

Richard Ford, notified of the trouble, impetuously took off from New York trying to reach London and contact the others. He came back soaking wet and shivering, not yet having developed anywhere near the necessary range.

Vickie herded the recruits into the ranch house twelve hours later after catching an almost immediate flight from Heathrow, followed by hops through New York and Denver to Missoula, where the chastened Ford was waiting with their biggest SUV to pick them up. She handed her charges off to Brenda and took up station in Jander's room just as he was waking up.

"How's Pavel?" were his first words.

"He's pretty sore, but otherwise fine. He's downstairs getting acquainted with the cats." She hesitated, then sat beside him on the bed. "I'm sorry," she sighed. "I was trying to do your job, trying to read the new people. I should have been watching the normal traffic." She paused. "Did you…"

"Yes. And I've been dreaming about it ever since. Maybe when I've had more experience as a leader I'll be able to handle something like that without getting anyone killed."

"It's my fault," she said miserably. "I failed, not you."

He sighed. "No." The silence grew. "Tell you what. We both screwed up. It's too tough for either of us to handle, so let's share it." He ran his fingers up and down her arm. "We have to take the bad with the bed." She tried a feeble smile and took his hand. "And as much as I hate to think of it, they won't be the last. Pavel is right. It's a dirty business and we don't have any idea what we're getting into. None of us does."

She rolled onto her side with her back toward him and drew his arm around her. "It's horrible."

"It's necessary, sometimes. It'd be all good if we can force a criminal into a bungle and have either the law or his own kind take care of him, but there will be plenty of times we'll have to do the dirty work ourselves."

He pressed himself closer to her. "You told me weeks ago that if I meant the human race ill, you would kill me. You meant that, and I appreciate it, honestly. Now you know I'm no threat, but someone could be – I would kill Pavel, for instance, if he turned on us. We can't have one incident such as London soften us the point where we can't take the necessary violence. It hurt, and it shouldn't have happened the way it did, but they were bad people and the world is better off without them. Period. No recriminations, no guilt. Life and death both go on."

He pressed his face into her sweet hair. "I need your help."

She turned over and they held each other tightly.

CHAPTER 10

All the recruits were recovered from their trauma within a few days, including the delicate artist, Lorraine Ardelle. She had been so profoundly shocked that at first she had wanted to drop the entire matter and return to France. But after a long talk with the psychologist Vickie, and after seeing the healthy Pavel become a telepath with no ill effects, she decided to stay. She took the zap and waited for the results.

Pavel's wound turned out to be a surprise advantage to the Corps. Terry Kirkland discovered to her delight that an activated variant's nervous system could be repaired by transmutation instead of having to go through the normal slow healing process natural to basal human nervous systems. Pavel was set to rights in no time and threw himself with his native keenness into training under Vickie.

A few days later, Chelsea Winschell, the compact and lovely English barmaid, was helping Brenda in the kitchen when she reached into a drawer for a knife. Brenda shrieked and dropped a pan.

Denny, who had taken an instant liking to the diminutive blonde, rushed into the room so fast he came close to taking out three inches of wood above the doorway. "What happened?" he roared.

Jander entered at a more sedate pace, already knowing what had happened and intensely curious. Chelsea stared at the knife in her hand. "Now, how in bloody hell did I do that?"

"Her whole arm went through the counter!" Brenda cried. "Right to the elbow!" She jabbed her finger at the closed drawer.

"Calm down, everybody!" Jander had to raise his voice to be heard; by now the room was full. "Haven't you ever seen a ghost?"

Dead silence.

"Ghost?" Chelsea's voice was so flat the Jander had to laugh.

"What else would you call someone who can reach through a counter and pull a knife from a closed drawer?"

A breathless hush washed over them as the Englishwoman digested that, then she looked again at the drawer. "I can see the knives," she whispered.

"I'm not surprised," Jander grinned. "A ghost would almost have to be clairvoyant, otherwise you'd never know what you were walking into." He watched her stare around in utter delight.

"I want you to try something for me, Chelsea. Look through that wall for a rock on the ground outside. Got it? Okay. Now close your eyes. Can you still see it?"

The girl nodded, swallowing hard.

"Good. Now go get it. Wait a minute – be sure you take your clothes with you."

She gaped at him, then laughed her pub maid's uproarious laugh. "I'd bloody well better, hadn't I?"

"She can pass through solid objects," Jander explained to the others, "so of course she can float right out of her clothes. But as evidenced by the knife she took from the drawer, she can affect other objects she's in contact with. Coupled with this is probably some form of telekinesis, levitation, so she can move herself and other objects without sinking clear to the core of the planet."

Chelsea took a deep breath, exhaling it through her teeth. She stared at her hand, and watched as its outline softened. Her entire body and her clothing changed with it, becoming almost completely transparent. Denny stretched out a long arm, and drew back with a grunt as his fingers passed through her neck with no resistance or distortion.

The wraithlike figure wafted toward the wall and slipped through without leaving any sign of her passing. The others rushed to the windows – except for Lorraine, who stayed rooted to her spot and stared straight ahead in absolute shock.

The spectators saw the ethereal form touch a rock, which became spectral at her touch. She tossed it over her head and saw it solidify as soon as she released it. Gravity brought it back down to her, and the solid stone passed through her palm and thumped to the ground. She flipped herself head over heels to retrieve it, and again it became ethereal. Returning to upright she repeated the toss, but this time she willed the stone to transform as it touched her hand.

Jander watched the demonstration open-mouthed, dumbfounded by her instinctive control.

Chelsea floated back through the wall, solidified and dropped half an inch to the floor. She handed her prize to Jander with a triumphant flourish.

He grinned at her and slipped a hand around the back of her neck. "That was awesome!"

She copied his grin. "It felt perfectly natural, like I was born to it."

"And so you were," he said, then turned. "Well, Lorraine?"

The French girl was still staring at the wall. She stuttered something in French, ending with, "I could see her!"

"So I thought. You're clairvoyant."

"Sac... mon..." Her giggle was a touch hysterical as she looked down at her body and squirmed. Jander caught her muddled thoughts; among other things, she felt naked. She also wanted to disappear.

"You don't have to be a ghost to be clairvoyant. You can see through walls. Isn't that enough?"

"Mais oui, more than enough." She giggled again. Clearly she was looking through other things than walls.

But, as it turned out, that talent did not come alone. Before long she discovered that she could cast her – call it "point of reference" – a hundred kilometers away if need be, or she could do something no one else ever could, look down the back of her own neck. More, she discovered that her hearing worked the same way; wherever her mental eyes were, so were her ears.

Thus, one by one, they found themselves. Max Elser discovered that he could trace and interpret the path of binary impulses through a computer chip as easily as reading a book. He was also a computer engineer by education and developer by profession; Steele planned to use his dual talents a great deal.

The young Virginia Carter, southern in voice and manner, devastating in charm, was, like Pavel, a telepath. Kalanev, himself still a fledgling student of the mind tutored by Vickie, was set to the task of teaching the Macon-born beauty the mysteries of crime scene analysis and covert operations.

Only the Bavarian, Walter Rosenberg, was left to discover his variant talent. That occurred on the track.

The Corps had constructed a camouflaged athletics area in the rolling fields of the ranch. It was Jander's contention after the debacle in London that Denny was not the only one who needed regular exercise. So all of them at the ranch, and at this point about half were present, worked out every day on the tracks and in the well-equipped health club in the ranch's new wing.

The belated Montana summer was just beginning to grow into itself as five of them turned out for a run over the bridal path through the forest that doubled as a cross-country track. On a casual word they fell into an easy jog, which for Denny was a record-breaking gallop. He quickly pulled out in front and opened distance.

Walter, until recently a shopkeeper and rather out of shape, tried to catch the powerful titan and became more and more frustrated. He ran faster than his feet would allow, and was already gasping when he stumbled over a root and fell hard. Snarling, he tried to regain his balance, tripped over his suddenly baggy sweatsuit and scrabbled in a heap. He snapped strong jaws and tore off the sleeve of his shirt.

Jander, loping along in his wake, saw what was happening and shouted, breaking into a sprint. He reached the struggling form and grabbed him, needing forcefields to contain the suddenly powerful form. "Take it easy! Calm down before you hurt yourself."

Denny heard the commotion and glanced back, then slammed to a halt and stared open-mouthed.

Jander was working over Walter. "Here, Max, help me get him out of his clothes. He's likely to choke to death if he goes back to normal."

Max just stood there, mouth agape and eyes exploding from his skull. "I don't believe it," he muttered.

"Why not? We have ghosts and witches and alchemists, why not a werewolf?"

He managed to extricate the struggling form from the tangled fabric. Walter stood tottering on four legs, his intelligent brown eyes staring at Jander in total bewilderment. Jander noted that he still had his full mental ability, confused as it was by greatly altered senses; but otherwise, he was a normal looking, if rather large... gray wolf.

"Lycanthropy," breathed Brenda, the last of the five to reach the scene.

"Right, another form of personal transmutation such as Wade's, but limited to one form. A metamorph, as opposed to a multimorph. Turn your back; he wants to change."

She did so, staring over her shoulder until the last instant. Walter became his old, stocky self and struggled into his pants. "I will not do that again, as long as I live!"

"Sure you will," Jander chuckled. "Using your talent is as natural to you as it is to any of us. Granted, you may have a few superstitions you'd be better off without..."

"Jaa-*hah!*"

"... but you'll get to like it after a while. You'll be able to run rings around that ape, there." He poked a thumb at the gobsmacked Denny. "You just have to practice running on four legs."

"But what use is a hound to the Omega Corps? And how can I switch forms in public? I can't carry my clothing with me all the time, and I certainly can't run around naked."

"We'll figure something out. As for your usefulness, a dog can go a lot of places a human can't and be completely ignored, except that you're twice the size of a German shepherd. And think of the offensive capabilities of a mouthful of fangs." Jander clapped him on the shoulder. "This raises possibilities I thought were beyond us, and adds to our potential a great deal."

The German searched his eyes. "You're not just saying that?"

"Absolutely not," Jander assured him. "Come on. Get out of those pants and we'll pace you."

"Jander!" They turned to see Jake bearing down on them at a canter on his roan gelding. He pulled the energetic horse up to a prancing halt and leaned forward on the saddle horn. "I just got a thought from Vickie. She has Pavel on the landline from London. He says he has something important for you. Vic says he sounds plenty excited."

Tossing him a puzzled frown, Jander flew to the house. The others followed in their various ways, with Denny easily keeping up with Jake's accomplished horsemanship.

The landline connection was a bit fuzzy after bouncing from satellite to satellite over an ocean and most of a continent, and made more so by a scrambler at each end. "Pavel?"

He never would have imagined that Pavel's first words were premeditated, but they comprised a label destined to stick to Steele forever. "Lord Orion! I am in London, examining the repercussions of our little escapade last month, and stumbled across something that I am certain will interest you." His precise syllables failed to hide his agitation.

"Do they suspect something?"

"No one that I have been able to discern has missed those two devils, and your cleanup was effective enough that Chelsea's disappearance is considered an unsolved kidnapping. But that is not why I am calling.

"I have found," he paused for effect, "an alien."

Jander froze with the landline pressed against his ear, goose bumps springing up all over his body. He pulled in a deep breath, then said, "By that I don't suppose you mean a non-Britisher."

"Correct. He is a vice admiral of the Stellar Confederation Fleet. And he is looking for us."

CHAPTER 11

J ander's shock gave way to impatience. "Cut the drama and report, mister."

Pavel's faraway voice was clipped. "About eight light years away an explorer named Vice Admiral Nil Spart intercepted a high-order impulse from what he knew was a low-order planet – ours. I would surmise that it was the first use of the activator. He came here to investigate. He landed his starship, the well-armed cruiser *Kaltim*, in the Congo River basin and traveled to the most metropolitan city within reach, London. He intends to stay here until he finds the source of that impulse and those that have followed."

Jander's whirling mind nonetheless processed the information in purposeful precision. Taking the Ukrainian's cue to use code names, he started inventing them on the spot. "Cobra, keep monitoring him. Try to pinpoint the exact location of his ship, its size, armament, safeguards and crew. Find out his motives, why he wants to find us so badly. And check to see if any more of them are running around loose. I'll be over with Alpha and a full complement as soon as I can get there. Is the Ghost's old flat free?"

"Until the end of the month, yes."

"Good, wait for us there. Get to it!"

"Yes, sir." He hung up.

Jander dropped the phone into its saddle and spun to the waiting group. "Vickie!"

"Yes, sir." No one was surprised or even noticed the title from such an unlikely source.

"Contact Arden and Terry in Los Angeles. Get them here. Jake, Ginger, try to reach Thelma in New York. Get her here with Richard and Carmen. Max, Lorraine, Chelsea, all of you change for London. The Omega Corps has its first case!" He left for his room to change.

Jake looked at Vickie, said "Whew!" and started thinking.

Within fifteen minutes they were gathered in the dining room. Jander recounted his conversation with Pavel, gave them a moment to regain their composure, and went on, "So the first order of business is getting to London. The teleporters will carry us, with a few stops along the way – it's a heavy load. I will support us during transit in a bubble of force until Arden and Richard are ready to jump again. Once there, I expect Pavel will have the location of the ship. Vickie will stay with me in London; the rest of you will jump to the ship's location.

"You will go over that ship with a sponge, studying the computer assuming it has one, the machinery, any maps, charts and documents, and the minds of the crew, and cramming the information into Carmen's eidetic memory. Thelma, you work on the crew. Ginger, you will be the funnel, reading Max while he reads the computer, collecting what Lorraine, Chelsea and Terry see, linking them to Arden for his engineering analysis, and shooting the whole mess to Carmen. Don't worry about understanding it, querida, just remember it. We'll probably have to build a whole new order of computer to figure out half that stuff. It will be a long, hard job, but it must be done as quickly as possible. If our interview with Spart is successful, we'll be down to help with no one the wiser."

"You mean you're just going to walk in on him?" Jake asked.

"Why not? Can he hurt me?"

"I don't know, can he?"

"After what happened the last time I saw London I'll be on my toes, believe me. And if anything goes wrong I have you here to back us up. Keep the heavies on hand in case we need help. Walter, get busy practicing your bite. You might need it." The German woofed at him and grinned. "All clear? Let's go!"

The task force of eleven variants stepped out into the yard. On a word they hopped into the air, and found themselves enclosed in a transparent, flat-bottomed cylinder of force. All joined hands, and the two teleporters linked minds through Vickie and concentrated. They all felt an eye tearing instant of mental confusion, and the group found themselves suspended high over the city of Toronto.

Richard looked down and clutched at his stomach.

"Uh, b-boss…" His discomfort was echoed by a chorus of gasps and groans.

"Sorry." The floor and the lower meter of wall became opaque, so the two could focus without the disconcerting sight of five thousand feet of nothing.

Four jumps later they were crowded into the London flat. The teleporters got the location of the spaceship and took off overland with the spy party, traveling jump by jump through secluded spots selected by Lorraine.

Pavel brought Jander and Vickie up to date on the alien admiral. "The Confederation Fleet is essentially an armored police force," he said, speaking aloud to distill his thoughts. As experienced as he was in his own métier, telepathy was still new to him. "Their First Law is that no one may interfere with underdeveloped planets, of which Gaea, as we are known to them, is one. Spart is here to ensure the enforcement of that law." He seemed not the least bit put out at being called "underdeveloped".

"And he thinks we could not have originated the activator?" Jander prodded.

"In essence, yes. From his thoughts I gather that the energy radiated by our machine is akin to some sort of psycho-mechanical educator, acting contrary to design from our viewpoint, perhaps. He is quite concerned that the barbarians of Gaea might get enough knowledge to take their savage ways to the stars." Now he was being ironic.

"By the way, if I may be permitted the liberty,

might I suggest that you have been remiss in not investigating that mechanism a bit more thoroughly?" His fatherly grin took out the sting.

"In this case you may take the liberty. I kicked myself clear across the Atlantic with that thought."

"What is he going to do when he finds us?" Vickie asked.

"First, he has no idea as to the age or origin of the machine, or the type of people using it for that matter. His concern is that some galactic criminal may be recruiting an army or something equally undesirable. Second, he has no idea that the mechanism is not in fact being used as an educator, at least not in any way he is familiar with. How those details will affect his thinking I cannot guess." He fell silent and waited, knowing that as a thinker he was far outclassed by these two.

But Jander valued his experienced judgment. "How would you suggest we approach him?"

Pavel frowned. "I was not expecting a direct approach. Your plan so far is good, studying him and his ship from a distance and learning what you can."

"But we can't keep it that way. As far as I'm concerned, he's the one interfering in human affairs. I want him off our backs." He gave the older man a lopsided smile. "Preferably with a minimum of conflict. With all our talents we're not quite up to taking on a galactic fleet." With that magnificent understatement he flopped on Chelsea's former couch and stared at the ceiling.

Vickie passed the time by searching for and locating the alien mind. "Why, he's not even close to human! His thoughts are so alien I can hardly read them!"

"Da," Pavel said. "I had my difficulties, also. However, the physical form is quite human. No one would glance at him twice on the street. But if you look closely at his wrists, you may see a difference in the arrangement of the bones and tendons. In addition, his species does not have the constantly growing facial hair we human men have. He is quite conscious of those differences in appearance. The mental divergences are likely from social evolution, quite distinctive even from our own diverse cultures. One would assume that with practice we will be able to read such minds with ease."

Jander slipped into their thoughts unnoticed, studied the differences and revised his thinking somewhat. "Pavel, you will stay here to cover our safe house. Vickie, here's what we'll do…"

VICE ADMIRAL NIL SPART, born of the Stellar Confederation planet Sabar, sat with his feet up in his rented flat, glancing often at a table full of odd-looking electronic receivers with multiple plasma displays. All of them had been idle since he had sneaked them in three days before.

His ship's approach was cautious to the Sabar-like third planet of the yellow dwarf star the Confederation called Kitaote. His crew had detected a very recent flurry of quantum impulses from somewhere on Gaea. The pulses were similar to a stimulator designed to feed data directly to the brain, a tool well beyond Gaean technology. Spart and his ship were the axes of a triangulation designed to intercept and trace those high-order emissions should they recur.

In the meantime he sat in the room surrounded by books, magazines and a Gaean-manufactured wireless laptop, avidly catching up on this planet's history and science. He had taken a thorough educator course in Gaea's history and affairs before landing, but the last survey report had been nearly a century old.

Since then, the Gaeans had strode their moon and sent robots to visit other Kitaoten planets, built several crude space stations and observatories, and sent sub-light probes to the far reaches of their stellar gravity well. But while they had made astonishing advances in electronics, there was no mention of a practical means of cyber-cortical stimulation.

As a society, although plagued by fanatical ideologies, greedy oligarchs and fiercely competitive political systems, they had struggled with limited success toward planetary unity. They could be an asset to the Confederation in a century or two. If they survived.

So engrossed was he that he did not notice the slight breeze past his cheek. In the bedroom behind him, a bolt was magically thrown and a window swung open by itself, to close again a few seconds later.

Undetectable within an energy shield, Jander and Vickie glided over to the door and peered into the sitting room for their first look at an alien lifeform.

As Pavel had said, the Sabarian was quite humanoid in most respects, with light skin, blue-green eyes and a hominid skull and face topped with graying blond hair as he approached his second century of life. He was somewhat under six feet tall, with a broad chest, trim waist and a normally proportioned pair of legs.

The arms, however, had shorter forearms and wrists that were longer and far more flexible than a Gaean's, hinting at extra bones and more supple ligaments. He was absorbed in a hardcover history book, occasionally tapping queries into his laptop to cross-reference the unfamiliar.

Vickie secreted herself in a corner of the bedroom and settled in for some heavy thinking. Jander, still invisible, floated into the other room and fell to examining the alien instruments. He probed with the analytical section of his protean brain, feeling for the forces employed, studying their use.

He examined the batteries with particular interest. The stored power was derived, as far as he could tell, from solar accumulation, so amplified and compacted that it almost had a life of its own.

The instruments themselves were rather basic, most of them being direction finders on a wavelength much higher and more vibrant than any wireless transmission he had ever imagined. He filed in his mind that the targeted frequencies matched the emissions he had sensed from the ancient activator.

Satisfied that he would not be surprised himself, he dropped his shield. "Good morning, Admiral."

Spart started strongly, sending the book flying. He leaped to his feet and spun around. "Who are you?" he demanded in proper Queen's English. "How did you get in here?"

Steele smiled blandly. "I'm the man you're looking for. I came in through the window."

"Up six flights?"

"We Gaeans are quite adaptable, don't you know," Steele said, mocking him with the same accent. Without waiting for an invitation he found himself a chair, pushed aside a scrabble of magazines and sat down, crossing an ankle over the other knee.

Spart's jaw tightened at the affront, but any objection quickly died in the face of the younger man's words. "What are Gaeans?"

Steele kept smiling, but only with his lips. "Don't try to play games with me, Admiral." He extended his hand palm up, letting the sleeve of his loose shirt drop and flapping his hand so the other man could see the Gaean structure of his wrist. "I know exactly who you are. So far, your activities have not yet been brought to the attention of government authorities, but a few of us are aware of the Stellar Confederation you purport to represent."

Spart stared at him wide-eyed. "How did you learn this?"

Jander gave him credit for not trying to deny it. "We have people in my organization who are good at such things."

"And what exactly is your organization?"

"The Omega Corps. An international cartel of specialized Gaeans organized for and dedicated to the cause of justice and law enforcement."

The Admiral sent a reproachful glance at the laptop and research materials scattered around him. "I don't recall hearing of such an organization."

"Because officially we don't exist. No government finances us, no head of state grants us power, and not one average citizen is aware of our existence."

Spart was about to ask more questions, so Steele interjected, "Your investigation is a threat to our planet's development, Admiral, and I do not intend to allow you to interfere with our affairs."

Spart blinked, taken aback by having his own motives thrown back at him. But he did not achieve his high station by being slow on the uptake. He turned his chair and resumed his seat, then tried an attack of his own. "Where is the educator?"

Jander was about to feign ignorance by asking what an educator was, but caught a swift notion from Vickie. The psychologist urged him to maintain his superiority by appearing omniscient. He made a mental note to thank her later.

"We have no educator. Are we capable of building one?" His eyes roving over the piles of written material.

Spart studied his verbal opponent carefully, formulating his next moves with the analytical insight of a career strategist. A jumble of questions settled into order in his mind. If it was not an educator, then what was it? How did it come into his possession? What was it used for? What were the results? When was...

Steele, linked to him through Vickie, had no intention of answering any such questions. He waited until the admiral was about to draw breath to start, then moved to derail him.

"Tell me, sir, what would happen if the Confederation came to know that your identity had been discovered?"

Spart remained silent, but Jander could see his cold stop in Vickie's mind. A jumble of answers flew through his consciousness as the implications sank in. Ruin at the least, incarceration probably, perhaps even death for piracy. "That would never happen," he said at last. "Who could possibly inform them?"

"Suppose, just suppose, that I had the knowledge and ability to construct a craft capable of interstellar travel? And suppose I mentioned that it was my identification of you and your purpose here that made me realize it would be worthwhile to do so?" He raised a single eyebrow, deadpan insolence clear on his face.

The Admiral's mind whirled. Typically for him, his own ruin was secondary to his thinking. But these anarchical barbarians, with spaceships? These untutored savages could, and quite probably would, cause enormous chaos, maybe even war. Such a threat was why the First Law was formulated in the first place. The Admiral was appalled.

Being a fair diplomat, however, and a first contact enthusiast, he kept his face impassive. He was well aware that saying the wrong thing was far worse than saying nothing. This offensive Gaean had the upper hand, he knew. How he had the upper hand, he did not know. But despite his opponent's apparent naive frankness Spart was aware that he was facing a highly intelligent and able tactician. He had the Admiral tagged right down the line; he was outgunned and he knew it.

Steele raised himself out of his chair. "Well, since it seems you no longer want to talk…" He started to turn away.

Spart pushed himself to his feet and held out a restraining hand. "Wait…"

Jander stopped and faced him, deliberately making himself imposing with his greater size. "Yes?"

The Admiral realized he had nothing to say. He was outmaneuvered and completely impotent, and this supercilious barbarian knew it. He stood silent, glaring angrily.

Jander gave him a bland smile, turned and strolled to the bedroom door, then turned back. "Remember my warning, Admiral Spart. Any attempt at interference will be met with equal vigor. I'll return when I'm certain of your intentions."

He stepped into the bedroom and closed the door behind him. A moment later, Spart growled an expletive and followed. The room was empty, the window locked.

VICKIE WAS STILL GRINNING when they reached the flat. Pavel leaped to his feet and held out his hand. "Magnificent! The best you could have done. Perfect!"

"We're not through with him yet," Jander warned as he tapped his fingers into Pavel's palm. "We've given him a lot to think about. He has a vague idea of what he's up against, and he's certain that whatever he does about us will be wrong. We'll let him stew a bit and stir him up some more.

"Right now," he continued, "I want to go down and take a look at that ship. Keep abreast of things until I get back." He headed for the window.

"You're just going to leave him sitting there?" Vickie asked.

"For the time being, yes. He's an honorable man, Vickie, a good man. I want to see what conclusions he reaches on his own. If he tries to do anything active, like contact his ship for anything but a status report, let me know immediately. I've got a tracer on your mind. Just concentrate on reaching me, and I'll hear you."

He winked at her, clapped Kalanev on the shoulder, then stepped through the window into midair and disappeared. The curtains fluttered as if in an updraft, and he was gone.

HE RETURNED SEVERAL HOURS LATER, kissed Vickie and gave Pavel a tired nod, and sagged onto the sofa. "That is some job," he sighed. "The ship is egg shaped and seventy meters long, chock full of computers, machinery and six species of people, and every bit of it is way beyond my wildest imagination. "Still, I was able to take some of the load off Carmen and Ginger. And these guys have some stuff I had to analyze for myself. And hey, if you think Spart is hard to read, ask Thelma about Hasgondi. Pacifist bears."

He shook his head and chuckled. "Sabarians, Leosans, Hasgondi, Dwatans, Kanitaks, Fthlonians, plus five other species in the Confederation that aren't in his crew. All working as a team with no prejudices, just mutual appreciation of their distinctive contributions. Man, we have so much to learn."

Vickie flounced down beside him, wide-eyed and eager. "Tell us about it!" Pavel took a chair opposite, an adventurous gleam in his ice-gray eyes.

Jander rubbed his temples. "Mind you, when I said it would take an entirely new type of computer to understand all that, I was understating, though I didn't know it at the time. I'm nowhere close to knowing how they do most of it – or why, for that matter. But I can speak in generalities…"

"We might not understand even those," Vickie interposed.

"…and maybe catch the essence of it. Their primary

energy source is solar, or stellar. The outside of the ship is studded with multiplex accumulators, which can catch visible light, photons and other particles from vast distances. Light speed doesn't affect accumulation because no matter how fast they're going, stars in their line of flight are always radiating in opposition to their velocity. That's basic physics put to good use.

"Once caught, the energy is amplified and concentrated again and again, kind of folded in upon itself like a Damascus blade, until it's many times as potent as any solar power we have developed. An extremely efficient power source – no worries about supply, no problems with bulk storage other than emergency batteries, and since it starts out as energy they have no problem with matter conversion and waste.

"But the drive engines..."

He sighed and rubbed his temples again, then dropped his hands as Vickie took up the task. "The drive is a different story, a holdover from the intergalactic bronze age. It seems out of place in the rest of the ship, inefficient and wasteful. It's a process that I'd have to call nucleonic. They take all that beautiful free energy, bombard an alloy of heavy metals with it, recombine the soup into unstable matter and spew it out of the ship – bits and pieces of split atoms and energy in a concentrated blast.

"The manufactured solid fuel is very dense and heavy, so they can carry only so much because the mass to be moved limits either the size of the engines or the distance they can travel – so diminishing returns limits the size of the vessel. However, this unlikely mess does propel a standard cruiser sized ship at a speed of about six gravities per second squared, and since they enclose the ship in a quantum infusion field that creates a bubble of normal space to counter the mass-time differential, they get places in a hurry."

Jander interrupted his narrative to take a bottle of water from Pavel, who clearly had noticed the exhausted rasp in his commander's voice. He took a long pull, the stretched out on the sofa. Vickie shifted to pillow his head on her thigh, and he sipped at the bottle as he continued.

"The problem is, when they pass the speed of light they're blind and deaf to anything outside the bubble. But this is where more technology comes in. Their sensory equipment captures faster-than-light particles – there are quite a few – and converts them into an accurate reflection of conditions outside the bubble, through what I'd have to call quantum entanglement capture and replication.

"Their point-to-point communications is also through quantum entanglement, where a particle stream created in the transmitter is simultaneously duplicated in the receiver, so the stream exists in both places at the same time. Again, don't ask me how they do it." He smiled ruefully. "Compared to the youngest technician on that ship I'm a ten-year-old coal miner. We're way outclassed."

"Technologically, maybe," Vickie soothed him, "but I can't believe we don't match them intellectually. Look at the job you did on that Admiral. It's only a matter of integrating that higher knowledge of theirs – a matter of time, not capacity."

"By the way, how is our friend?"

"Done to a turn," she chuckled. "Made as a bull and ready to lock horns."

"But he is more dangerous now," Pavel said. "He now has an idea of what he is up against, and he is quite capable."

"So? The most brilliant strategy can't work against someone who knows it word for word," Jander pointed out.

"So, what are your intentions toward him?" Vickie asked. "What good is it if he hates you?"

Jander clucked at her. "Think a bit, psychologist. You can't hate someone you don't hold in good regard – and it's his respect I'm after."

Vickie reddened, but kept silent. She knew that he would not have said something that cold if he had been anything short of exhausted.

In any case, Kalanev stepped to her rescue. "So perhaps he respects you. But by the same token, he still hates you. You have merely proven yourself dangerous."

"Not at all. I've just proven myself clever. My next task is to try to gain his confidence..."

"So he'll trust you to handle things intelligently here on Earth – er, Gaea," Vickie interrupted, determined to regain her self-esteem. "You'll have to tell him something about us, and about our methods. You'll have to convince him that we're doing the right thing."

"And that will be difficult. His number one law will get in the way. Without that high-order meshcap there would be no activated variants." He failed to stifle a yawn.

Vickie stroked his forehead, her eyes gazing askance at the wall. "And since the variants are a product of higher technology the number one law has been broken. But surely he can see it was accidental?"

"Ignorance of the law is not a defense," Pavel pointed out. "He may wish to confiscate the activator."

"That's my greatest worry," Jander agreed. "If he demands that I even let him see the thing I'll refuse. And unless some compromise is reached, he may want to take it from us by force."

"Can he? If he does that, he'll be guilty of breaking the First Law himself." Vickie saw the implications and grinned.

"And that's my number one defense," Jander smiled up at her. "If he's sincere – and we've both studied his character enough to know he is – his only recourse would be to leave bad enough alone."

He handed the empty bottle to Pavel and stretched with a groan. "Well, I'd better get some rest before I tackle him again. The ship team is taking staggered breaks, which sounds like a pretty good idea to me. Keep an ear out – and please, please find me some breakfast."

"Not enough food for thought?" Vickie quipped, and moved to let him settle his head into the pillows. In seconds he was asleep.

CHAPTER 12

Spart paced back and forth in his crowded room, still irritated but no longer fuming. He had gone over the conversation in his mind again and again, analyzing and calculating and squirming with self-accusations of ineptitude. But he had calmed down enough to reach a few conclusions.

He paused at the window overlooking the humming street below, staring with a bit of distaste at the primitive vehicles fouling the air with combustible carbon fuels. He bent his right hand to scratch his right forearm where the unfamiliar native cloth had irritated his skin – a physical act a single-jointed Gaean could never do – and went over the brief encounter one more time.

The barbarian was good, no doubt about it, but he lacked sophistication. The idea of him scratch building a starship was just that, a wild idea. The admiral could see that even though small groups of Gaean scientists may have gained enough knowledge to theorize a faster-than-light craft, they were too divided to pool their information. The fractious governments and avaricious corporations funding the research were too busy trying to find more efficient ways to enrich themselves and overpower each other.

Besides, the barbarian did not actually say he could build one. He could discount that part of the exchange as bluff.

But the implications were tremendous. His opponent had hit the important point right on the chin: if he took any direct action against the self-styled Omega Corps it would be a Confederal crime. In fact, even his discovery and contact by the Gaeans could cost him his career at the least. He had not even told anyone in his crew about the contact; to do so would have implicated them as complicit, and he had too much love and respect for them to risk dragging them down with him. So, he was bound by his personal sense of honor to bear the burden alone, which would coincidentally protect the Gaeans as well. The thought of having his own integrity used against him rankled.

Still, he could not just walk away without having a better grasp of the extraordinary chain of events. His information lacked on two important points. One, if the high order mechanism was not an educator, then what was it? Two, what was the function of the Omega Corps? It was all well and good for them to call themselves a law enforcement agency, but freelance? And he had disconcerting thoughts of other all-powerful law enforcement agencies in Gaea's recent past that had committed horrendous atrocities.

For the time being, he decided, he had to wait. To search the planet for an organization no one knew about would be futile. The barbarian would come to him, and he was fully prepared to be forceful.

"Good evening, Admiral."

Spart yelped and spun so fast he almost fell. The barbarian was standing right behind him with that familiar bland smile. Furious at being caught off-guard, and even angrier at losing his dignity, Spart exploded.

"What the bloody hell are you trying to prove? Your childish games of hide and seek are not impressive. If you call yourself intelligent you could at least conduct yourself with civility. Do you have any sense of propriety on this planet?"

"It's my planet, bucko. Mind if I sit down?" Vickie, hidden in the bedroom, barely suppressed an eruption of mirth.

"Does it matter if I mind?" Spart stabbed a finger at a chair.

Steele ambled over and dropped into it, swinging an idle leg over its arm. Magnanimously he waved at another chair for the admiral. "I see you have found your voice since last we met. Perhaps you are now ready to discuss our mutual interests?"

"I can see no points of mutual interest." Spart defiantly remained standing.

"Oh, but we have several," Steele returned mildly. "For instance, there is the mechanism your instruments detected. I should at least tell you it isn't contemporary. It was found in a wilderness area within a segment of a craft of alien origin. The condition of the materials indicates that it had been buried for thousands, perhaps tens of thousands, of years."

He gauged the slow change in his adversary's face, from belligerent to analytical. "So you see," he continued in the same non-aggressive tone, "it's really a Gaean artifact, whatever its origin. No contemporary resource delivered it into our hands, so it is quite beyond your jurisdiction."

"You're quibbling." Spart took his seat, needing all his energy to think. "In point of fact, it is not a product of Gaean technology, and its use constitutes a violation of our First Law, that the progress of a barbarian planet —" he saw no reaction to the pointed slur — "may not be altered by any form of extraplanetary technology."

Jander raised an eyebrow, "How can you say that? You have no idea how or even if it is being used."

Spart kicked himself mentally. This was the most discomfiting dialogue he had ever been involved in. Suppressing a growl of irritation, he said through gritted teeth, "All right, then, just how is it being used?"

Steele pulled his leg from the chair arm and sat up straight. "Human evolution is in a state of transition. In the last few thousand years there have been stories in our legends about people with mental and physical talents beyond the ordinary. It is likely that these gifts will become more evident and even common in a relatively few centuries. Currently, these abilities are naturally manifest in a very few Gaeans, but in a large minority the potential lies dormant, waiting for evolution or technology to activate it."

He paused to allow Spart to digest that. When the admiral nodded, he continued.

"Technology came first. The alien mechanism, possibly a malfunctioning educator, stimulates that portion of the human genome in which the dormant abilities lie. A very select few have been exposed to those energies, and trained to use the variant talents resulting from the exposure. The result is the Omega Corps, a clandestine group of activated human variants who work beyond national boundaries for the benefit of all mankind. I am called Orion, and I am honored to have been tagged with the rather grandiose title of Lord of the Omega Corps."

Spart listened to every incredible word, eyes narrowed, gauging the sincerity of the man before him.

"An admirable endeavor, if true. But that is a lot of power to be gathered into one group."

"Very true, and that is a constant cause of vigilance for me. However, with the increase of variant potential in our species, we've also seen a marked increase in practical intelligence. I'm sure you'll agree," he said carefully, "that cooperation is a function of intelligence."

"Of course," the Admiral said slowly. The gentle dig was not lost on him. "However, your recent history would belie that. Conflict is constant. And it is quite easy to give in to the temptation of forcing cooperation if one has the power to do so, in the erroneous belief that the strongest are destined to lead."

"A rather odd choice of words, Admiral, that presumes the Omega Corps is dictatorial in its intentions. We most emphatically are not. We have been following your First Law without knowing of it, as a function of logic. Forced cooperation is an excellent breeding ground for insurrection. Any attempt at dictatorship would mean not only our lives, but also the lives of any who appear to have our potential.

"In our not too distant past thousands were murdered – horribly murdered – for suspicion of witchcraft. And throughout our history, some of it very recent, millions have been slaughtered just for being different from the ruling class. The last thing we need is a bloodbath in which countless innocents die simply because they appear to have variant potential. That would set us back centuries."

Spart glanced at his reading material and nodded. "So, what do you see is your function?"

"To blunt the impact of activities which are detrimental to mankind. You were right when you said that this is a barbarian planet. We prey on each other and our environment; we kill each other for foolish and petty reasons; we rob from the poor to reward the rich; and we're breeding ourselves clear off the planet. It's way too much to stop, or even impede greatly, but it's not hopeless. We intend to ensure that it does not become so.

"Our goal is survival, of humanity and the planet

it lives on. The Omega Corps will never be noticed by history if we do our job properly, but it will make possible the hope that someday our descendants will look upon this era as the beginning of an enlightened age."

Steele settled back in his chair and waited. He did not expect the admiral to be much affected by his rhetoric, but he hoped his intentions would strike a chord.

Spart met his eyes with a steady gaze of his own. "You are an unusual man, Lord Orion," he broke the long silence. "A prosaic idealist. How do you expect to keep a large minority of your population secret?"

Steele was relieved that Spart had called him by name, with honorarium. That made him a respectable person rather than a problem. He suppressed a smile as Vickie projected a vision of herself doing backflips. "I doubt we'll ever activate more than a few hundred, and we have only a handful so far…"

"Seventeen." The Admiral was happy to beat his opponent to the punch for once. The knowledge that Steele had led him to it would have killed him. "We intercepted seventeen impulses."

"That is the beginning, yes. We are only now organizing into an effective force. As yet we have done little, nibbling at the fringes of organized crime and the like. We are handicapped by the fact that we can't work directly."

"And that is your most positive argument as far as I am concerned. That is the point that convinces me to allow you to continue. I would like to see that starship."

"I'm sure you would." Steele had seen the request coming and was prepared for it. "I'm afraid I must refuse. I stand by my contention that the ship and the activating mechanism are the property of Gaea. You have my word that they will not fall into the hands of anyone outside the Corps. Either you trust me with them, or you hunt for them yourself – and that," he warned, "I will oppose."

"I'm sure you would," Spart repeated Steele's response, smiling for the first time.

Steele, through the mental probes of Vickie, saw his thoughts working toward asking about their variant talents, and rushed to change the subject. "So, what will be your report to the Confederation?"

"As little as possible." Spart turned to the new problem. "I suppose I can explain those impulses as experimental radiation. They are indeed only somewhat similar to educator emissions, and I can see from my research that you've made tremendous scientific progress since your development of atomic energy – particularly in the area of electronics."

He looked up, his face impassive yet somehow pleading. "I'm taking a great risk with you, you know. If this encounter becomes known to my superiors, I would face the equivalent of your court martial."

"As you pointed out this morning, how could they learn? I don't want them to know about us either." Steele smiled back and stood. "Very well, then, we are agreed. You will not interfere with our operations as long as I don't openly interfere with Gaea's development."

Spart nodded. "As if we'd never heard of each other."

"I'll take my leave, then." Replicating the Sabarian trait of abstaining from long goodbyes, Jander bowed and walked to the bedroom, closing the door behind him. The admiral followed and tugged at the knob; after a few seconds it came unstuck and he peered into the room. As he expected, it was empty.

CHAPTER 13

Spart took off in a jungle-searing blast of non-toxic nucleonic plasma two days later, still embarrassed by how little he knew. He did not even know the Gaean's real name, for pity's sake, or what it was that made him so special. As the *Kaltim* rumbled upward within its stealthy defensive screening the Admiral stood on his circular bridge and glared down at the planet, suspecting it was going to prove troublesome but impotent to do anything about it.

Jander followed with his spy team to the edge of space, each of them probing and analyzing to the last. He was pleased with the amount of information they had gleaned, unsuspected by any member of the diverse crew. His head buzzed with a massive jumble of unfathomable science advanced enough to be magic, and his companions were in no better shape as he brought them back to earth to rejoin the ground team. Little Carmen, her eidetic memory crammed with esoteric lore, was fast asleep before they touched down.

Computopathic Max was as fatigued as the rest, but his bloodshot eyes burned with excitement. "We must begin our new computer immediately. I can now see what we have missed in the past. Our brain will be the greatest ever built!"

Jander smiled tiredly. "Let's get some sleep first, shall we? Ready, boys?" The exhausted Arden, with Richard, who had had nothing to do but go for supplies and cook for several days, linked through the reasonably fresh Pavel and took the team in easy hops back to Montana. Ignoring Jake and the other eager variants, they collapsed into beds.

The next day Jander got together with Jake, Max, Arden and Denny, who was back from a mechanical repair contract he had been unable to escape. "Our first order of business is, as Max says, to develop our quantum cybernetic computer. I want to blend our theoretical take on plasma-based multilinear resonance with the Confederation's means of force-freezing decoherence.

"I also want to couple it with a two-way variation of the Confederation's mechanical educator, so we have both input and output. I think we can design a cyberbionic telepath, at least for communication with our quantum machine, converting synaptic impulses to qubit electrical impulses that the computer can interpret. That way Carmen and I can unload before the turn of the century."

"Where are you going to build this monster?" Denny asked. "Putting it here is too much like putting all our baskets in one egg."

"That, I hope to know in a few days. We're going to field two teams led by Vickie and Thelma, to hunt up a centralized city with a large office or commercial building for sale. We'll locate the computer deep underground, hidden under plenty of safeguards. But we'll still be using this place to build the starship."

"Gaaah. Wait a minute." Jake let his breath out in a blast. "You mean you're going to duplicate the whole ship?"

"Oh, hell, no. Ours will be completely different — bigger, faster, far more powerful than anything the Confederation has in space." He looked at the faces of the astonished quartet and continued innocently, "What's the matter?"

Jake squeezed his eyelids tightly together. "Okay. I have no objections to having a spaceport in my back yard. I already have a werewolf." He released something between a giggle and a cough.

"Of course!" The German was waking up. "That's why you demanded we study the ship so thoroughly. I thought you would be preparing a defense, in case they tried to confiscate the activator. But won't you be breaking your word to Spart?"

"Nope. I promised we wouldn't interfere with the course of human development. I said nothing about galactic affairs." He grinned. "But that's way, way in the future. Now to the business at hand..."

STEELE TOOK THE TIME to investigate the activator and its effect on variant brains. With a measure of knowledge gleaned from Spart's *Kaltim*, which was equipped with dynamic educators for several species, and guided by his own gift of wave analysis, he and Jake built a shielding mechanism that would keep the radiation of activator energies from escaping to be picked up by Spart or anyone else.

Then he meditated long and hard on what his eidetic memory had recorded as he had read the Corpsmen before, during and after their activation. He formulated a few tenuous theories, but was far from satisfied with the results. He had no idea how the activator worked, or what part of a variant potential's nervous system it worked on.

He sprawled in that recliner, sans helmet, and pressed the motive switch time after time, feeling the energies bouncing off his analytical screens, pausing in thought after each manipulation. He commandeered the minds of Terry and Lorraine, seeing what they saw, studying their mental pictures of the console for hours. He ended little wiser than he started. He could not understand it; he could not duplicate it; he could not formulate any theory or even vague idea about the energies employed.

He and Arden pored over every inch of what remained of the ancient spaceship, not much more than the control cockpit now stored in the barn, looking for clues that would describe the beings that had flown it. They found nothing there to help; with almost nothing of the wreck left intact save the structural metals of the control room they had no real vision of the physiognomy of its crew, much less how their brains may have been structured. For all they knew, the activator might have been in perfect working order for a mind other than human.

Or, it might even have been brought to Gaea to do exactly what it was doing, to advance the potential of the human species. The fact that only the activator had survived the untold centuries lent credence to that dumbfounding theory, and led to many hushed conversations around the dinner table.

Finally, with much trepidation, he let radiopathic Jake volunteer to sit in the chair and take the zap again. Nothing happened. The machine worked as it always had, but Jake experienced no pain and no discernable change.

It was psychologist Vickie who suggested they try activating a normal mind. Jander decided to kill several birds with that stone; they envisioned several other experiments to determine the effects of variant powers on normal minds and bodies. They started looking for a likely subject.

"HENRY SANBURG."

He mumbled in his fitful slumber, the thin, foul-smelling pillow smothering the sound.

"Henry Sanburg."

He awoke at that, staring into the darkness. His death row cell was empty save for himself.

"Henry."

He rolled over and dropped his feet to the floor, the

utilitarian bunk creaking under his shifting weight. "Who's there?"

"Do you wish to live?"

Henry jumped at the disembodied voice that seemed to come from right outside his cell. The voice was low, gentle, solemn. "Whuh –"

"You will be executed in a few days for a murder you didn't commit. I offer you life for service."

Sanburg stumbled to his feet and stared about him wildly. "Who are you? Where are you? What do you want from me?"

"I am called Orion. I am standing right in front of you, though you can't see me. I need someone for a variety of hazardous tests that could prove fatal – but only perhaps. I offer you that chance to live. If you remain here, you will most certainly die."

"You mean… like a lab rat? You're gonna work on me?"

"In a way, yes, though I assure you we have no harm intended. I can't tell you who we are, or what we will do, yet. But I can tell you this: among the many tests you will be sent the edge of space, floating in free-fall orbit without a ship, and survive. In another, major test, you may become one of the most intelligent and talented people alive, assuming you survive. In exchange, and regardless of success or failure, you will be given a new identity, a new home, and everything you will need to start a new life."

He paused to give Sanburg a moment to digest that, then added, "And I guarantee you this: whether you come with us or not, whether you live or not, the man who committed the homicide you are accused of will be properly punished."

Sanburg sagged back onto his bunk. That put an entirely different slant on things. If it were just for himself, his despair would have made it a hard choice. But to clear his name, to avenge his girl... He would owe this voice his peace of mind. To have his life too would be... heaven.

It did not cross his mind to doubt that Orion could deliver. One does not question a reprieve.

"How do I get out of here?"

Vickie, monitoring his mind, nodded, and Steele dropped his shield of invisibility.

The effect on Sanburg would have been comical in another situation. He leaped to his feet and staggered backward, almost falling as he lost his balance. He stood on wobbly legs, back pressed to the cold cement block wall, gaping at the three people before him.

He saw a tall, commanding figure in a silver-snapped western shirt and knit slacks under a leather blazer, all in black, who could only be the leader. Beside him was a beautiful blonde, radiant in a knee-length green frock cinched with an ivory sash. At his other side was a clean-limned, well-toned Black man in burgundy shirt and charcoal slacks, whose eyes were filled with solemn compassion. It was the most impressive trio he had ever seen.

The woman glided forward and focused her hazel eyes on the lock of his cell. The lock gave a quick series of clicks and the door swung open with a slight rasp. The three stepped inside, the door closed and locked by itself behind them, and Orion and the other man held out their hands. Sanburg took one each. The woman linked with the two men, then the Black man closed his eyes and threw his head back in the very picture of intense concentration.

Sanburg felt a tugging at the base of his skull, and in an instant the four were standing in a cool, dry living room softly scented with cedar. His hands were released, and he lurched to find his footing on the hardwood floor.

A diminutive Hispanic woman lounging on a couch looked up from her laptop, tossed her mass of dark curls back from her sparkling eyes, gave him a fleeting smile and returned to her reading. A tortoise-shell cat that seemed used to people popping in and out gazed at him languidly from the back of a sofa by the window.

"That was the first experiment," Orion caught his wide-eyed attention. "You are educated and imaginative enough to understand much of what we do. That's one of the reasons we chose you. What you just experienced is teleportation, instant transference of matter from one place to another. The test was whether Hermes, here, could transport a nonvariant person. You will be meeting many people with extraordinary powers; what we do with you will be the gauge of our effectiveness. Do you agree?"

"Uh, y-yeah…." Henry stared around him, dazed.

He had a pretty good idea of what had just happened, and his mind was filled with such awe that it bordered on shock.

Orion smiled. "I can sympathize with your feelings. We all felt the same way the first time we were exposed to such things. But you'll get used to it, as we did."

Sanburg was much relieved by that admission of mortality.

Thus, Henry Sanburg became the official lab rat of the Omega Corps. He was thrown through the air at remarkable speeds by lovely Alpha and the energetic, red-haired Vesta; he was flashed for hundreds and thousands of miles by the pragmatic Hermes and another, cheerful man called Mercury; his deepest thoughts were probed by Alpha and Binary and Peachie and Cobra and others; he was deliberately damaged by Chloe and healed better than ever; he was even subjected to being walked through by the nerve-wracking Ghost. And he stared at himself in perfect reproduction by the Mimic, and watched himself grow old by proxy.

And through it all, he was treated with respect, compassion and camaraderie, accepted as one of the family even though he never learned their real names. He was made a participant in the experiments rather than a laboratory rat, a state of affairs that in time made him a willing subject no matter how outlandish the circumstances.

Over the weeks, the soul that had been battered by deep loss and injustice slowly turned from fragile despair to healthy self-esteem. He came to look forward to every adventure with the eager anticipation of a pioneer, and enjoyed every minute of it.

But his most amazing experience by far was his trip through space.

"This is the most dangerous test," Orion told him. At that declaration, Sanburg sprouted goose bumps. "My forcefield projection is by far the most complex and difficult to master of our abilities. This test will be two-fold; whether I can control my power at great distances, and whether the force sphere will remain airtight and protective in airless, pressureless space. Are you ready to try it?"

"No, but what the hell," he grinned. By now, Henry was well accustomed to flirting with death.

"Jump, then." Sanburg hopped, and stayed up, suspended three inches from the ground. He stretched his arms wide and then upward and found a perfect sphere, perhaps eight feet in diameter.

Orion continued, "I want to keep the sphere transparent, so you'll be able to see outside. It will be altered to protect your eyes and health from the sun and other hard radiation, and you should have enough air in there to last through the test. Have fun!" With that, he propelled the sphere into the air.

"He's scared to death – left his stomach ten feet off the ground," Vickie told him softly. "But otherwise, he's all right – underwear's still clean, anyway."

"Keep talking," Jander grunted. "I can't spend all my time on the sphere. I'll always have to deal with distraction. How well can you read him?"

"Perfectly." She paused, then went on for conversation's sake, "As we've discovered, interference from other minds is the biggest obstacle in telepathy. When the target mentality is atypical, like Spart's, detection is pretty easy. So is finding familiar, isolated minds like the mail carrier or the local sheriff. But attempting to find one particular mind in a crowd, or sort out the impressions of the whole bunch, can be hard. I can read Henry so well because he's the only one up there." She grinned. "As he's well aware."

"Any discomfort?"

"No, I'm fine."

"Him, knucklehead," he grinned at her deliberately innocent face. He had asked for distractions.

"Oh... not yet. From his visual impressions I believe he's in the high stratosphere. The sky is getting dark and stars are becoming visible. He's panting a little from the excitement. He'll use his air up pretty fast at this rate."

Jander altered the screen to allow the thinning oxygen from the high atmosphere to replenish Henry's air supply. "Keep monitoring. I need to know all his impressions."

The experiment continued, Sanburg rising higher and higher toward the darkness of space. Steele made the screen more and more complex as the external atmosphere diminished to nothing and the radiation of the exosphere increased. Vickie kept up an animated patter as she studied the mental impulses of their subject hundreds of kilometers above. No breathing difficulty; no eye damage; no tingling sensations; he's starting to enjoy it; the shield is rigid, no give. Item after item was checked off; the test was successful.

Sanburg reached the apex of the flight and stared upward at a view only astronauts had seen, the full magnificence of the boundless galaxy. Vickie passed along that he was having to wipe away tears at the sight.

Steele looked into her mind to share the view, and almost lost his concentration in the process. With that as a warning he decided they had all had enough. He brought the sphere back down, taking care that the shielding stayed strong enough to reflect the heat of re-entry.

He was sweating with the effort by the time Sanburg came back to earth. Still, he had enough energy to ask, "What did you think?"

Sanburg pulled him into an unabashed embrace, speechless with awe and wonder.

"I ASSURE YOU, THIS IS the final test, but it's by far the most vital," Orion told him. They were standing in the hidden cellar room and Jake, alias Binary, was adjusting the activator's meshcap over Sanburg's head. "The machine seems to normalize a person to his highest variant potential, and you have none. If my theories are correct, nothing will happen.

But I'll be honest with you; if I'm wrong, you might as well never have left Death Row."

"Just promise me, that if I end up getting the Chair in this chair, my Deanna's murderer sits here next." Sanburg's tone was light, but his eyes were grim and steady.

"I guarantee it." Steele offered his hand, and Sanburg gripped it with both of his. Jake and Vickie settled themselves into Henry's mind. Terry – "Chloe" of the Omega Corps – stood by for medical assistance. Henry settled his shoulders into the recliner, nodded and closed his eyes. Orion hesitated a moment, remembering the torture of his own first time under the cap, then pressed the button.

Jake roared a guttural scream and reeled across the room, landing huddled against the wall with his arms wrapped around his head. Vickie passed out on her feet, collapsing in a boneless sprawl. Steele, listening in through both their minds, shouted hoarsely and fell to his knees, pressing his hands to his temples. The agony was almost as great as when he himself was activated.

Little by little, the agonizing shock faded to a dull ache. He opened his eyes to see Terry kneeling before him. "I'm... all right," he managed to say. "The shock... Vickie?" He moved on his knees to reach her.

"Unconscious, but undamaged. Jake is already recovering." The doctor moved past them to check on Sanburg, probing with her microvoyance. "He's dead," she reported flatly. "Poor man. His brain is heavily damaged, much more than a simple electrocution. His spinal cord is almost liquefied, and you can see the mottled skin. The shock must have been tremendous."

"It was," Jander said softly. "I'm sick about it. He deserved better than that."

Terry nodded, and extended a gentle hand to close Henry's eyelids. Vickie rolled onto an elbow and shook her head, then smiled at the solicitous Steele and dropped her cheek to his reaching palm.

"Well, so much for my theories," he said. "It's clear the mechanism is lethal to someone without the right junk DNA."

"Not necessarily," Jake said from across the room as he staggered to his feet and leaned on the wall. "One test doesn't prove or disprove a theory. We need another subject."

Jander met his bloodshot eyes, then looked at Vickie. He did not probe their minds; he did not have to. "Call Richard. Have him collect Ginger and go snatch up Jennison."

A few days later, after Chloe's tender reconstruction of his damaged body, Henry Sanburg, along with the similarly repaired Cedric Jennison, was found at the latter's South Houston address. The two had engaged in a fierce battle that neither survived, but the escaped death row inmate had forced a written confession out of Jennison before they had fought.

The experiment was confirmed; the real killer answered to the justice of the Omega Corps.

CHAPTER 14

In the following months the Omega Corps grew rapidly. Steele flew all over the world, discovering, studying and judging variant after variant. The select few were shipped to Montana, where they were activated, trained and set to work. He found thousands, everywhere; but he chose only the strongest, those with the greatest potential, and most who already had higher education or experience in some useful subject. Telepaths, transmutators, teleporters, clairvoyants, eidetics, telekinetics, spectralists, sports and variations, all had their part in the growing organization.

Included in the basic training was a boot camp developed by Carter Long, a telekinetic transitioned Marine instructor aptly code-named Badger. Orion, Alpha and Cobra all contributed their expertise to the program designed to include not only mental and physical training but instruction in combining their variant talents into teamwork.

Everyone from Orion on down took the grueling ten-week course, with quite a number, Lorraine and Brenda among them, receiving additional weeks of conditioning drills needed to meet Badger's merciless Marine standards.

In the end, every Corpsman regardless of

occupation had the same confidence, discipline, combat readiness and team spirit glowing in their eyes and bearing. Personality conflicts were inevitable, of course, but the mutual respect and support that bound them together was unquestionable.

Even during training, the recruits were put to work in their chosen specialties. So crowded and busy did the ranch become that Steele and the Ansons, with Denny Connors' mechanical skill and the help of the trainees, collaborated to devise a domed shield to project a holographic image of a tranquil hobby ranch. From the air it depicted the plowing and sowing of a largish truck garden and the wanderings of farm animals, including the three horses cropping the pastures and being ridden by the homesteaders.

Beneath the dome, concealed from the casual sight of aircraft and satellites, grew workshops, training fields, and a barracks for the dozens of recently activated Corpsmen. Still, the traffic in and out of the complex was too heavy to hide all the activity with any great success, so the search for a less conspicuous headquarters pressed forward.

A suitable building was found in due time. Pavel, with Ginger and Chelsea in his team, found a huge mixed purpose high-rise in St. Louis, with plenty of room above and unobstructed, geologically stable bedrock below. Old tenants were found new homes, well-screened shopkeepers were installed on the street level to make things look normal, and a large portion of the Omega Corps moved in above.

To the delight of the locals, the crime rate in the historically tough city started to drop, which in turn reduced the vigilance of law enforcement and gave the international cast of the Corps more freedom of movement.

Below ground, the bedrock was transmuted to far more dense tungsten and steel, and the resulting heavily armored and shielded subterranean levels became offices, laboratories, clean rooms, studios and machine shops far in advance of any other facilities on the planet. So extensive was the excavation that all their power needs were met by geothermal energy, bypassing what would have been an enormously conspicuous drain on the city's facilities.

Meanwhile the members of the Corps infiltrated far and wide, appropriating heretofore dirty money and purchasing the most advanced machine tools and mechanical components available – and some that were not available.

As they had expected, the computer had to be built from the ground up. The Confederation's approach was rooted in microwave-based quantum technology, made possible by the brilliant nanoscience of the Squn, a small species that looked a bit like wingless bats.

The wizards of the Corps added their own dazzling wrinkle, using microscopic plasma cells to focus the motion of the microwave pulses carrying the quantum code. The result was an almost intuitive cyber-mechanical processor carrying data at near light speed.

Besides being smarter, faster and far more capacious than any computer before it, the plasma-based linkage made possible the fulfillment of Steele's fervent wish, the input-output educator meshcap. Jander, Jake, Max Elser, and others pooled their genius to create a pliable helmet similar to the activator, which could be used by any activated variant to converse mind to machine with the mother mechentity, fondly if irreverently dubbed "Putie".

Even Steele, despite his impenetrable mind shield, was able to link in with a conscious effort, proving the fundamental difference between organic telepathic contact and the helmet's cybernetic transference.

When the computer and the I/O feeder were ready the spies of the Corps penetrated everywhere, searching for the most advanced ideas and devices developed by anyone on the planet. A sojourn to a secret lab, a sitting with the brain-picking meshcap, and Putie was a bit more wise.

EARS ALERT TO THE SLIGHTEST SOUND, the huge gray wolf crept forward along the wood-chip-covered walkway between fragrant gardens. Intelligent eyes and sensitive nose searched every step along the night-darkened pathway, the only sound of the beast's progress the occasional scrape of cautious claws marking the path.

Walter Rosenberg, metamorph, was nervous and

wary. He was in a minefield.

Behind him at the edge of the forest, two human figures watched him anxiously through night-vision goggles. Tsin Li-san, a telepath from Lanzhou in central China, had been unable to locate the brain holding the key to the minefield layout. Since a teleporter could have landed them right on top of one Walter was called in, so that the Chinese and his Italian companion could reach the hidden lab and pick its brains both human and mechanical.

Geraldo Belocci was the computopath of the team. He had already used his tablet to create interference with the electronics operating the security surveillance, so they were vulnerable only to physical threats.

Walter paused under the cover of a small stand of fernleaf bamboo, turned and wagged his tail twice. The two human-form Corpsmen crept up to him, carefully avoiding Walter's scratch marks. They settled down next to the wolf, their foreheads beaded with sweat in the cool autumn air.

The bushes rustled, and the German's human voice whispered, "That was the easy part. The whole area in front of us is alive with mines."

"Can we get through it?" Belocci had been activated quite recently and still had reservations about variant skills.

"I've done this sort of thing before," Walter assured him. "The explosive the Chinese use is pretty distinctive – to me, at least. I can smell it meters away." His body contorted and he again stood on four legs, canine senses alert. Long gone was the superstitious, timid shopkeeper of so many months before. Doppelwulf of the Corps had become a seasoned and capable team leader.

With utmost caution the three skulked forward, the wolf in the lead. Jerking abruptly, Tsin hissed a warning. The group froze as the crunch of boots grew behind him. The Chinese gestured reassuringly, and before long the sound faded. <*"Routine patrol, outside the minefield,"*> he telepathed. <*"They missed our tracks."*> They went on toward the dimly lit building ahead.

"Here," Belocci whispered aloud. "The computer is right under us."

"But the people are farther ahead," Tsin answered in kind. "Too far to unscramble from each other."

Wolf became man. "We split up, then. I'll lead Tsin further in."

The Italian sat in the moon shadow of a tall clump of ferns and closed his eyes. Man and wolf moved away and were soon lost to the darkness.

Tsin placed his hand on the animal's back. They exchanged long looks, and Walter sat, nose and ears on guard. Tsin, eyes half-closed in concentration, lips moving to unheard words, swayed to the rhythm of his erstwhile countrymen's thoughts. After a while he sighed, patted the head of the beast beside him (Walter never did grow to like that), and they started back.

Suddenly Li-san tensed, gasping. Damning himself for his necessary preoccupation, he sent, <*"Geraldo's been spotted. He's sitting right in the middle of the garden like Buddha. I was too busy to notice the guard."*>

<*"Link with me."*> The man-wolf studied the situation, then trotted to the left, nose questing a safe path. Tsin shot a thought to the computopath, telling him to set up a diversion.

Outwardly calm but squirming inside, the young Corpsman started swaying back and forth. Now that he knew where to look he could see the guard behind a tree, weapon ready but not quite pointed, peering at him in scowling curiosity. In the dim light the Italian's dark hair and complexion served to camouflage him as Asian.

Still swaying, Belocci riveted the soldier's attention while a low, dark shadow crept closer and ever closer. When he was six meters away, Rosenberg charged.

The guard caught the movement and spun around, but he had no time to react. The powerful beast slammed into him, taking his breath away and hurling him backward. His head and shoulders collided with the tree and he collapsed, out cold.

Geraldo rose and started forward, but was stopped by a low growl. The recollection of where he was sent new shivers down his spine. Keeping carefully to the cleared way, he eased himself out of the minefield. Tsin and the wolf met him at the edge, and they ran through the night toward their rendezvous with a teleporter.

THE EXCAVATION IN JAKE'S west pasture gaped under the energy dome that shimmered with the forces that hid their activities. Among them was a feat of stunning mental strength. The huge slab of bedrock cut from the depths by Jander's mentally created forcefields was forty meters by twenty, and half a meter thick.

Jander, hovering in the air beside it, raised it up from the deep by force of will alone. He needed every bit of his concentration to lift what was by far the heaviest and most awkward object he had ever tried to move, and it taxed him to the limits of his ever-growing command.

He suspended the eight hundred tons of rock with a multiplex forcefield that supported the weight by shifting the spacial geometry beneath the slab. By generating a superconductive energy force around its edges, he maneuvered it against the pressures of gravity, mass and the gusting June winds for more than a thousand meters to its destination. He guided it to the precisely leveled depression dug into the rocky soil and lowered the slab into its new home, exactly on the mark.

As it crunched home he relaxed his forcefields, and was rewarded with no further shifting. It was now a solid foundation for the three-story classroom and training facility that would be clad in rock from the same underground source. He waved to his cheering support team and wafted himself skyward, looking for a place to catch his breath.

He alighted on the galvanized steel roof of the ranch's gambrel barn and made a seat by straddling the crest. As his mind rolled over his most recent feat of magic searching for improvements, his eyes took in the busy scene around him.

The enormous pit started two hundred meters beyond the open-air garage across from the ranch house and extended another three hundred meters toward the forest, in an oval that was almost four hundred meters across. He watched a pair of telekinetics fly out of the depths, each of them suspending a ton of pulverized rock destined to be blended with the compost of last year's autumn to form new topsoil throughout the woods. Finding places to put the excavated rock had been a constant challenge, but that phase of construction was winding down as the underground hangar neared its design dimensions.

Some of its machine shops and foundries were already operating, turning out girders and plates of the immensely strong alloy called nanosteel developed by the planet Nokilo. The planet's jet-black denizens with two hundred degree body temperature were the premier metallurgists of the Confederation. The dense, non-conductive alloy they pioneered would form the one hundred fifty-meter spherical shell of the first starship of Gaea.

The physicist Jander, along with engineers Arden

and Denny and many others, had decided on the spherical shape in expectation of developing a gravity drive manifesting the superconductive energy fields he had just employed.

All the known spacefaring species within and without the Confederation used the nucleonic method of bombarding heavy metals with stellar power and blasting it out as a volatile soup through massive stern engines, which limited the size and shape of the ships by balancing the mass of the fuel against the energy needed to propel them.

But since the Corps ship would be using its accumulated power directly to push against its own mass, a sphere would better provide the stability to make the geometry of the push more uniform.

The great advantage was that the ship would have motivators pointing in all directions rather than straight aft. Changing course would not require turning the entire ship.

The drawback was that they could conceive of no possible way to build a solid sphere that could mount all the motive engines, stellar energy collectors, weaponry, defensive generators, sensor accumulators, and other trappings needed to make the ship function.

The solution was to build a sphere with twenty identically equipped hull sections built of convex panels that would bulge toward the spherical shape. The hundreds of mechanical accessories would be sandwiched between those thousands of thick nanosteel panels.

All of that would take a colossal assembly area, which was presently a big hole in the ground.

Jander heard a light thump and scraping behind him, followed by a breathy voice. "Whoa, baby!"

He looked back to see Richard standing wide-legged with his back to a cupola. "Hey, guy. Still got a problem with heights?"

"Yo, I don't apologize for bein' a ground animal." Richard crouched and inched forward, extending a bottle of water in his right hand. "I caught your act from the kitchen window and thought you might need this."

"You're not wrong." Jander took the bottle and popped open the flip cap. "You didn't have to bring it up here, though." He took a long pull.

"Well, Max is lookin' for you. Something to do with Monty's quantum matrix." Monty was to be Putie's opposite number at the ranch, housed deep beneath the barn in a heavily protected vault. "He says the nanowave ion trap isn't up to par yet, and he thinks you might be able to reinforce the shielding enough for the electronics to kick in and block the external noise."

Jander swished water around his mouth, swallowed and nodded. "I had to do that with Putie, too. I thought we had that licked by now, though. I don't want the whole operation to be dependent on me." He watched an eighteen wheeler emerge from the forest entrance to the ranch and turn onto the road toward the pit. "We have that new guy, Feliks Radschck, who I know is a topnotch electronics expert. Let's see what he can do with it."

Richard nodded. "I know Feliks. He's on another project that I'm a part of, but I figure Max can prob'ly steal him for a day or two." The Corps now had one hundred seventy-three members, half working or training in Montana and half operating under Jake's command in St. Louis.

"Good. I need to zip up to Vancouver and look at another mechanical engineer. If I can recruit him it'll take some of the burden off Denny."

"Yeah, I guess that is your first job. Okay, I'll hunt down Radschck and bring him to Max."

"Thanks, bro. I appreciate you doing all this." He drained the bottle and handed it back.

Richard shrugged. "Glad to help. Gotta do something 'til my education catches up." He waved a hand in farewell, rose cautiously on the high roof and vanished.

Jander took a last look around, then wafted into the air and headed west.

THE LETTERING ON THE DOOR alleged real estate; intelligence indicated the funding of insolvent borrowers at ten percent interest per week, payable in flesh or in favors as required. The office was deserted, faintly illuminated by light from the hall outside the milky glass entrance.

Two silent shadows, one tiny, the other huge, climbed the glass to block out the light. The small one became fainter, and suddenly it was within the office. Chelsea Winschell solidified and unlocked the door for Denver Connors.

"You make a good thief." Denny grinned.

Chelsea stuck her tongue out at him and looked around. "So where's the bloomin' safe?"

"Over on that flowerin' wall. You'll have to fish around for the ledger book."

She walked through him, the top of her head barely reaching his ribcage. Two shadows, one set of footsteps, advanced to where an oversized oil painting of the New York skyline was mounted flat to the wall. Chelsea squinted, focusing her fixed-reference clairvoyance, then stuck an arm into the painting and brought out three thick sheaves of paper. "Money?"

"We can use it." Denny riffled the deep stack and stuck it into a pocket. "One less scalp for the loan sharks."

"Your metaphors are —"

The light snapped on. The two whirled to a door leading to a back office, to see a dark, well-dressed man with one hand on the switch. The other held an automatic.

"What you doin' here?" He trained his gun on the obvious threat. He tried a sneer to cover his feelings about one so large, and growled, "This here's a private office, and you'se trespassin'. Gimme one good reason I shouldn't put you down like a dog."

"Oh, no, please don't hurt him!" Chelsea, the very picture of fearful young girlhood, rushed toward the gunman with open arms and a frightened expression.

The thug contemptuously raised his empty hand to shove her out of the way.

Chelsea kept right on coming. She stopped when his arm was halfway through her body, waited for the expected change of expression, and calmly said, "Boo." And leaped!

Shrieking wildly, the little ghost whipped up and around the terrified gunman, flashing over and through him, now and then gaining substance to slap and scratch at his face. Connors stood grinning as he watched, marveling at her speed and ingenuity.

The thug was much less appreciative. He loosed an impossibly high scream and folded, jerking violently in an effort to land a blow against his tormentor. In no time he was reduced to a gibbering, whimpering husk of frazzled nerves, incapable of pulling a trigger or even pointing a gun.

Denny ambled over to him, picked him up with one massive paw and underhanded him toward a window a dozen feet away. The gunman did not even scream as he and the shattered glass plummeted eleven stories to the alley below.

Chelsea stuck her head out of the painting. "Is it 'safe' to come out?"

"Witch. While you're in there, grab that ledger book. We gotta scram."

"Hmph. See if I accept a date with you again."

SERGEANT ARMSTRONG SLEPT SOUNDLY in his quarters, while Sergeant Armstrong tended to his duty at the radar installation. The bogus sergeant watched his screens and dials carefully, adjusting the controls to vary the sensitivity. His mind was wide open as he observed the strange ghosts flickering through the monitors.

Far above, Steele read Wade Gayland's mind and altered his personal screen accordingly, searching for that pattern of force that would be most efficient and economical at blocking the radar's sophisticated sight. Satisfied, he swooped toward the ground and into the building through a skylight he jimmied open with a thought, and tapped the Mimic on the shoulder. "Let's go," he muttered.

Used as he was to variant antics, Wade still jumped at the disembodied touch. He held out his hand and felt it taken, then he was inside Jander's screen and shared its protection. The interference that had blurred the surveillance cameras cleared up as mysteriously as it had begun. The pair flew out of the camouflaged military base and headed south.

"I assume you got what you wanted," Wade said.

"Uh-huh. I'll pound it into Putie and we'll wind up with a stronger anti-detection screen."

"Can you do that with all your powers?"

"Let's call them talents, okay? I hope so — antigravity for the ship, weapons systems, improvements on defensive screens, will come out of my force projection. But that's still in the future. Right now, I want to be able to move forward with construction in Montana without sending satellites and radar into a tizzy. The Confederation's limited stealth capacity is so integrated with their deflector shields it's useless for planetary purposes. And the stopgap stuff Jake and I came up with out of thin air is pretty porous."

"Pun intended, I presume. So when do we start on the ship?"

"The underground hangar is almost completed, and the shield we'll develop from tonight's fun and games will hide the sight, sound and radiation of our development and testing nicely. The ship's outer hull and a lot of the interior can be done right away, but I'm far from satisfied with the technical aspects of the drive. When we go out there I want us to be the meanest mama in space."

"Why? Why do you want to go out there?"

Jander shrugged and looked up at the night sky toward his namesake constellation. "Because it's there…"

Wade snorted through a nose that was already reverting to his own. "That's it?"

"Not quite." He still gazed upward, his inner sight going beyond the visible stars. "Nietzsche wrote, 'when you look into the abyss, the abyss also looks into you'. Out of context to the subject, maybe, but the vastness of the universe makes it appropriate.

It's not just... there, I guess, not just a destination. It's calling me. I belong up there. I, we, can make a difference, up there."

Wade followed his stare, his own eyes taking on the same faraway look. After a while he said, "Save me a seat."

THE WORKSHOP NINETY FEET below the streets of St. Louis was packed with machine tools, work benches and all manner of building materials from sheet metal to electronics, all of them idle for the first time in weeks. The room was deserted but for the small team of Corpsmen standing before a pair of elevator-sized booths covered on three sides, roof and floor with a latticework of exposed circuitry designed to generate and channel an entirely new approach to quantum entanglement.

Richard Ford switched his attention from one booth to the other in a steady rhythm, his hands alternating between rubbing his ripped biceps and running over his well-defined abs. His weight training regimen was transforming his soft cab driver's body into a solidly sculptured work of art, which in turn was increasing his stamina, range and confidence. "You sure this thing'll work?"

"It has worked," Arden Anson assured him. "We've tried it on all kinds of inert matter, then with plants, a few crickets and cockroaches, two turtles, a rat and a good-sized dog. All of them came through with minds and molecules unchanged."

"Or so it seems," Terry Kirkland said. "We have no way of anticipating any secondary long-term effects, and we certainly can't know what it will do with an intelligent mind, much less an activated one."

"But Sharon Gibson has told us the animal brains suffered no ill effects," Feliks Radschck put in, "and the huskie is a pretty intelligent dog. I think we're ready to flip the switch."

"Of course you do," psychologist Phyllis Rydell retorted. "You helped build it. Me, I'll believe it when I see Richard survive it."

Ford stared wide eyed at her. "Well, thanks a lot!"

Arden laughed in his high tenor, which helped Richard's mood not one bit. "Hey, pal, I truly believe it'll work, and it's my design – with a hell of a lot of help, of course – but I was a teleporter long before you were, and I trust it."

"Then you test it!"

"No," Feliks said firmly. "If something goes wrong, Arden might be your lifeline. If you honestly don't want to try it, I'll go."

"But we need a teleporter for this," Phyllis objected. "That's the only comparative control we have." She reached out a pale hand to touch Ford's arm. "And Richard, I apologize for my poor choice of words. I wouldn't have okayed this if I thought there was even a marginal risk. And you can bet Vickie and Jander would have killed the project before it started if they thought you'd be facing any hazard at all. Feliks and I will be in full rapport with you, with Terry and Arden, when we go."

"So five brains get fried instead of one. That makes me feel a whole lot better." Richard paced nervously between the two booths, peering into each of them with exaggerated care.

"What are you doing?" Arden asked.

"Lookin' for flies."

The Americans burst into laughter, followed by the Polish Radschck when Rydell flashed the movie reference into his mind.

"That can't happen," Arden assured him. "We both know teleportation doesn't work that way. Believe me, we're good to go."

Richard, nerve restored by his own sense of humor, closed his eyes with a sigh, then turned to the man who had taught him how to teleport. "Okay, let's do it." He moved toward the booth on the left and stepped in.

Arden turned to Phyllis and tapped his temple. She linked minds with the telepathic Feliks, then the two of them opened the channel to Arden. Terry was next to join, and when the four of them were in full rapport, Phyllis led the gestalt into Richard's mind.

The teleporter drew them in, gratefully reaching for the calm assurance of Phyllis, the sincere comfort of Terry, the staunch confidence of Feliks, and the strong and abiding camaraderie of Arden. Their five minds now one, Richard was ready.

He reached for the front corner of the booth and

pressed a button, then stepped to the center. Two seconds later an instant of flickering created a short-lived aura around his form, and he was in the other booth.

Arden gasped and Feliks inhaled sharply, but the combined mentality of the five Corpsmen remained meshed. Terry immediately started a systematic search of Richard's physical nervous system as Phyllis did the same to his thought processes.

Feliks and Arden concentrated on tracing the quantum entanglement impulses that had raced through Richard's entire being, along with his clothing and the carefully chosen items in his pockets. Richard himself did everything he could to make the examination thorough, searching his own mind for the sensations of the trip and its effects on his consciousness.

Arden whooped and spun in a full pirouette, fist punching the air. "It worked!"

Phyllis smiled much more sedately. "So it would seem." Terry, still searching Richard's physiology, nodded agreement.

Richard leaned his shoulders on the back wall of the booth and threw his head back in relief. "Yeah," he said softly. "Yeah, it did. A touch slower, just a touch, and with a little kick in the back of the head, but nothing anybody can't handle."

"Yes, that tiny delay raised activity in the brain stem," Phyllis agreed. "It's kind of like you feel when you teleport to the far edge of your range. We'll have to see if that increases with distance."

"Right," Arden said, sobering as he followed the implications. "If it gets worse with distance, we could have a problem. But we did prove the theory."

Feliks grinned and slapped his boss on the back. "We did indeed. Ladies and gentlemen, we have an electronic teleporter."

"THIS IS TOUGHER THAN it should be," Denny rumbled. He and Jake, the latter temporarily back at the ranch for his electronics expertise, were sitting at matching keyboards in front of six large wall-mounted monitors in an underground room. The air still had the musty smell of pulverized rock.

The three top monitors displayed three-dimensional images of circuitry enlarged to visible size, flashing with slow-motion streaks of microwave connections. The lower left monitor held row upon row of static quantum code, while the center one held the same code with annotated corrections that changed as the circuitry images on the monitors above it flashed through their contextual relationships. The sixth monitor on the right had an entirely different set of code.

"No, it's just as tough as it was when we started. That's the problem." Jake turned his head toward his big friend, though his eyes never left the changing code on the top center monitor. "We're trying to blend our quantum code − a new field for us, mind you – with two sets of Squn code that has been developed over centuries." The Squns were the foremost nanotechnologists of the Confederation. "Of course it's an imperfect fit. I'm beginning to think we'll have to keep the three technologies separate."

Denny grunted and leaned back, his oversized chair creaking under his ever-increasing weight. "I don't like that idea. Three systems means three times the equipment, three times the power drain and three times the maintenance."

"Well, we already have five times the ship on the drawing board. It's not like we won't have room for it." He tapped a key, and all six monitors froze. "Let's explore it, at least. I don't want to fail this badly without an alternative."

"Well, okay. I don't like to lose either, but even less would I want to let Jander down."

"Likewise. Now, the goal is to get the defensive, stealth and compensator screens all working simultaneously for our spherical ship. So, let's look at the compensator first."

He leaned forward and set his left hand on the speedball that served as a mouse for Putie's extreme sensitivity. Thanks to the quantum entanglement communications system pirated directly from the Confederation, the connection to the supercomputer in St. Louis was instantaneous and unbreachable.

"Okay, here's the compensator." The pair of monitors to the right sprang to life. "The Confederation has, shall we say, 'given' us the spiral warp generators they use to infuse nearby space with a quantum tachyon mass-time compensation field. That not only creates a bubble of normal space at hyperlight speed velocities, but radiates that bubble up to a whopping two million kilometers. Anything within that sphere is influenced into the same relative velocity as the generator source. That allows interactions such as fleet maneuvers and liaisons at hyperlight speeds, and offensive and defensive weapons can be used without losing any of their effectiveness. The sphere is dropped when velocity is reduced enough, which allows approach to relatively static destinations such as planets."

"I'll take your word for it," Denny said. "That code is way the hell out of my basket."

"Same here, but Putie's got a handle on it – and Jander, too, since the new inner sphere is his idea. Now, most ship losses at hyperlight are when that mass-time compensation field generator – let's call it the warp sphere for brevity – fails, and the entire crew becomes a coat of paint between the squished bulkheads from the sudden influence of inertia.

"A ship within the combined sphere of two or more can survive it because the other ships cover it, but we'll be solo for the most part. So, we'll be adding a smaller warp sphere extending just beyond our defensive screens that will flick on if the outer sphere even starts to weaken. And we can use either one at choice."

As he spoke the three-dimensional image on the

upper right screen flickered with the slow-motion passage of energy waves. "Since the inner sphere occupies the same spherical plane, plus a hair, as our defensive screens, we can hide our electronic signature and wander through another ship's sphere undetected outside of six thousand meters, six kilometers. No ship in known space has the energy capacity to generate two spheres, but Jander and Putie calculate we'll have enough accumulators and batteries to do it."

He sat back. "Your turn."

"Right." Under Denny's guidance, the top center monitor came to life. "Here's the multiplex shield that is an advancement of the one that's hiding us here. The one above us prevents our energy transmissions from being detected, and it hides us from view with a hologram. The shield for the ship will be a whole lot more inclusive, not only masking our signature but also preventing penetration by anything that could detect our emissions, from lowly heat to the many forms of hyperlight particles we call tachyons but have a lot of identities to the Confeds. Let's call it the baffle screen for the hell of it. Thanks to Jander – again – we can be completely undetectable any time we want to be."

With a few keystrokes he reduced the size of the circuitry image and materialized a silver-blue sphere beside it. A white line flowed in slow motion from a section of the circuitry to englobe the sphere with a shimmering aura. Other lines of other colors came from different sections of the mechanism to the globe, each of them adding its flame to the aura until the sphere within faded to invisibility, then the aura itself disappeared leaving a blank space on the monitor. "Voilá, we're completely hidden."

"But still vulnerable." It was Jake's turn to reach for his keyboard to activate the left-hand display. "Here we have the tandem defensive shield used by the Confederation. It's impervious to material objects to a high degree, bouncing any projectiles or space rubbish off to the side of their egg-shaped ships. It also deflects energy weapons like their nucleonic cannon blasts – which are basically concentrated pulses of the same energy that propels the ships. But it's limited in strength by the amount of energy their batteries can supply, so in a protracted battle or if they're hit with too many simultaneous blasts, it can fail.

"We can bolster it in a lot of ways, not only because we'll have at least fifty times the battery capacity, but we'll have another manifestation of Jander's power that will expand the frequencies to overlap and reinforce each other.

"Our newest Jander wrinkle is this." He highlighted a section of the display. "This will absorb any energy that hits the shield and deflect anything more deadly than visible light. The visible will be allowed to come through, which our energy accumulators will absorb into the batteries and make us even stronger."

"Which is a hoot and a holler," Denny said, "but

there are two problems. First, it alters the screen so radically we'll have to divorce the collision shield from the energy shield and generate it separately. Second, the modified energy screen does the exact opposite of the baffle screen, absorbing instead of deflecting. They cancel each other out and either make us detectable if we use the deflector, or a lot more vulnerable if we use the baffle. The recipes are too different to cook in the same casserole."

Jake nodded. "And then we add the inner spiral warp sphere just beyond the same diameter from the ship. The warp bubble conflicts with the defensive and baffle screens because it's an infusion globe rather than a horizon." He waved a hand to encompass the entire array before them. "Trying to combine all this into one technology, even with qubit polarization, is way beyond even Putie's reckoning."

"That's it, in a nutshell. So here we are, breaking our heads over how we can blend the four technologies, when in practice we simply can't."

They stared at each other for a long moment, each looking for ideas in the other's eyes, then Denny shrugged and broke away. "Well, if we can't, we can't. We've got enough so our gang can develop them in parallel, so let's clean up this kitchen and move on. We've got a helluva tight schedule to keep."

Jake sighed in resignation. "I agree. Let's package it for Jander so I can get back to St. Louis." He grinned. "After lunch. You've definitely got food on your mind!"

THE MONTANA AIR WAS CLEAN and cool, perfect for working out in the athletic fields. Denny had taken a bit of time off from his various duties and was concentrating on juggling four sixteen-pound shot while Vickie, astride a palomino mare named Honey Bucket, held him precisely eight feet, three inches from the ground.

Behind her in the distance were the huge ranch, the barracks, the new building under construction, several training fields, and the deep excavation for the underground hangar with blocks of bedrock floating up and out of it. Dozens of people, some of them floating through the air, moved about at purposeful speed.

The hunter who happened upon this astounding sight gaped slack-jawed and terrified from the cover of a tree. Dropping his rifle, he turned and ran.

Vickie heard the scatter of sound and turned in her saddle and caught sight of the intruder. She grimaced, wondering how their security sensor screen had failed to detect him the instant he had penetrated the perimeter. Irritated, she dropped the titan who had installed it with a deliberate ground-shaking thud, engendering a guttural grunt as one of the iron balls landed on his foot.

"Stop!" Vickie shouted.

Something clicked in her brain, and the hunter halted dead in his tracks.

Surprised at herself, Vickie sent a command through her brand new mental door. <*"Come here."*>

Denny, who had felt the backlash of that order, straightened his huge form and watched in awe as the hunter turned and staggered flat-footed toward her, terror in every line of his face.

<*"Be calm,"*> she directed him. <*"You will not be harmed or changed in any way, but you must recognize that this is not a place you may trespass."*>

With the coherent thoughts went a soothing flood of empathy, reaching the hunter on an emotional level she never before had tried to influence. His face cleared, and he waited impassively to do her bidding.

She leaned across the horse's neck and drove the commands deep beneath his conscious mind. <*"When I release you, you will walk away with your rifle and retrace your steps to the fence. When you cross the fence, you will forget what you have seen and experienced here. And you will forget the sensations of my mental contact. Should you ever look this way again, when you see our fencing you will obey the warning signs and you will not trespass. Go!"*>

The hunter turned and stumbled away, picked up his rifle and disappeared into the woods without looking back. Vickie probed his mind as he walked away, without finding the slightest psychological hint of what had just taken place.

"Well, I'll... be... jiggered..." Denny rumbled.

Vickie pursed her lips as she patted the neck of the sidestepping mare. She remembered what Jander had told her months before: *"There is something in your brain that I haven't figured out yet. It has to do with telepathy, but of a different order, and immensely powerful."* Now she knew what it was: mental projection, telehypnosis.

All she said was, "I wish I'd had it in London..."

CHAPTER 15

It was one year from the day that Brenda Anson had given name to the Omega Corps, and the two hundred twenty-one members gathered in the St. Louis headquarters to celebrate the occasion. The spacious meeting hall was an amazing hodgepodge of ghosts and werewolves and witches, flying genii and disappearing phantoms. Even Steele's cat, who had tortied her way to becoming the unofficial mascot of the Corps, was seen engaged in flirty conversation with a zootelepath.

Jander, with Victoria on his arm, strode into the room and took his place at the podium. Vickie joined the other members of the high command seated at tables on the low stage behind him. Jake was there, along with Arden, Terry and Denny; and Pavel, who looked and felt terrific since Terry's crack medical team had transmuted several decades off his age. The cellular regeneration restored not only his youth but the lightning reflexes he had lacked in London. No one with the sense of a turnip would now dare to challenge the cross draw of the Cobra.

One by one the other Corpsmen spotted Jander on the low stage and walked or trotted or flew or teleported to tables in the vast hall. Steele held up his hand for silence.

"Ladies and gentlemen, and whatever else you may be at the moment..." he paused for the inevitable laugh, "We are here tonight for three reasons: one, to celebrate the anniversary of the conception of the Omega Corps; two, to make that concept official..." he was interrupted by cheers, "...and three, to plan for the future, specifically to announce the start of construction of our faster-than-light spacecraft."

Hushed whispers hissed through the room, then the shouts and cheers began. While all were aware of the construction in Montana, that they were so far along with the planning was news to all but the central cadre of the Corps. Not because of mistrust – Steele knew every mind in the room clear to the soul – but because their proof of concept had only recently come to full fruit. After months of research, Putie and the geniuses that fed her at last had the information to suggest an approach.

The uproar died down to murmurs, and Jander continued. "If you agree, the first two reasons can wait, and I will tell you about our plans for Gaea's first journey to the stars..."

Again he was interrupted by applause. He waited them out, then went on.

"The schematics for the general outline of our starship are already complete, and as you know we've close to completing the construction of the hangar in Montana. The ship we'll be building will bear no resemblance to the egg shape favored by the Confederation."

He turned and nodded to Arden, who tapped the keys of his laptop. A graphic image of the new ship ballooned onto a huge 3-D plasma screen at the back of the stage.

"The shape will be a sphere with a total of twenty hull sections. Each of the six square equatorial sections will meet with an adjacent quadrangle at the tropical lines, and each of those will taper to the hexagonal poles. All of them will be formed from convex nanosteel plates to make the hull bulge more toward the spherical shape. The ship will look like a gigantic faceted jewel, one hundred fifty meters in greatest diameter and not quite that from pole to pole."

More murmurs escaped the audience. The spheroid would be many times the volume of Nil Spart's *Kaltim*.

Jander let them resettle, then continued, "The reason for this diversion from accepted galactic design is the method of propulsion we'll be using. The spacefaring species we know of use a nucleonic method of bombarding heavy metals with stellar energy and blasting it out as near-solid force. But with a combination of Gaean and Confederation technology, and with the mechanical manifestation of some of our own abilities, we hope to develop a practical method of harnessing the superconductive energy needed to produce gravitic propulsion."

Murmurs started through the assembly. He caught the thoughts of some of the more scientific minds in the crowd. Gravity in itself was weak relative to the other dynamic forces in the universe, yet energy generated between superconductive plates exerted the most variable effect on any mass that produced it. How could it be harnessed as a motive force?

"It will be the most difficult, perhaps impossible, part of the construction," Jander agreed with their thoughts. "We've got many weeks and months of work ahead, and even that might not be enough. Still, the potential is too great to ignore. If our theories hold up, we might be able to travel through space at a constant acceleration of ten gravities per second squared or more – speed of light in half an hour."

That was almost too much for finite, even variant, minds to comprehend. The gallery sat stunned, grappling with the concept of almost unlimited speed. When he could see in their minds that they were succeeding, Jander went on.

"We've developed our own version of the spiral warp generators that infuse nearby space with a mass-time compensation field. That allows us to achieve hyperlight velocities. Now, the infusion field creates a bubble in space where the normal physics of dark matter don't always apply, particularly regarding the inertia created by velocity. If the separate inertia compensation generators within the ship fail, that inertia crumples the ship like a car in a compactor. We'll have a redundancy of inertia compensators to keep that from happening.

"Most ship losses at hyperlight are when the mass-time compensation field – we call it the warp sphere – fails, which throws the ship back into normal space at hyperlight speed. No one knows what happens then since no results of such a failure has ever been found. The theory is that it creates a brief black hole, so you can imagine it must be quite an adventure."

That brought a brief nervous laugh.

"Now, a ship in convoy is within the combined sphere of all the others and is protected, so they survive just fine. But since we'll be out there on our own with no other ships to cover us, we'll be adding a smaller warp sphere extending the same diameter as our defensive screens that will flick on if the outer compensator sphere weakens. And since it occupies about the same spherical plane as our defensive screens, we can use it to move through another ship's sphere undetected – more on that in a moment. No other ship in known space has the energy capacity to pull that off.

"We're pirating the Confederation internal gravity converters, also. The principles involved are entirely different from those of a superconductive gravity drive, which is why they don't have the drive. Those compensators are built into the internal surfaces of the ship to allow any enclosed space to have what-ever internal gravity we code into it.

"Let's return to the shape of the ship. Arden, if

you would, please..."

The view on the screen zoomed to one of the hull panels. "Each quarter of each of the twenty hull sections will support a gravity drive cone with its meters-long tail pointed toward the center of the ship. In effect, each engine pushes against the mass of the ship itself. Therefore, while the concentration of six cones on each of the pole sections gives more boost toward the 'up' and 'down' directions, the presence of four drive cones on every section allows for superior maneuverability. Vocalize, key in or even think a directional command depending on the control medium you're using, and the ship's flight path can be changed without having to turn the entire ship."

The image on the screen zoomed back out and simulated a series of dizzying maneuvers. "This is still theoretical, of course. Development is a long way off.

"Our power supply will be modeled after the Confederation's method of solar accumulation, but modified to accept wave radiation from any source. This means that if an adversary tries to zap us with some kind of ray, including anything akin to the Confederation's nucleonic blast cannon, we will be deflecting the force of the attack but gathering the visible frequencies as useable energy. Any opponent, instead of damaging us, will be feeding us instead!"

Someone in the audience hooted with delight, drawing cheers and laughter from the rest. Using the enemy's strength against them – that was something they could understand!

Steele held up his hands. "But of course, any fueling system has its limitations. Even though our supercapacitor battery banks will be able to store enough energy to power a planet, you can only push so much water through a fire hose before it bursts. So, concurrent with the accumulator screen will be a much stronger defensive shield, again based on the wave refraction and molecular cohesion shields the Confederation uses but enhanced by certain forces I am able to generate mentally. Anything the accumulators can't absorb, including natural radiation such as gamma or photon that would otherwise fry us in short order, will be deflected by the spherical defensive shield and diverted harmlessly off to the side.

"A parallel shield will be proof against everything physical, from rocks to explosives to kinetic projectiles. We're going to be the toughest nut to crack in the known galaxy!" That was greeted with more applause.

He nodded again at Arden, who threw up the color-coded graphic of the screen system that he, Jake, and Denny had sweated over for weeks.

"Just beyond the accumulator and defensive screens, and on the same horizon as the inner warp sphere I described earlier, will be a third, multiplex shield with properties entirely unlike anything known to Confederation science. Built into this one shield will be several functions derived from variant talents. Among them are applications to make the entire ship invisible to any kind of wave sensors, from radar to line of sight to x-rays to hyperlight quantum particle sensors. It will also refract any sensory probe that would detect our own defensive screens or the inner warp sphere. It gobbles up a tremendous amount of power, but we will be undetectable whenever we wish, without interfering with either accumulation or defense. We've been calling it the baffle screen for lack of anything better."

That brought another round of applause. As it died away Jander waved another gesture to the engineer, and a new schematic popped up on the screen.

"Our primary offensive weapons will also be based on my power of molecular cohesion. On each hull section will be four housings for forcefield projectors – six on each of the hexagonal poles. Half of these will be of a pulse type, which will spew out solid spheres of coherent energy even stronger than the kinetic defensive screen, accelerated and rifled like a rail gun through the nonconductive nanosteel barrels. These will be swivel mounted when run out for action to facilitate aiming over an overlapping range, so every point of the galactic compass will be covered.

"Since the spheres are basically 'fire and forget' projectiles they will eventually lose cohesion, but until they do they will be able to punch through any barrier, matter or energy. The diameter of the spheres will be something short of two meters and the half-life range will probably be six or eight hundred thousand kilometers.

"The other primary weapon will be a beam projector, which will send out a hollow cylinder of force that can be directed at will, like a quarterstaff. Range and diameter, about half that of the pulse cannon, but as they are directed rather than fire and forget they'll be more versatile. We might even be able to rocket a kinetic mass through them like a cannon barrel, but that's kind of like a finger flick after a haymaker."

"Oh, the best range of the Confederation's nucleonic blast cannon is eighty thousand kilometers, or about one eighth of ours. Their armament is in the form of bolts of nucleonic energy far more concentrated than their drive. That amounts to half a kiloton of explosive force but doesn't have the penetrating power of our weaponry.

"But enough about me," he grinned, and took a pause to let the laughter pass. "As you all know, many times I have called in one or several of you to perform for me, so I could analyze your powers. The results are theories wildly different from any science known throughout the galaxy, giving rise to a bewildering variety of what can generously be described as gadgets. Here's a rundown of what all of you have contributed:

"Teleporters: You've already given us the telebooth for quick transport. Step into a booth, punch a few buttons and zap, you arrive in a receiving booth at your chosen destination. We already have quite a few telebooths and larger telepads in use both here in Headquarters and in Montana, and before long we'll have quick access to anywhere on Gaea.

"As for the ship, more powerful telepads with open destination controls will be used to transport crew and cargo to coordinates as far as twenty thousand kilometers. To return, just key a code into the keypad on your wrist to wake up the 'porter that sent you, and you're right back where you started. Let's give our resident hopheads a round of applause!"

When the crowd subsided again: "Now from all you mental types, the radiopaths, computopaths... The Confederation, and independently, some species outside the Confederation, have developed two methods of hyperlight communications. The first is quantum entanglement, where variable quantum particles can be made to exist in two different places. That's long-range, point-to-point communications with no time lag. The second method is a tachyon broadcast, a slower and less secure method of communications that allows modulation of faster than light particles. Compare them to cell phone versus radio. Now, we have yet to figure out any way to intercept entanglement, but a quantum manifestation of variant talents has helped help us translate any of the radio, microwave or quantum particle supra-light messages, coded or otherwise, that we might intercept. We'll be the most well-informed ship in space!"

More applause.

"Clairvoyants: Our quantum capture sensor equipment, though for the most part copied straight from the Confederation, will be enhanced with variable point of reference extrapolation that will give us a far better picture of what's beyond our warp sphere. Actually, that will be our only view of the universe – no windows are possible because it's been proven by many species that no organic nervous system can perceive the hyperlight environment outside a warp sphere and remain sane.

"Telekinetics: No progress yet with a tractor beam, but by reducing the strength and velocity of the beam projectors we can sure push things. The beam projectors will have controls to reduce their force of impact and allow a variable shove that can be as gentle as we might need. If we can reverse the process, we can make things come to us.

"Telepaths: Along with the I/O helmets we use to talk with Putie and her kin, we now have instrumentalities that can distinguish between normal and variant nervous energy. That gives us the security of building our special equipment with 'signature' sensors, so that they can only be used by variants. Anywhere we go, on Gaea or throughout the galaxy, we will be able to operate with the confidence of knowing that our superior technology will never be used against us."

That got another round of applause. Jander joined them, letting them know he was aware that none of it would have been accomplished without all of them.

"That is our progress so far. Any questions?"

He could not have stirred them up more if he had materialized a giant frog in the center of the room. The most persistent question he could hear was, "Can I go?"

He held up his hands. "The ship will have very comfortable accommodations for a complement of at least three hundred – more, if cabins are shared." He could not resist a glance at Vickie, who smiled and winked. "We won't lack for space, so everyone can have their own place to call home. All of you who want to may go, and plenty more besides."

"What do we do when we get there?"

Jander paused in honest confusion, then chuckled. "Mimic asked me a while back why I wanted to go and all I could think of was 'because it's there'. I may be a little odd, but I'm still human, with a normal human curiosity. I just want to go out and look around. Isn't that enough?"

"Plenty!" The thought was louder than the word.

"Some of you are wondering why, if we're just going to be looking around, we have a ship powerful enough to destroy star systems – literally," he went on. "That is a direct result of what we pulled from Vice Admiral Spart's thoughts and memories – the galaxy is full of nasty people. The Stellar Confederation Fleet is pretty much a police force, and they're having as much trouble as any such force anywhere. Thus, while our numbers will be too small to be threatening, we will operate from a position of overwhelming strength.

"Whether we use that strength as the Omega Corps is doing here on Gaea depends on what we find. How we handle ourselves will always be a series of tough and dangerous decisions. But with so many great minds, especially Alpha and Cobra, as my advisors, I hope to be able – and be trusted – to make those decisions.

"Which brings us all back to the second reason we are here tonight."

He paused and cleared his throat. He could see in their glowing faces that they were expecting more great news, which made what was coming next the toughest thing he had ever had to do. He avoided exposing himself to their thoughts as he took a deep breath and continued.

"Wherever we may go, and whatever may happen to me, I want the Omega Corps to remain a strong and dedicated force for justice on Gaea. Jacob Anson, Binary of the Corps, has already decided to remain here with his wife and soon-to-be son. I have seen in several of your minds the decision to stay. Believe me, that relieves me of a terrible load, the idea that I would be guilty of a breach of faith by leaving – whether the world in general knows it or not.

"I am an adventurer at heart, preparing to embark on the greatest adventure of all. But I can't be two places at once. For me to hold on to my leadership of the Corps would not only be impractical but unfair to all of you. Therefore, it is my decision that the pride and pleasure I have enjoyed as Lord of the Omega Corps may no longer be mine. I propose to hand the torch to Binary, and that you acknowledge him as your lord."

He pushed himself away from the podium with a nod to the stunned Jake, and took a seat next to Vickie She reached for his hand and gripped it with firm reassurance. It had been their decision, not his alone, and they both knew it to be sound.

But no one else, not even the leader-elect, knew of their decision before tonight. And to judge from the hushed murmurs from the audience, no one else had ever imagined it. An Omega Corps without Orion? Impossible!

It was Jake who had the final word. He pulled himself to his feet and found his way to the podium, passing behind Jander without looking. He steadied himself with both hands on the dais and spoke in a breathless but firm voice.

"I want you all to know that I was the first to pledge himself to the service of Lord Orion. I will never retract that, nor will I ever accept any authority above his or Lady Alpha's, including my own. If he wishes to delegate to me the honor of directing our operations here on Gaea, I will proudly and in all humility accept that challenge. But I will never accept his title. In all of space and time, on Gaea or in the farthest corners of the galaxy, there will be only one Lord of the Omega Corps, Jackson Alexander Steele, and only one Lady, Victoria Lee Cunningham." He bowed his head in stubborn resolve.

The crowd began to rumble, then shouts of support rang out. In no time the place was filled with clamor as the assembled variants worked themselves up to near riot emotion. Jander and Vickie stared at them, then at each other, utterly nonplused.

Denver Connors leaped up from his chair, sending it to the stage with a crash. His bull roar of a voice cut through the chaos like a thunderclap. "All, HEEP!"

A powerful mental hammer from Cobra brought the command to every variant in the hall. They stopped whatever they were contributing to the chaos, spun to face the stage and snapped to attention.

Jander and Vickie stared at each other, then rose and stood with them.

Binary stepped away from the podium and faced Alpha and Orion, proud determination in his glittering eyes. Then, in a burst of honest and overwhelming emotion, he went to his knee before them.

CHAPTER 16

Steele pushed back from his console and rubbed tired eyes. So many details! Specialized generators, converters, stress points, compensators, a million and one things to be checked and rechecked. Shoehorned into Putie's vast cybernetic brain were what seemed like gigs and googols and yottabytes of hard code, schematics, diagrams and animations, each one seeming somehow incomplete. For weeks he had been absorbing and studying them, getting more and more frustrated.

He crumpled a printout and pitched it at Cindy, who accepted the offering with a joyous flurry of nimble paws. She, too, had received the gift of renewed youth thanks to transmutation, and it showed in every bright-eyed moment of her pampered life.

Vickie breezed into the office fresh and sprightly. "Hi, god."

"Oh, shut up." That moment at the banquet, when every single Corpsman followed Jake's lead and knelt to them, would live in his mind as the most embarrassing of all time. "You're in this, too, you may recall."

"But I'm only the number two divinity." She twisted through a graceful pirouette that made his heart leap and hooked a thigh onto the corner of his desk. She reached with arched back and poked the old-fashioned laser mouse out of his reach. "Can't you delegate anything?"

"We only have nine eidetics. You need a total memory to handle this mess – besides the education."

"Says who? Alexiy has the navigation down pat – he can get that console to direct him to the pearly gates without half a thought."

"No fair. He can talk to the damned thing." He sighed and reached for that maddening leg. "Maybe you're right. We should take some time off. Let's get married."

"*What??*" She fell off the desk and staggered to her feet.

"I'm serious," he assured her. "I want you to know that I haven't looked beyond the surface of your mind since London, so I don't know if the idea would appeal to you or not. Those thoughts are yours and yours alone, and that's the way it should be."

He stood and spread his arms helplessly, suddenly not at all the confident Orion. "No, that's not quite accurate. I want it that way because if you don't feel as strongly for me, I don't want to know about it. But I can't stand having you around all the time driving me crazy just by being alive. I need to know, and I'm afraid to look. So like any human being, I doubt and I wonder. Do you love me enough to marry me? Knowing we could live a thousand years?"

She faced him, close, not touching. "Jander." Each word, every syllable was a symphony. "Between us

we must never have any doubts. Look now, and see
how I feel. And please, never, ever hesitate to touch
my mind again."

THEY SPENT THEIR WEDDING NIGHT in a luxurious Corps-owned bungalow on the shore of Kauai,
isolated by distance and foliage from any neighbors,
news or communications. The sighing of the breeze
through the sheltering fronds was a soothing back-
drop for the sweet birdsong and whooshing ocean
that filled the warm air.

Jander stretched luxuriously on the sateen sheets
and reached for his bride. "You know what I think?"

"Whatever it is, it'd better not be business."
She levitated her silken hair and tickled his neck.
"Besides, how should I know what you're thinking?"

He chuckled and pulled her to him. "Not exactly
business, no, but it does have to do with the ship.
What's the thing you like best about our Montana
site – or this place, for that matter?"

"Mmmm... the trees, the birds, the natural
things." She snuggled closer, exhilarating to the feel
of skin on skin. "That's the only thing that bothers
me about this business, the thought of being cooped
up in a tin can for months. I'm a country girl."

"My thoughts exactly. So why don't we take the
library, study halls and collections out of the recrea-
tion section, break them up into more topical divi-
sions and scatter them around the ship, and use that

three-level space to carry our own park?"

"Park?" She thought about it. "From a psychological standpoint it would be an ideal addition. A little bit of Gaea to carry with us, where we can relax and feel at home. And it'll contribute to the recycling system. Hmmm... we can add a few wind vents to simulate breezes, diffuse the lighting with mock clouds..."

"And add speakers to simulate bird and insect sounds," he added. "As natural as we can make it without having to worry about varmint control. About nine or ten meters of vertical space, so we can have some decent trees. And gardens, fountains, maybe even a brook..."

Vickie sensed the subtle change in him and poked his ribs. "Worry about the logistics later, god. Right now, just dream about it."

"Call me god again and you'll find yourself six swimming miles from Sri Lanka." He poked her in retaliation, and logistics were forgotten.

DURING THEIR MUCH-NEEDED world tour/vacation/honeymoon, Jander and Vickie took the time to discover, research and recruit more variants. Before long, Montana and St. Louis, and the dozen or so branch offices scattered throughout the globe, were swarming with very strange people. All over the world journalists were becoming more optimistic, pointing out item after item of social advance and wondering why.

Meanwhile the gigantic ship took shape deep beneath the Montana ranch, its bulkheads and decking, passages and infrastructure multiplying as construction pushed it toward the hangar doors above.

An enormous telepad received raw materials from other telebooths and pads hidden near resources around the world. The foundries, labs and workshops deep in the bedrock turned out mechanical and electronic components by the ton, to be assembled within the cavernous interior of the ship and connected with countless kilometers of filament cable.

Arden and Denny, the chief developers, kept a close eye on all of it. Beneath the barn, even deeper underground than the hangar, Putie's younger sister, Monty, kept track of the engineering details while Putie herself housed the theoretical base. Between them, the two mechentities not only databased the entire project but provided the foundation for what would soon be the brain of the ship itself.

Jander, with his eidetic memory and deep knowledge of quantum and mechanical physics, provided the genius that was their fodder. Most of the theoretical conundrums were no match for the combined power of cybernetic certainty and brilliant human intuition.

Vickie took her wifely duties seriously, to such good effect that Jander no longer worked himself to exhaustion day after day. But there came the time when the superconductive gravity propulsion system could no longer be deferred. Steele had put off the confrontation, fearing with no little cause that he would be thwarted. Failure would not only mean serious delay but would force the redesign of the entire ship.

Months went by as telepath-led teams searched for the most innovative theories from Gaea's greatest minds. Weeks were spent as Vickie and a panel of psychologists struggled to dissect the gravitic manipulation that was the essence of telekinesis and levitation. Jake and Max and Feliks and Denny and Arden and a dozen other engineering, electronics and mechanical specialists examined and judged every qubit of accumulated knowledge.

Hours and days passed as half a hundred variants joined through telepaths to brainstorm a line of science no one in the galaxy had ever dared to explore beyond theory.

And during and around and through the massive effort, Jander watched, listened, read and absorbed as much as his prodigious mind could stand.

At last, he sent everyone away and sequestered himself with an I/O meshcap in a shielded St. Louis room, with only Cinnamon and Putie for company. He sat at a desk surrounded by monitors, donned the meshcap to establish firm rapport with the mighty quantum plasma mechentity, and set to work.

Time passed unnoticed as he immersed himself in intense concentration, jetting idea and theories through the feeder at the speed of thought. Again and again he seized on what to him were brilliant and innovative solutions to impossible problems, only to have gaping holes shot in them by Putie's cold impartiality.

But slowly, certainly, the gaps and chasms were filled, and deep within the mechentity's plasma memory grew a massive schematic of such inconceivable complexity that not even the eidetic Jander could envision its full scope. Together they broke it down, shaped it into components, filled in details, hammered at connections, with few breaks and only brief snacks delivered by a silent Richard.

For almost two days they concentrated together, determined human and the tireless mechentity, until at long last they had a coherent plan that could be read and understood by those who would build and operate it.

Jander stood and stretched, and leaned over Putie's widescreen monitor and gave it a strong hug of genuine gratitude. Yawning, he gave the snoozing cat a couple of strokes, dragged open the door to the sanctum and pushed himself outside. He sagged into a chair, gave his anxious cohorts a wan smile and a tired nod, and fell asleep.

Pavel, remembering a day well over a year before when Jander had saved his life at similar cost, threatened to shoot anyone for the privilege of carrying him to bed.

AS ALWAYS AFTER TIMES of stress, he awoke to the sight of Vickie standing guard. As always, his first thoughts were not of himself. "Does it work?"

"How the hell should I know?" she grinned as she stretched out beside him. "But if it will make you feel any better, Denny is so happy he cracked Brenda's maple table with his fist. That guy's getting rather large, you know."

"Six-fifty is bantam weight. When he's big enough to bench press the ship, I'll call him big."

"Don't blink." She levitated him to slip an arm around his neck. "By the way, since that big nanosteel disco ball is on all our minds lately, we shouldn't just call it 'the ship'. It ought to have a name."

"And you, of course, have thought of one."

"Of course. I was thinking, especially considering who it will be carrying, that we should call her the *Angel*."

"Remember Sri Lanka," he retorted, then thought about it. "*Angel*. Hmmm… I like it. The guardian spirit. Has the right ring – and I don't mean for your reasons. Lady, you've got it. *Angel*, it is."

"Who you callin' lady?" She sank her teeth into his shoulder.

CHAPTER 17

Jander stood, hands on hips, on a high balcony overlooking the huge underground hangar, eyes scanning the activity as his ears and mind concentrated on Carmen Rodrigues. The petite Puerto Rican was leaning on the railing beside him, eyes half closed, reciting the daily report in a practiced monotone. She did not have to travel from St. Louis to make the report personally, but in deference to her lord she always did.

Corpsman Rosita had created the job of Jake's executive assistant and quickly proved herself beyond invaluable, administering the day-to-day operations of the organization with sharp-tongued wit and tenacity. While she carefully kept herself outside the chain of command, she was without question the glue that held the organization together.

"Hey, Chief!" Denny Connors strode out of a hole in the ship onto a scaffold sixty meters below, carrying a ten-foot I-beam on his shoulder. Carmen stopped her recital in mid-word, her expressive eyes spearing the source of the interruption.

The engineer was oblivious to her mercurial temper. "Take a look at this steel," he called in his usual roar. "I think it's under." Hooking a forearm under its end, he tossed the massive beam into the air.

Jander caught it in a forcefield sheath and floated it the rest of the way. Setting it down on the balcony, he materialized a yellowish ball of energy and pressed it against the beam. The ball got more and more tenuous until it sank into the steel. "Seven percent under," he called, and wafted it back. "What do we need a three-meter beam for, anyway?"

"Bracing for the aggies."

Jander winced. It had to happen. He knew that "ambient internal gravity generator" would soon have a nickname, but he was hoping in vain for something else. This would spark a brand new generation of atrocious humor.

"Check out all that last shipment. I don't want to lose a Corpsman every time we change directions. See if we can use this stuff as fodder for the nanosteel process."

"Gotcha. Say, how many aggies does it take to lift..." A flash of lightning leaped from Jander's finger and sheared off an inch of wooden brace. "Okay, okay!" Nonchalantly shouldering hundreds of pounds of steel, Denny hopped back into the ship.

Carmen was reciting again when Jake came up. "We got some trouble, boss."

"We must have, if it yanked you out of St. Louis. What's up?"

Jake looked sour. "The Admiral's back. Sitting on his keister in London, waiting for you to show up. He wants a progress report." Vickie strolled up behind him, alerted to his presence by the proximity of his powerful mind.

"Progress report," Jander repeated disgustedly. "Terrific."

"Do you think you can snow him twice?" Vickie asked.

"Not with the same tactics. He'll be on guard." He frowned and leaned on the railing. "Maybe I should turn Ginger loose on him. That little darlin' could charm a bear out of his honey."

Vickie sniffed. "What am I, a salmon?"

"You, on the other hand," he went on in the same reflective tone, "are the epitome of womanhood, the Excalibur of feminine pulchritude, the ultimate and exquisite culmination of millions of years of..." A wrench leaped from a nearby toolbox and waved over his head. He pretended not to notice. "Besides, bears like salmon." Vickie growled at him.

"But you've given me an idea," he grinned. "Let's go to London."

SPART WAITED ALONE IN his hotel room, knowing full well that Orion knew he was back and was planning another irritating ambush.

More than a year's worth of news magazines were stacked on the table beside his Gaean laptop. He had studied them with every sense alert and had found not the slightest hint of the Omega Corps or variants of any kind in the media, but the mood was different. Negative reports were fewer and less dire.

In fact, he could sense a new tone of optimism, of peace and security, that this turgid world had never before known. Even the air he breathed was cleaner as the damage to the climate was on its way toward reversal. He could only be impressed by the barbarian's progress.

But he wanted the inside story, the part that only Orion himself could provide. He wanted to be certain that the Gaean's machinations had caused no possible harm. And most of all, he wanted to know who and what Orion actually was.

"Good evening, Admiral."

Spart gasped and jerked so strongly he nearly fell out of his chair. He snapped his eyes shut and his lips moved in a silent jumble of curses. Finished, he rose and looked behind him. The irritating barbarian stood close by the chair, and beside him was…

…the most perfectly beautiful woman he had ever seen on this or any other world.

Terry had aided in enhancing Vickie's ethereal beauty to almost angelic levels. Her hair was a gossamer ash-blonde cloud that shimmered with her every swaying motion; her dazzling hazel eyes and rich lips were subtly framed to draw out their every taste of feminine glory. She was wearing a shimmering blue silk creation of exquisite simplicity, which floated around her every sumptuous curve as if magnetized by her translucent – and very evident – skin. The fabric work of art had no visible seams or fastenings – it looked like it was designed to be torn off. A sublime, elegant, nail-chewing, lip-biting, eyepopping masterpiece.

Steele indicated his femme fatale with an immaculate sweep of his arm. "I would like you to meet my Chief of Staff."

Vickie smiled her most languorous smile and breathed in her most musical voice, "I've heard a good deal about you, Admiral."

Spart was thoroughly overwhelmed. He did not know that he was under the subtle touch of her hypnotic power. She did not know that it was unnecessary.

Steele himself was having a bit of trouble. Even though her mental power had no effect on him, the physical attraction he felt the first time they met was just as tremendous, just as dazzling as it had been then. Compared to the sheer animal seduction Vickie commanded, Ginger was the salmon.

But duty called. He skirted past the hard-working hypnotic section of her mind and slipped into contact with the telepathic. His friendly smile broadened a bit at what he saw.

Vickie was laying it on, her marvelously contoured torso swaying as if to faraway music. "I hope you had a pleasant trip. Space must be such a remote place to work. May I sit down?"

"O-of course, please do," he beamed. Any American male would have seen right through that line, but Spart was so much putty. With the delicate use of her telekinesis Vickie settled with impossible grace into a chair. Exuding the very essence of comfort, she wriggled demurely. The result was devastating.

Steele pinched himself mentally. "To what do we owe the pleasure of this visit, Admiral?"

Spart tore his eyes from the captivating vision long enough for a glance in Steele's direction. He was having trouble with his tongue. "It occurred to me even when I was here last time that I know next to nothing about your special talents, and the activities of your organization. In fact, you deliberately steered me away from the subject. Who are you, exactly, and what are your abilities?"

The speech was obviously rehearsed. His heart was not in his words – and there was no question where it was.

"Lord Orion will do. You may call the lady –" who flickered expressive eyelashes and parted her lips slightly, and made other tiny feminine motions designed to melt granite – "call her Lady Alpha. As I told you before, we are positive variants of the basic human genome, somewhat more adaptable than the norm, a bit more intelligent and proficient."

"That tells me nothing." He was staring, he knew he was staring, but he could not help it. "Of whom, or what, does your membership consist?"

"Why should I tell you?" He gave Vickie an eyebrow sign and she crossed her legs with agonizing elegance, each caressing the other in luxurious and delightful tenderness. Jander licked his lips and went on in the same calm tone, "What is the motive power of your ship?"

"Nucle–" He caught himself and turned to face Steele. "Are you trying to pump *me*?" He was beginning to get that old feeling, that he was being manipulated. Vickie sensed that she was losing her audience and took a deep breath. The slight sound caught the Admiral's attention, and the effect of the lung expansion on her silk-swathed anatomy completely derailed his train of thought.

"I'm just pointing out that we are under no obligation to provide you with any information," Steele said quietly. He was starting to sweat; he wished he could tell her to ease up. "After all, by your laws this conversation shouldn't be taking place."

"Nevertheless," Spart said distractedly, "I feel responsible for your actions. It was my decision to allow you to continue."

"Was it, really?" Steele asked reasonably. "How could you have stopped us without interfering? You might try to take the machine, but you could hardly kill us all."

Vickie exuded the appropriate odium to that horrid thought, and Spart agreed fervently. "Of course not."

"Then what is your purpose here? Spying on us will do neither of us any good. You indicated when last we met that you trusted me to handle things here in an intelligent manner. Have you had second thoughts about that?" He knew his argument did not hold together too well, but at this point he had no real need for verbal fencing. Whatever Alpha wanted, Alpha got.

"No, I trust you, and I would never do anything to cause you any harm." His face was turned toward Steele, but his eyes were locked on Vickie, and his tone gave his words an entirely different slant. He was solidly hooked.

"Then we will take our leave. I would like to stay and further our acquaintance –" the words were Jander's, the expression Vickie's – "but as you know we are very busy."

"Of course." Spart leaped to his feet and watched in utter fascination as the maddening siren unfolded herself and rose in one magnificent flowing, hip swaying motion. Spart bowed almost to the knees and kissed her hand; she twitched it upward oh, so slightly as his lips touched, and his heart stopped. He stood paralyzed as they strode and glided to the bedroom and closed the door. He sank into his chair drained of all energy, not bothering to see if the room was empty. He knew it was.

Hand in hand, they floated out the window. Steele's throat was parched. "My gawd, woman!"

For the first time since they had met, he heard her giggle. "That was exciting!"

"Exciting!?" I wanted to tear your clothes off!"

"Well, who's stopping you?"

CHAPTER 18

Alpha and Orion stepped through the open double pocket doors onto the almost-completed Bridge in the center of the great sphere that was the *Angel*. They found an unoccupied haven in the triangle defined by the command chair and the two subcommand consoles behind it, and looked around.

Everywhere on the Bridge, computer specialists, engineers, electronicists and systems technicians bustled in purposeful confusion, dodging piles of complex components and miles of almost invisible filament cable as they worked to build a coherent whole out of the chaos. When finished, the Bridge alone would far surpass any mechanical installation ever conceived.

"It should be ready for the maiden voyage by our second anniversary," Steele observed.

"Ours? Or the Omega Corps'?"

Jander squirmed. No answer could get him out of this with decorum. He opted for the safer course.

"Ours. Things have gone faster than I expected. The only big thing left is the ground support, and the shielded ATVs are coming along quite nicely. Because of space considerations we'll have only a few larger vehicles, basic solar-powered trucks for the most part.

"For combat support, we'll have twelve Banshee fighters about twelve meters long and armed with twin twenty-centimeter pulse cannons. They're fully shielded except for baffle screens – the fighters aren't big enough to squeeze them in. We also have two Banshee-T trainers so our experienced pilots can pass on their skills.

"For personnel and cargo, we have six unarmed sixteen-meter Sprite shuttles, with a max crew of six plus your choice of either passenger seating for another six, or two hundred cubic feet of cargo. I wish we could have something larger, but we're limited by the size of the hangar deck."

"I heard Arden has a bigger prototype he's joyriding around in," Vickie said.

"Not exactly, but yes, he built one that has a baffle screen and prototype warp generators, mainly to test the stuff we're working on for the *Angel*. He and our best candidate for helmsman, Nwoye Lam, and a few others have been to Jupiter and back and they say it's a blast."

"I envy them. Oh, have you figured out that force projecting handgun yet?"

"It's being tested on the rifle range. We've got it down to the size of a Colt 1911, but with a longer barrel for more accuracy at a distance. It generates a five-millimeter force bubble small enough to zip through anything. The power cartridge is the same solar concentrate battery we've developed for everything else. It's good for fifty shots with an effective range of over two kilometers with no recoil and no loss of trajectory. Anyone trained by Carter Long or Pavel can lay down a pretty serious curtain of fire."

"Five millimeter sounds tiny, though."

"Yes, it is. We had to compromise to keep the generator hand-sized. But it evens out – that caliber will zip through anything like a needle through canvas. Anyway, you can select single, triple-tap or continuous fire depending on the target. I wish we could have made the thing simpler, though. It would take a Ph.D. and ten years' experience to fieldstrip the thing."

A raven-haired spectralist took a shortcut through Vickie's hip on her way to a destination unknown, flashing a fleeting grin of apology as she passed.

"That reminds me," she said. "Terry organized a team and came up with wonderful nanosteel blend fabric that can stop anything physical – except for your toy, that is. Anyway, Thelma's having the time of her life designing a set of uniforms that'll give us maximum coverage and still be stylish."

"Why? It's not like we're going to go out in public like a bunch of superheroes."

"Not here on Gaea, no, but we're not building this mobile planet to have someplace to hide."

She turned and sat in one of the subcommand chairs. "We have two reasons for uniforms. One, we'll be meeting other intelligent species and we'll want to look properly organized. And much more important, it will give the members of the Corps a sense of belonging, that we're all a part of the same big family. That's what uniforms are all about. There's a lot of pride and comfort in belonging to something greater than yourself."

Jander's expression softened as he gazed at her. "You couldn't be more right. Thank you. Sometimes I get so caught up in the hardware I overlook the human element."

She smiled up at him. "That's why we're a team. When we go out there, you'll make us safe and I'll make us sound."

He reached out to touch her hair. "Deal."

He stepped back as the spectral technician wafted between them, and watched her slip inside a console against the portside wall. "It's a good thing we're variants or we'd never get this beast put together. Let's get out of the way and go see if the engineers have finished the reason for all this cabling."

VICKIE FOLLOWED HIM off the Bridge to step into a temporary telebooth across the passageway. Jander punched their destination into the keypad and they were in another booth outside the ship.

Heavily braced scaffolding rose all around them, supplementing the meters-thick tripod landing legs that were nonetheless far too slender to support the massive weight. When the gravity engines were installed and operational, they would counter the mass while the tripod would serve to level the ship.

Dozens of Corpsmen were levering complex mechanisms into their gaping cavities in the thick nanosteel hull. A Sprite hovered near a huge hatch in an upper quadrant, balanced on Aaron's proof-of-concept superconductive gravity engines. The cones in its chassis glowed a deep red-gold to maintain the hover, while the stern drive engines were idling dim. Many more such cones pocked the entirety of the shuttle's skin, a few of them occasionally brightening to keep the craft stationary.

Dug into the bedrock all around the cavern were eight stories of workshops, forges and labs turning out the myriad components of the starship. Jander and Vickie strolled through the chaos into a corridor that stretched deeper into the bedrock. They passed through a wide pair of automatic doors into a chamber with walls and ceiling covered with bell-shaped transmitters.

The doors closed behind them as they advanced, and both felt a slight tingle as the transmitters electronically cleansed them of contaminants. The tingling stopped by the time they had traversed the room, and the next pair of doors opened for them into the clean environment of an electronics workshop.

Denny looked up as they strolled into the big assembly room. "Hey, good to see you, Chief. Come to see our finished product?"

Feliks Radschck, the Polish electronics wizard, looked up from his bench and did a stiffening double take when he recognized them.

Jander gave him a casual wave to put him at ease. "You bet. I hear you two have gotten the integrated hull arrays about ready to go. We just visited the Bridge and it looks like the infrastructure is almost ready, so..." He raised an eyebrow.

"So, every component is alpha tested and we're a go for mass production," Denny finished the thought. "All that's really left is the interference check on the full array, and Feliks was about to kick that off. Wanna watch?"

"Absolutely. No pressure, but our lives will depend on this effort." He grinned at the nervous Radschck, who was still getting used to the casual friendliness of its Lord and Lady. "I can't wait to see how you solved the field compression problem."

Denny swept a hand in Feliks' direction, passing the lead to him. Feliks glanced at his monitor that displayed a complexity of circuits and said, "Yes, we solved that by centering the tablicy – pardon, that is 'array' in Polish filtered through Denny's accent. We center the array around the warp sphere generator. As you recall, one of our big problems was that the different types of defensive shields were interfering with each other, which weakened them all. But by putting the warp sphere generator between them, the backwash from the infusion sphere dampens the frequency leaks and allow them all to live in a mutually clean environment."

He pointed rapidly at different sections of the monitor. "That also gave us a safe place to put our network technology – sensors and communications." His fingers jabbed at another series of components.

That lost Vickie, whose knowledge of nanotechnology was layman at best. "Perhaps if you show us the array itself, we might get a better grasp of it."

Radschck straightened and faced them, turning his back on the monitor as if to hide it. "Of course. We have the alpha test array in another room. Follow me, please."

He spun and hurried toward a broad door in the stone wall, leaving the others to follow. Vickie, ever compassionate, sent him a subliminal telehypnotic pulse to calm him a bit and give his considerable intellect a chance to take control. His pace was much slower by the time they entered the demo room.

He was relaxed enough to grin as he waved both arms at a complex array mounted on a nanosteel frame. It was a mass of copper, gold and stainless steel transmitter antennae, concave tungsten, aluminum and bismuth receiving dishes and other combinations of the two, all arranged in a disk shaped conglomeration over two meters across. In its way it was a beautiful construct, and would add to the jewel-like glitter of the *Angel*. In contrast, scattered behind it were dozens of separate hard drives, some of the huge, that housed the operating code and were connected to the disk by scores of cables.

Feliks found a laser pointer on a bench and flicked its green dot on a broadcast dish within another, larger dish in the center of the array. "This is the warp sphere generator, or generators since there are two of them. The inner dish is for the sphere that will cover us at about the same diameter as the defensive screens. The wider disk underneath it generates the long-range sphere that creates a bubble two million kilometers in diameter. You can see that all the other components encircle them and are therefore safe within their electronic shadow."

The laser moved to a smaller dish at the lower left, this one with a heavy conical antenna of gold in its center. "This is the baffle screen generator that makes us undetectable to every type of sublight and hyperlight sensor system."

He shifted his aim to the next dish a third of the way around the circle, one with a broad convex center. "This one generates the collision shield that protects us from space debris, kinetic weapons and other physical intrusions. This..." the dot moved to the top of the array and another dish with an elaborate horn-shaped antenna. "... is the energy deflector, that will protect us from any wave form weapons but still allow the sublight visuals and hyperlight particles our sensors are looking for. Since it's around the corner from the baffle generator they won't interfere with each other."

"That was our biggest headache," Denny put in. "Jake and I really wrestled with this, as you know, but Feliks came up with the simple solution that made us look silly."

Feliks ducked his head at the praise. "Well, I had

a fresh viewpoint after all the hard work done before me. But it works so well that we were able to incorporate all our sensor and communications receivers into the same array."

The pointer flared again. "Here is the sublight sensor transceiver, that collects visible spectra for display on our monitors. That includes anything within our warp sphere when it's active. Over here," the laser moved around the perimeter, "is the hyperlight sensor that captures the particles we collectively call tachyons but have a lot of different names in Sabarian, Leosan and Squn. Angela – " the *Angel's* quantum cybernetic mechentity, still under construction – "will convert those into views we can comprehend from the environment outside the sphere.

"Next is communications." He pointed out three more separate areas around the array. "This is the tachyon broadcaster, that sends out a general signal kind of like hyperlight radio that can be picked up by anyone in the galactic neighborhood. Over here is the tachyon receiver to pick up other people's signals. And finally, this construct both transmits and receives quantum entanglement signals, which are point-to-point communications."

He stepped back, allowing his audience to take in the entire array. "Now, this outer ring, here," he waved the laser along the edge of the disk, "is the projector for teleporting the entire ship. It infuses the inner warp sphere, which itself is an infusion bubble, with the quantum entanglement energies that will move everything within the infusion sphere to a location dictated by the relative strength of the infusion. If infusion is heaviest on the southern end, for instance, the ship would be teleported in the northerly direction to a distance based on the strength employed."

"Wow," Vickie's melodic voice warbled through several notes. "How in the world could you test that?"

"It wasn't easy," Denny told her. "We had to take our Sprite beta shuttle into the asteroid belt, send the 'porter out in a miniature model of the *Angel* and trigger it telekinetically." He grinned wryly. "Then we had to find the damned thing. We won't know how well it really performs until we get it installed and can test it in the ship."

"What?" Vickie bristled and speared him with The Look known to women everywhere. "With three hundred human guinea pigs aboard?"

"It's no more dangerous than the telebooths," Denny said hastily, genuine alarm in his eyes. "The mice we had in the test model came through it fine. Believe me, if we didn't think it was safe we wouldn't even install it. It traveled farther than we thought it would, is all."

Vickie relented enough to turn down her glare. "Well, it's my job to worry about our people. The last thing we need is half the Corps with scrambled brains."

Jander nodded to acknowledge her point. "I've gone over it thoroughly, hon, and so has Putie. The only question is the range, not the safety."

Denny added. "Let's face it, this is all new technology. Since we've thrown so much of our own talents into this stuff we've advanced Confederation science quite a distance, so of course there are a few unknowns – but safety isn't one of them. We've tested the hell out of everything, believe me."

"And," Feliks dared to join the conversation, "since all of these distinct units are either in the shadows of the warp sphere generators or integrated with them, every product of the array we use will be cleaner, stronger and more coherent than anything the Confederation has. For instance, once we get a couple hundred of these installed on our hull, we know we'll be able to triangulate sensor scans to give us a more three-dimensional picture than a smaller and less spherical ship can produce. The same is true for the teleporter. With a little practice and calibration we should be able to hit our target destination within a hundred meters."

Vickie nodded reluctantly. "All right, you've made your point." She stepped back, trying to quell her irritation, and watched as her husband turned his attention to the glittering disk.

Jander's eyes traveled over every inch of the array, finding the position of every component and calculating their impact on each other. After a few absorbed minutes he raised his hands as if to embrace the entire display. "Okay. What are you using to power the test?"

Denny answered, "We're using the accumulators we installed in the southern pasture. I'm told the cows like the shade, by the way. For this test we're filtering out the spectrum from our yellow sun and going strictly with stellar energies. That's what we'll be picking up through the warp bubble when we get out there."

"Good thinking. Feliks, do you mind if I monitor the test through your mind?"

"Not at all, sir. You can compare what we expect with what we get."

Steele nodded. "That's the idea, plus I'll be feeling for the energies generated with my analytical screens – and, I hope, containing anything that goes wrong."

"Dobre. Good." He sat down at the computer station facing the array and started typing. "I will begin by activating the electronic shielding built into the walls of this chamber, which we expect will keep the energies we'll be generating from escaping... done. I'm connecting the power now. I won't start the alpha test until you direct me."

"Fine. I'll follow the sequence in your mind and tell you when to I'm ready for the next step." Jander pulled a rolling chair from its parking space against a wall and sat down about four meters from the tablicy – in his mind he had already adopted the Polish term for the array.

Feliks tapped a pair of function keys. The big monitor on the wall adjacent to the disk came to life, displaying a detailed graphic of the array. Near the depiction of each component were bar graphs that would measure the power that would surge through the components as they were activated.

Vickie found herself a chair next to Feliks and joined her telepathy to his, then extended her link to Denny so that Feliks could concentrate on his monitor. Jander rolled himself forward a bit as he spent a few seconds to orient himself to the display.

"You may begin."

"Ten percent power to the inner warp sphere." Feliks hit the command key, and he – and Denny, through Vickie – studied the results on the monitor. One bar graph leaped upward as the inner dish in the center of the tablicy emitted a net of tachyon particles that permeated the entire shielded room.

Jander felt a pressure on his analytical screen and compared it to what he had felt from the counterpart he had sensed idling in Admiral Spart's grounded *Kaltim*. It matched. "Positive results, guys. Do you agree?"

Both engineers confirmed his impressions, and the sequential testing continued. One by one, the defensive shield elements, the sensor receivers and the communications network transceivers were powered up and run through their paces. After each round of tests, the power was increased and the test repeated.

A few minor adjustments were made on the fly, but overall the alpha test sequence ran its course as an unqualified success. Each and every component of the tablicy was up and functioning with no interference from the others. With every positive result Denny's grin grew and his chair arms twisted out of shape under his grip.

As the final test, Feliks powered off the warp sphere generators central to the entire array while leaving everything else active. That would allow them to approach a sublight destination and match speeds with it.

In an instant the orderly emissions crowding Jander's brain turned into an agonizing soupy jumble. He gasped and clutched at his head, struggling to shield himself from the confusion.

"Outer sphere, now!" he gritted, and Feliks, who had the next command ready, snapped on the larger of the central dishes.

Vickie sent her chair flying and knelt beside her husband. "Are you all right?"

Jander took a few seconds to gather his overtaxed wits. "Uh… yeah. You were right about that interference, guys. I think we'll have to reinforce the housing around every component so we can operate safely at sublight speeds. If we don't, whenever we approach a destination we'll be deaf, dumb, blind and naked as a rock."

"Shit." Denny looked at Radschck with a pained expression.

Feliks never noticed, his mind already working full speed on the problem. "Tak. Yes. How stupid of me. A third dish is needed, a very thin one surrounding the other two. That one will always be powered up to shield the other components, but will not extend beyond the radius of the array. That will also give the wider sphere generators the single task of creating the bubble instead of also protecting the other components. We will have to sink the triple disk deeper into the array so that the new disk will do its job without itself interfering with the other operations. Tak. That will work."

Jander rose and clapped the engineer on the shoulder. "That's a damned sight better than my idea. Make it so, and let me know when you're ready for another alpha test."

"I knew we kept you around for a reason, Feliks," Denny grinned. "Let me know if you'll need a bigger divot in the skin of the ship, I'll postpone the manufacture of the affected hull plates until you get your measurements."

The electronics expert beamed under the praise and nodded. "Yes, sir. I'll get started right away."

Jander extended his hand. "Sounds good, guys. Well done, both of you. Keep us posted on your schedule."

"You bet." Denny accepted the offered handshake, then watched in approval as the grinning Jander took Feliks's hand in both of his. Vickie gave the Polish genius a kiss on the cheek, which left him flushed, and patted Denny on the chest as she and Jander left the room.

CHAPTER 19

Hand in hand, exchanging greetings with every Corpsman they passed, Jander and Vickie strolled up a long passageway that ramped toward the surface. They used a conventional elevator to reach the glassed-in mud room of the ranch house. A pair of enormous panels covered with natural sod hid the hangar from view behind the garage. The only external sign of the installation was a slight convexity under the pasture.

Brenda looked up from her position on the couch as they came through the living room and rested her tablet on her own far from slight convexity. "Jake wants you to call him in St. Louis," she said. "Something about a summit meeting."

"Thanks, Bren." Jander led the way upstairs to what used to be Jake's ham radio room, now a more than world-class communications facility. He dropped into the comfortable chair in front of one of the three consoles and Vickie pulled up a chair from another. The touch of a few keys, and Jake was looking back at them from his office in St. Louis.

"Hi, Lord 'n Lady. How's the ship?"

"We might beat Brenda. What's this about a summit meeting?"

Jake glanced down at something out of range of

the screen. "Well, we had a meeting of dons right here in St. Louis," he said. "Seems they wanted to meet in a city where organized crime was no longer terribly active. Couldn't have picked a better place."

Steele nodded. "Thanks to you. And what did they have to say?"

"Let's be frank. These goons are not dummies. In fact, a few of them show undeveloped variant potential. Not that we want them in our organization. Anyway, they seem to suspect there's something operating here that's more than just bad luck. Our little dodge of mixing nauseating impurities into their drug shipments is getting stale as a result. Too much horse they know is purebred is being gelded. I wanted to meet with you to see if we can figure out some other way to compromise the stuff."

"To tell you the truth, that one's been bothering me. The only other way I can see is to destroy the growing fields. But that would not only point to an organized assault of international origin, it would disrupt the economic balance of the area. And unfortunately, a lot of people subsist on the honest manufacture of opiates. Heroin isn't the only product."

"My thoughts exactly. We can't be seen burning the fields time and again. That would be just as bad as sugaring the horse in every shipment. And unfortunately, we don't have many governments fighting the illicit trade to the extent that we can secretly help them, like we've been able to do with cocaine and meth."

"So?"

"So how about a series of nice, neat natural disasters?"

Vickie perked up. "Like floods in Burma. Earthquakes in Turkey. But would be tremendous damage, people killed, the lives of thousands disrupted. Remember the First Law; we must above all refrain from damaging interference."

"But the damage would be profitable to them in the end; that's the beauty of it. The U.N. – with our under-the-table help – has recently conceived and put into operation a viable agency modeled after the Red Cross, disaster relief that can be used anywhere on the globe. People would be fed and housed, and things would be put back to normal in a few weeks – with one crop gone."

Vickie held up a staying hand. "No. No way. Emphatically not. There is so much more to disasters than land damage. People's homes, their belongings, heirlooms, everything that makes them a family could be lost. I won't be a party to that kind of misery."

"The Corps can see to it that it's kept to a minimum," Jake argued.

"No, we can't," Jander said. "Not only is Vickie right about the personal losses, but it will send us too deep toward forcing our ideas on the world. We can't go around disrupting weather systems and manipulating the environment."

"Why can't we? There's a lot of potential benefit, too," Jake said.

"Because of the First Law. Too many unexplained phenomena would mean too much activity. Someone would be bound to notice. We have enough trouble staying anonymous as it is."

"But think of the progress..." Jake's voice faded as he saw the hardening look in his commander's eyes.

"Jake, I hope I never have to say this again. Our goal is stability, not progress. We've activated about six hundred Corpsmen. Half will go with me; the other three hundred will remain in your command. This is the maximum I will allow to operate on Gaea, and it is your responsibility to make certain that every one of them understands the constraints under which he is required to operate."

"Those constraints can be summed up in one dictum, and I want it to be our core value, now and forever, cast in nanosteel and embedded in every wall:

"We are not gods. We will not act like gods."

His voice did not rise, but it carried the unyielding dominance of nature itself. Jake slowly sank back in his chair. The power in Jander's eyes burned the words indelibly into his mind.

Jander took a deep breath to regain his temper. "We are pledged to ensure the survival of the species. We are not here to lead them; we are not here to push or coerce them in any way. And we sure as hell won't do anything to cause them harm because we think they'll end up better for it. They won't. Any reforms or advances made by the world at large must be and shall be by their own efforts and decisions."

Jake listened in silence, then bowed his head. He felt the weight of the world descend on his shoulders, and a small portion of his chastened mind wondered at Orion's ability to hold up under the pressure of walking such a thin line.

But he had no thought within him of backing out. If this most competent of all men believed he could carry the load, he would carry it, proudly, with no doubts and no recriminations.

"As you wish, Lord Orion. I will make sure they understand."

"The heroin," Vickie reminded them softly.

"Yes." Jander caught Jake's eyes. "Your plan is a good one, carried out with extreme moderation. Subtlety is the key; the disasters have got to appear natural. A landslide in Afghanistan diverts a stream and the water floods out acres of poppies; if it's managed well that would be the only damage."

Vickie chipped in, "Monsoon rains loosen the soil under a cliff; a few tons of rock crash down on a road and delay shipments for days."

Jake picked it up. "A boatload of horse is under way near the coast of Indonesia; a sudden downdraft during a storm tears off the hatch cover and the hold is drenched."

"All good," Jander nodded. "Make it a contest. The most productive idea wins a weekend pass at our Hawaiian bungalow, or some such. Meanwhile, we can continue our efforts to get stronger sanctions from the U.N., as long as we remain within Corps parameters. The details I leave to you." He smiled. "Good practice."

Jake nodded. "Yes, sir. What about the junk already in the pipeline?"

Vickie suggested, "How about grabbing a page from the boys themselves? Hijack it."

Jake's face spread into a slow grin. "Now why didn't I think of that?"

"Too simple," Jander said, with an elbow nudge to Vickie's shoulder. "We've been thinking too much about our own talents and not enough about the methods they've been using for centuries. You can break eggs without making omelets." He jerked a thumb at his wife. "We'll get our resident psychologist on it."

"Sure. I haven't been in action for ages," she grinned. "See you in St. Louie, Jakie."

"With open arms." He cut the connection in the face of Steele's mock frown.

Jander sobered and drummed his fingers on the console. "Was I too rough on him?"

She slid her hands around his neck and massaged his shoulders. "Not at all," she said. "Jake can be a bit impulsive. The Corps wouldn't exist if he wasn't, but that's besides the point. You would have had to glue him down sometime. And you did it well, giving him authority and humility in the same breath." She looked troubled. "But whether he can control the others I can't guess."

"I'm sure he can. Jake is a supremely able administrator, much better than I am. If anyone steps out of line he'll make their heads spin. I'm glad we have him, and every member of the Corps respects him the same way." He smiled up at her. "I should know."

"That's right, I keep forgetting. You can read us as well as we can read normals. How often do you use it?"

"On the surface, every once in a while, just to get a picture without verbal translation. But deep thoughts I leave alone. I remember us discussing that a long time ago, and I still feel that way – normal conversation level is my usual limit. If I didn't trust them, they wouldn't have been activated."

"True. And it does take a lot of effort to read…" Abruptly she jumped to her feet with a look of alarm on her face, and rushed for the stairs. "Call Jake back. Brenda's water just broke!"

CHAPTER 20

The ship was at last completed and christened the *Angel*, by Victoria Steele and a flying liter of fine champagne. The mighty spheroid looked and gleamed like a gigantic jewel. The hull, constructed of Nokilonian nanosteel, shone a tempered silvery blue in startling contrast to the fluctuating red-gold of the fractal holograms disguising the gravity drive cones, and the almost painful silver-black of the stellar accumulators. More than two hundred tablicy disks added their multicolored sparkle to the dazzling display. A few of the great cannons protruded through their wide circular hatches, swiveling through broad arcs as the gunnery engineers made a last-minute check of their turrets.

The last of the eager crewmen stepped into telebooths, flew to hatches or rode the angled elevators within the ship's trio of splayed landing stabilizers, and made their way to their stations within the ship. Each wore the utility uniform of the Omega Corps designed by Thelma Grant with help from Brenda and Terry Kirkland. Slacks of nanosteel blue-gray secured by a black utility belt were tucked into boots of matte black, and a hook-and-loop secured shirt of the same nanosteel hue with red and gold accents at the neck and cuffs completed the outfit. The left breast of the shirt sported a black-bordered platinum shield outlining the stylized insignia of the Corps: a blue Omega enclosing a red scale of justice topped by the golden symbol for infinity, signifying their tacit motto: Justice for All.

None of the Corpsmen, including the top command, wore any kind of rank or specialty insignia. It was Alpha's suggestion that the Corpsmen establish from the start that wherever they went in the galaxy, they were the Law, each an authority unto himself. Rank would be irrelevant to any outside the Corps.

In everyday life, even on duty, the crewmen were allowed the civilian clothing of their choice and culture, if it was practical for the job at hand. But on this day of days the basic utilities were worn in respect for the occasion, though they were accessorized with many individual choices of headgear such as westerns, berets, turbans, outbacks, hijabs, hairbands and others mixed in with the uniform standard nanosteel blue flat caps.

They had no ceremony planned to accompany the launch, and no celebration other than the camaraderie of brotherhood that filled the underground hangar. Corpsman from all over the world had dropped whatever they were doing to see the ship off. Even the youngest potential, Alexander Cunningham Anson, gurgled politely in his mother's arms.

Jander, who himself was cradling his cat, leaned over his godson's tousled red head and probed gently. "A strong variant," he told the beaming Jake. "It'll be interesting to see if he gains power naturally or will have to be activated."

"Activated, I hope. Can you imagine a telekinetic two-year-old? I have enough trouble with this one." He threw an arm around his wife. Brenda telekinetically shoved a strand of red hair up his nose and caused a stifled sneeze.

Jander chuckled and held out his hand. "I wish you were coming, Jake. If it weren't for you there wouldn't be an Omega Corps, and no *Angel*."

"Don't blame me, blame whoever crashed that old ship." He took the offered hand and gripped it strongly. "We're gonna miss you, buddy."

"We'll be back, don't worry about that. But a test flight might be detected, so we're just going to let 'er rip and see what happens. It may be quite a while."

"Well, when you get back the Corps will be just as you left it, and the world will be a little bit better."

Jander stared for a long time into his friend's eyes, not probing, just remembering. Then he turned away, gave Brenda a hug (prompting a feline kiss from Cindy to A.C.) as Vickie so treated Jake, then the two of them stepped into the telebooth. There they lingered, looking over the Omega Corps assembled.

Arden was there, staying to run the shipyard, and Lorraine Ardelle, Carmen, Thelma, Max, Ginger Carter. So many Corpsmen, new and old, three hundred of the finest and most talented men and women the planet had ever produced, had come to see the ship off. Their Lord and Lady waved, and as

Vickie reached for the keypad the entire assembly broke into a cheer that echoed from the bedrock walls in resounding waves.

The Captain and his Chief of Staff materialized in a telebooth in Engineering on the lowest deck, and felt the tingle of the quantum pulse that Angela, the ship's governing mechentity, generated to cleanse arrivals of any parasites and wildlife that might hitchhike in and contaminate her environmental systems. Every telebooth to the outside world was so protected, designed not only to discourage Gaean threats but any intruder not of Gaean origin they might pick up from other planets. Anything below a certain complexity either would be rendered harmless or forcefield trapped for examination. A pulse curtain of the same energies guarded the external hatches, and more were at the entrances to the Park to keep the resident natural lifeforms from escaping.

Jander and Vickie rode an elevator to the Bridge Deck, taking the slower conveyance to give them time to collect their thoughts. Some members of the crew had an aversion to the momentary twinge in the head the telebooths delivered, so the designers had added three pairs of conventional elevators and several stairwells to ease their minds.

Jander smiled a bit as they silently rose. The ship had twenty-four decks, of which the command level was thirteenth. By mutual if silent agreement the otherwise pragmatic Corpsmen had chosen to label it simply, "Bridge Deck". Communications, sensors, armaments control including the individual gunnery consoles, two conference rooms and the offices of the commanders were also on this deck, along with one level of the theater-meeting hall.

Hand in hand, they strolled up the long ramp that led to the hatch leading to the Bridge. The broad double pocket doors slid into the bulkheads on either side. As the commanders crossed the threshold Angela announced, "*CAPTAIN ON THE BRIDGE!*"

The hatches closed behind them to unite the two halves of the Corps crest on their inner surface. The ramp outside was designed so that the hatch opened onto the raised command surface at the rear of the Bridge. Orion took the master's chair a few meters forward of the hatch, and Alpha settled into the leftmost of the two consoles diagonally behind him. Denny Connors, called Kodiak, the Chief Engineer and third in command, was at his engineering control station on the first deck.

The Bridge, like the ship itself, was a convex hexagon in shape, and loosely modeled after the set of an old television show with an international following. Before him, a broad step down from the command seats and to his right, was the helmsman's console, occupied by Nwoye Lam, an energetic Nigerian telekinetic. To the left was the navigation console where computopath Alexiy Pashkov held sway.

The communications station with telepath Tsin Li-san was dead center a bit beyond them, and forward to the right and left were the sensors station, with spectralist Kurino Yukio in the seat, and armaments commanded by Pavel Kalanev. A three-dimensional holographic imager/map table, currently inactive, was centered between them in front of Tsin.

Computer diagnostics and engineering readout stations, environmental monitors, auxiliary craft tracking, and backup stations lined the two bulkheads to port and starboard of the command chairs.

Facing them all on the forward bulkhead of the hexagon was the huge multipurpose 3-D command monitor, and below it were two wide plasma screens reserved for ship's status and situation readouts. Dozens of smaller monitors, each one reserved for its own sector of the outside universe, splayed over the bulkheads left and right, separated from the wall stations by a secondary personnel hatch on either side. Each monitor had a color-coded frame with an alphanumeric label that indicated its viewpoint north to south around the ship's spherical hull.

Among the present scenes were the hundreds of variants lining the balconies or floating in the air less than fifty meters from the ship. Steele reflected that if anything went wrong the entire Corps could be wiped out. He considered calling Jake to have them get clear, but decided that most of them would stay in the danger zone anyway, orders or no orders.

He filled his lungs with the untainted air the *Angel*'s ultra-efficient environmental systems provided, and let it out slowly to calm his nerves.

He touched a stud on his chair arm. His command console popped through a hatch in the deck and rose to comfortable work level before him.

"All stations, report." Angela opened a broadcast to every command station throughout the ship and repeating his words after her standardized half-second delay. *"Accumulators, active." "Artificial gravity, on." "Environmentals, operating." "Sick bay, standing by..."* One by one the remote stations signaled their readiness, followed by the Bridge stations, then Denny's booming bass declared his engines' status to conclude the ritual.

Steele's console confirmed their status. They were ready to go.

"Communications, request the opening of hangar doors."

"Hangar doors open, aye." Tsin Li-san leaned forward into his hush field and spoke into his console's microphone to pass the message to ground control. With agonizing slowness the two huge slabs of camouflaged tungsten steel above them dropped six meters underground, then slid sideways into their housings. Bits of soil and grass from the disguising pasture showered down with the light of the summer sun.

"Helm, bring south motivators to grounding stasis."

"South pole and Capricorn drivers to grounding stasis, aye." Nwoye Lam gradually brought the gravitic motivator cones in the stern and the subtropical sections to life and slowly took the weight of the ship off the construction scaffolding. The spectators outside gave ground as the tons of steel and wood separated from the hull with deafening shrieks and groans.

"Prepare to lift off. Helm, let's begin at two meters per second."

"Two meters per second, aye." Lam burst into activity, black fingers and telekinetic mind flickering over his keyboard. "Ready, sir."

"Lift us out."

Eyes skimming over his console's bar graphs, left hand poised on his speedball to maintain the ship's mean position, the Nigerian caressed his right-hand joystick and eased his weight down on the pedal under his right foot. Slowly, meter by meter, the *Angel* eased upward. His monitor's graphics displayed the ship's equilibrium as they floated into the crisp Montana sky under his well-practiced touch. He double blinked at an icon in the heads-up display Angela kept steady above his line of sight of his head movements. The three landing stabilizers telescoped into their housings in the subtropical – Capricorn – sections of the hull.

When the ship was five hundred meters above ground, Jander ordered, "Baffle screens on."

"Baffle screens on, aye." At his armaments console, Pavel Kalanev pressed one of the scores of command keys arranged to either side of his keyboard. Instantly the *Angel* was undetectable as Feliks Radschck's brainchild began its mission. The *Angel* blended her way through the shield hiding the complex as the hangar bay doors began their return to the surface.

"Increase to sixty meters per second. No need to acknowledge, Mr. Lam. My console is quite adequate."

"Aye, sir." Nwoye waved a hand and returned to his board. The *Angel* shot upward and left the ranch behind.

Light as a helium balloon, she soared through the thermosphere and zipped into the vacuum. Lam eased his pressure on the accelerator to keep their velocity steady as they left the planet's gravitational pull in their wake. Angela automatically zigged them past a geosynchronous satellite and zagged back on course without Nwoye's or Yukio's guidance.

Kurino was not idle, nonetheless. Her eyes darted back and forth over her console's many small monitors until she was satisfied there was no further danger of collision. "Lagrange point one exceeded, Milord." They were beyond the farthest man-made satellites.

"Very good. Increase speed to point ten gravities squared. At eight kilometers, activate defensive shields."

"Passing eight kilometers, defensive shields on." Kalanev tapped a pair of keys, and the ship was now fully protected from space debris and radiation. Lam adjusted their velocity from relative to constant.

Jander stared fascinated as the moon appeared in a corner of the big screen and arched through the view, to ease off and display again on three of the smaller monitors as it fell behind them. Gaea itself, in all its blue and brown beauty, filled nine of the small screens and parts of several others.

He shook himself and got back to business. "Engineering. How's it look, Denny?"

"Purring like that cat of yours," the titan rumbled, breathless with emotion. *"Drive and accumulation are all green."*

"Well done," Jander acknowledged him and leaned back in his chair. He realized that the cat was indeed purring. Eidetic memory or no, he had not thought to put her in their quarters.

"Mr. Pashkov, plot a course to HR-8832 in Cassiopeia." He grinned. "It's a triple-star system with a bunch of planets. Sounds like fun."

The Russian computopath nodded and bent over "his" navigation console. Alexiy had assembled the thing almost atom by atom, and melded with it like a part of his own body. All the astronomical data of Gaea, and as much Confederation lore as the *Kaltim* had carried, was in its deep corner of Angela's memory. "Course plotted, sir."

"Shoot it to the helm. Mr. Lam, head us out at four gravities squared."

"Yes, sir! Second star to the right, four gravities squared!" Nwoye, code named Scatter, absolutely loved his job.

Jander sighed and looked over his left shoulder at Vickie. She returned his bemused smile with a mock frown. "If you're going to say we're on our way, I don't want to hear it," she said.

He grinned and called to Tsin, "Put me through to Montana, Li-san." A few seconds later, Jake's face flashed onto the forward monitor, with Brenda, Arden and Feliks behind him. "Hey, buddy,"

Jake fought in vain to control a whoop of joy. "It works!" Arden raised both fists above his head and pumped them in triumph.

"Of course it does. We built it, didn't we?" Steele's voice was overflowing with unsuppressed pride.

"Whither away, O Star Hunter?"

"Cassiopeia area first, then who knows? We're like tourists, with unlimited funds and unlimited time to spend them. No billionaire ever had it so good."

"You're telling me. Don't forget to touch base every two weeks. We're gonna be living for your updates."

"You'll get them. Take care of the planet for us, okay?"

"We're not going anywhere. Bon voyage, Lord Orion." Jake cut the connection before he got too sloppy.

Jander stared breathless at the big monitor, which now showed the brilliant pinpoints of inter-stellar space. They were already nearing the orbit of Jupiter, and Sol, or Kitaote as named by the Confederation, was a dwindling searchlight in a rearward monitor. As their increasing speed started to distort the view Lam activated the mass-time compensation field generators to create their inner warp sphere, and Kurino switched the sensors from sublight reflection to quantum accumulation. There was no apparent change in what could be seen, but he knew that outside the warp sphere was now a view of the universe no mind could comprehend.

He shook himself as free from the wonder as he could. "Attention, all personnel." As Angela repeated his words throughout the ship, he paused, still lost in the scene before him. The magnificent sight froze him into a state of overwhelming awe. He inhaled, his mind full of cobwebs.

"We're on our way..."

CHAPTER 21

Jackson Alexander Steele, Ph.D., Captain of the starship *Angel*, called Orion, Lord of the Omega Corps, the most powerful mentality, activated or otherwise, ever produced in the known history of Gaea, lay on his back beneath a spreading white oak and watched a squirrel chitter in the sheltering branches. He was the ultimate picture of pastoral relaxation. A Spanish guitar some distance away sent its intricate, muted ballad through the flower-scented air, adding a mood that approached benediction to the already beatific scene.

Vickie strolled over and settled beside him, plucked and chewed on a blade of grass. A gentle breeze rustled the leaves overhead and set her ash blonde hair into fluid motion. "Mind if I join you?"

He pulled a hand from beneath his head and caressed her supple back. He seemed to consider that answer enough.

She leaned back and they lay side by side in the comfortable silence of lovers. After a while she asked, "What are you thinking?"

He chuckled. "You're always asking me that. Must be a function of the subconscious, like Wade and his 'I agree'."

She wrinkled her nose at the hologram clouds

drifting through the sky projected overhead. "Well, it's not like I can read your mind or anything."

"True." He sobered into a contented smile and answered her question. "I like this place."

She snorted and folded herself half on top of him. "Why not? You designed a lot of it."

"And it's the second best idea I've ever had. Who's in charge of this little planet?"

"Denny. He's sitting in your chair and bending it all out of shape. The last I saw, Chelsea was keeping him company. You know, if he weren't so afraid of breaking her that might turn into something."

She rolled onto her back and looked up. A red squirrel, its tufted ears making it look perpetually surprised, stared back at her from the tree as it worked on a nut. "The squirrels were a nice idea."

"Um-hum. If Sharon can control them. The last thing we need is a ship full of puff-tailed rats." Sharon Gibson was a clinical zoologist, making full use of her zootelepathy. She could influence as well as read the thoughts of anything lower than a primate or higher than a frog in mentality. Squirrels were not her more cooperative subjects, and she was afraid she might not be able to guarantee birth control. "Oh, well, there's always Cindy."

"Ugh. You're mean."

"Just keeping the crew busy. Any idea where we are yet?"

"I'm afraid not. Alexiy is practically whipping his console, but we ran off the *Kaltim*'s maps completely."

"I should have known," he sighed. "Gaea is just beyond the fringe of the Confederation, and I wanted to stay as far away from them as possible during our shakedown. Unfortunately, I'm not bright enough to realize how fast nine gravities per second per second really is."

"You're not alone. And that's not even our top speed. Besides, jumping hither and yon every time we saw an interesting star played hell with our trajectory."

"Don't I know it." He sighed again. "From now on Angela will maintain a full log of our every move..."

"*Lord Orion from the Bridge!*" Denny's thunderous bellow sent the squirrel scrambling for cover.

Steele rolled onto his elbow. "Here, Kodiak. What is it?"

Angela picked up his voice and directed it back to the bridge; in turn, Denny's call was thereafter concentrated in a speaker built into the nearest picnic table. "*We have a clue to where we are – sort of,*" the titan said.

"What do you mean, sort of?"

"*Communications just intercepted a tachyon broadcast distress call in Confederation code. It's our old pal, Vice Admiral Spart.*"

Steele muttered a curse. "That clown is every-where." He pursed his lips, then pushed himself to his feet and went to sit at the table. "Distress call?"

"*Yeah. It's coded and scrambled, so he's looking strictly for Cornfed help. It says he's on an exploratory mission and ran into a fleet of nasties, eighty strong. I haven't talked to him; this was in his message. He's running like hell in the direction of the Cornfed frontier, which is near Gaea in this region."* He waited, not even thinking of suggesting a course of action. There was only one Lord of the *Angel*.

Orion himself was painfully aware of that fact. He looked to Vickie, who was gazing at him with complete trust. With no apparent hesitation he said, "Get us on a course in his direction designed to get us there fast and back down to their relative speed at the point of interception. I'll be right down." He got up from the table and headed for the hatch concealed in a bower, Vickie right behind him.

Connors rose as they entered the bridge, Angela announcing their arrival. "We're hauling ass," he grinned. "With the six polar drivers and all those on the southern hemisphere sections we've reached a speed well over twice that of the Cornfed cruisers. Contact in nine and a half hours, with polar switch for deceleration at midpoint."

"Very well, Commander, I have the bridge," Jander acknowledged and took the center chair, Vickie and Denny flanking him in the sub-command positions. "Let's not call them 'Cornfed' to their faces, eh?" The titan grinned.

Steele called to Tsin, "Let's have a rerun of that distress call, Li-san."

"No visual, sir, too far away for that with his equipment. Here's the translation from code to Sabarian, with our place names for reference. There's a zip-like file of the bad guys, too."

The hologram display area in front of him sprang up to display a starfield from the *Kaltim*'s point of view, with a broad scattering of pulsing green dots. The forward speakers opened with the Admiral's voice in his native tongue, with Angela supplying the star names in English.

"*VICE ADMIRAL NIL SPART COMMANDING CONFEDERATION EXPLORATION CRUISER KALTIM IN CANOPUS REGION. AM PURSUED BY UNFRIENDLY FLEET APPROXIMATELY EIGHTY STRONG NOT IDENTIFIED. ATTEMPTED CONTACT AND WAS FIRED UPON WITHOUT CAUSE BY TWO SHIPS. NO DAMAGE BUT SENSORS INDICATE NINE HITS NECESSARY FOR PENETRATION OF SCREEN.*

ACCELERATING AT MAXIMUM DRIVE LEONIS DIRECTION BUT CANNOT GAIN DISTANCE. REQUEST IMMEDIATE ASSISTANCE. VICE ADMIRAL NIL SPART COMMANDING CONFEDERATION EXPLORATION CRUISER..."

The message repeated; Steele signaled Tsin to turn it off and sat back in thought.

If he remembered his galactography — and assuming they were correct in their estimated position — any Confederation ship would not reach the *Kaltim* before several days had passed, and far less likely could a defending fleet be gathered in time. Long before that, Spart's fuel supply would be depleted to the point where the fleet was sure to catch up to him. The stellar accumulators were fine for gathering energy in deep space, but not relative to the fuel expenditure for the maximum output of that wasteful drive. Spart's small ship did not have the capacity to carry enough of the heavy metals they burned to propel the ship for very long at top speed. Unless they intervened, Spart was doomed.

He swiveled to face his officers. "Opinions?"

"Not opinions, no," Vickie said, "but maybe some observations. One, if I remember correctly, a trip from Canopus toward Leonis is within a few scant parsecs of Gaea." Pashkov at Navigation looked back at her and nodded. "If that fleet is an exploration party in force, they might get ideas. Gaea would therefore be in danger. Spart isn't the type to lead them toward a defenseless planet, but he's in no position to dodge.

"Two, his ship is, in his own words, an exploration cruiser. His computers were too limited to tell us whether the Confederation has any faster or stronger ships. Our intervention may not be necessary."

"Thanks, that one missed me. But with your help I got to know his mind pretty well, and he's an Admiral, remember. If they had *Angel*s he'd know. The do have big battleships, but they're as slow as the night before Christmas. Anything else?"

"Three. We owe him." She sat still with steady eyes, the better to put weight on the point.

Denny cleared his throat. "Four. The *Kaltim* can take nine simultaneous hits before she's breached, so that well-named unfriendly fleet has weapons not quite as strong as your basic Confederation cruiser. Chicken teeth for us. But Spart didn't mention taking a poke at them, so we don't know if we can hurt them, either."

"May I make a point, Captain?"

Jander swiveled to the analyst at the computer console. "Of course, Geraldo."

The Italian computopath sat erect, tapping his feet under his chair. "The Admiral indicated that he was being chased by an entire fleet. That brings up two possibilities: one, they have something to protect; or two, they are the body or even the vanguard of an invasion in force. If the first is true we may be able to reason with them. If the latter is the case, they may keep going Admiral or no Admiral — and as Lady Alpha pointed out, Gaea is right in the way." He paused and gave an expressive shrug. "And her third point is also true. If it were not for his help, as unconscious as it may have been, we would not be out here."

Orion glared unseeing, staring at nothing, until the young computopath began to fidget. Abruptly Steele jerked to his feet. "I'll have to think about this. Maintain course and speed, Alpha. I'll be in quarters." He spun and strode to the hatch, which Angela whisked open just in time.

"Aye, sir. First Officer has the Bridge." Vickie watched him go, chewing her lip. The psychologist knew what was going on in his mind. This was his trial by fire; on this one decision would hang the future of the Omega Corps, perhaps the entire galaxy – and he chose to face it alone. Not for the first time was she proud of her husband; not for the last time was she glad she was not him.

STEELE FLOATED THROUGH THEIR HOME suite on Deck 15 and threw himself down on their "rack", a king-sized gel-bed in the back room of their spacious apartment. Tucking his hands behind his head, he scowled at the ceiling. Cinnamon padded in from wherever she had been napping, hopped up onto Vickie's pillow and started to purr, tail twitching in a rhythm of its own. He relaxed into the soothing sound as he tried to organize his thoughts.

This trip so far had been a disaster. First, they had gotten themselves lost like a pack of cub scouts; now they were in a situation that would stump Odin. They had gone too high too fast; their knowledge and talents had outrun their experience by far. They were not ready for this.

But they were in it. Steele turned first to the implications. The decision Vickie believed was the most difficult was actually the easiest; the Omega Corps was about to become a galactic power. That fact was inevitable; strength like theirs was meant to be used. The real question was the method that would best serve to introduce themselves as interstellar players.

His first instinct had been to communicate with

Spart, to compare notes, and above all to try to steer the *Kaltim* away from the Confederation frontier and Gaea. Steele would have offered the immense power at his command to get the Admiral to sheer off.

But what would be Spart's reaction? To the Admiral, Steele was a barbarian, an undisciplined savage. He would at least need a demonstration to appreciate the *Angel*'s capabilities – and that was where Steele's machinations on Gaea came back to haunt him. Spart had no reason to trust him – or like him, for that matter.

But above all, he would be rubbing Spart's nose in the First Law, and worse, in front of his crew. Every one of them was familiar with Gaea, her people and her potential. The only one who had had direct contact was the *Kaltim*'s commander, and the advent of Gaean power in the galaxy would be linked to that contact. Spart would be ruined at the very least. That would not do; as Vickie said, they owed him. The fact that he did not know they owed him had no bearing on Steele's thinking; he doubted that any one of the variants under his command even considered disregarding that debt and going their own way.

So, direct contact would not work. But Steele had to have information: who were the nasties and why were they so nasty? Could he communicate with them? Not likely; it was obvious from their reaction to the *Kaltim* that they were not in this region of space to make conversation. So why were they here? Exploration, invasion, protection? The second possibility was the only one with a clear-cut solution. They had few options, none of them anywhere close to ideal. Immersed, he thought his glum thoughts as the minutes ticked away.

Cindy, still purring, edged closer and nuzzled his ear. He started, reached up to give her a few backhand strokes, and rolled to his feet. Strong, determined, with step firm and head high, he strode from the suite.

"CAPTAIN ON THE BRIDGE!" Angela announced.

Jander felt a spike of charged nerves as he entered. Vickie spun out of the command chair as if it was red-hot. He cleared her by inches as he dropped into it, tapped the key to activate his heads-up display, and blinked twice at the broadcast icon.

"Attention, all personnel. I'll bare the bones of our situation – we're in a pickle jar with the lid welded on. But we have the power and the resources to handle any situation in all of space – and we're going to use them!

"I'll see the following Corpsmen in briefing room B16: Portuna, Harmonia, Horsense, Seabhac. All other personnel to amber ready. Proceed!"

He clicked off his heads-up and turned to the bridge officers. "Pavel, you have the con. Alexiy, Nwoye, see to it that when we reach rendezvous we are the same speed and heading as that fleet. I want us baffled in plenty of time to arrive undetectable.

Kitsune, get as much information from your sensors as you can as we approach them." Kurino Yukio, the petite Japanese ghost, nodded sharply, eager to prove her skills.

Steele gestured his two top commanders and Geraldo Belocci, Corpsman Portuna, out the hatch and across the eight steps to the smaller of the two conference rooms. The three other crewmen were right behind them – the ship's transportation was that fast. Jander tapped a pad to slide the hatch closed and took his place at the head of the table as the others found seats along the side facing the monitor on the port bulkhead.

"Thank you. Our primary task," he began, "is to procure information. All else depends on that. You four will get us that information. We'll be within the warp sphere of the fleet, so we can sneak in under our inner sphere and they'll never know we're there. Angela, let's see the fleet from the angle of our nearest approach."

The monitor came alive with a display of the hostile fleet extrapolated from Spart's broadcast hologram, scattered in no disciplined order but driving with singular purpose. "We will get you as close as possible to an unfriendly ship, and you will get even closer by taking a baffle-shielded Banshee trainer clear up to their screens. You will wear remote feeder helmets and shoot your intel straight to Angela."

He pointed to Henry Wallace, a former ranch foreman from the Outback of Northern Australia who took the whimsical name of Horsense. "As telepath, Hank, yours will be the most important task. I'm sending Sharon along in case their minds are so alien an ordinary telepath can't read them. I don't expect results from you, Sharon, but I want to cover all the bases."

Sharon Gibson, known as Harmonia, nodded once. The clinical zoologist had a range of zootelepathy that surpassed everyone else on the ship.

"You will pilot unless you are needed, in which case you will turn over control to Quinn. I consider clairvoyant information secondary to mental. Geraldo, of course, will try to tap the computers. Pay particular attention to where they came from, what they're after, and how they intend to get it. Questions?"

"What if we're discovered? Do we shoot back?" Quinn O'Hearne asked.

"You won't have anything to shoot with, Seabhac. You'll be flying a gutted trainer with extra screening instead of a weapons console. That's the only way we can give you both the maneuverability you'll need and the necessary baffle screens. Denny, see to that, if you please."

"You got it," Denny nodded.

"I can't emphasize enough," Jander continued, "that I want you all back in one piece. If even a hostile thought comes your way, zig out of there fast. Anything else?"

No one spoke. He dismissed them with a wave and they scrambled out, headed for the hangar deck far above.

Vickie smiled her approval. "Good. Fine."

Denny waved at her and pointed to his temple. She opened a telepathic link and served as a conduit as Denny sent instructions to his chief mechanic in the hangar. "But that's only the beginning," he rumbled. "So we get our intelligence, hopefully without getting our tails singed. Then what?"

Steele opened his mouth, but Vickie beat him to it. "If they are an exploration or protection force, we try to reason with them, in their own language if possible. If they mean business, we get hostile, right?"

"In essence," Jander confirmed. "Most of all we get them off Spart's back, either by leading them by the nose until they get tired, or by testing our weaponry. But if we blast, we blast in a very special way. I don't want to just whip them, but scare the hell out of them. We back off a few light years, cut the baffle screens and come in like gangbusters, thrice as big as life and ten times as mean. When they lose, I want them to know they never should have tried."

"What about the *Kaltim*?"

"Let 'em watch. All they'll take back to the Confederation is a report of some mystery ship with twice the speed and twenty times the power of anything they've ever seen." After a moment he added, "I hope. Let me tell you, our trip so far has brought me down a peg. Or three. But I'm still confident, if no longer arrogant."

He looked hard at them. "I have a job for you two, difficult and permanent. Wherever we go, whatever we do, don't let me forget that lesson."

CHAPTER 22

Snug within her inner warp sphere, the *Angel* penetrated the vastly larger sphere generated by the fleet and approached under the protection of her baffle shield. A hatch at the top of an equatorial Cancer section slid aside and a Banshee-T glided out, the versatile Sharon Gibson at the controls. The agile little trainer, twelve meters long, slipped like a fish and skirted the ship to the other side.

Timed to the millisecond by Angela, the section of defensive screen farthest from the fleet softened, and the zootelepath blended her charge through the opening. Undetectable now, the Banshee-T circled the mother ship and used its superior speed within the fleet's warp sphere to worm its way between the hostile ships.

The four variants in their bulky environmental suits were crammed into the three-man trainer. Wallace and Belocci were folded in behind the spot where the instructor's seat had been ripped out to make room for the massive baffle screen generator. Denny's telekinetic lead mechanic had installed the hardware and snaked its wiring through to the tablicy discs attached to the hull. The mechanism was so greedy for space and power that the Corps' engineers had been unable to make it standard equipment in the smaller ships. Bolted in now as an emergency addition, it left the passengers barely enough room to sit.

Hank and Geraldo were already probing the chosen target ship, shooting their results through their feeder caps back to the *Angel*. Sharon and Quinn, pilot and navigator, also meshcapped inside their helmets, guided the unbalanced craft as close as possible to an alien ship.

Steele sat in his command chair, capped, assimilating the information as it came in. It was not very clear; the unfriendly's collision screens extended thirty diameters from the ship, and the Banshee could not penetrate without sending the cruiser into defensive frenzy. The variants had to try to unscramble fifty alien brains and scores of cubic meters of computer from an uncomfortable distance. Belocci, one of his best computopaths, was stumped; the processers and their code were too alien, too far away. Wallace was likewise frustrated despite his exceptionally long telepathic reach.

The clairvoyant information was by far the most complete. O'Hearne, the Irish metallurgist, had a good "eye" for what was vital and what was not; even though it would require the *Angel*'s computer to make sense of a lot of it, he had no doubt as to what constituted weaponry and screen.

Quinn also took time to "see" the crew; they were furred, slit-eyed and swivel-eared felids. They were bipedal, humanoid, and had no tails, but none of them doubted that they were an intelligent analog of cats. Their uniforms were simple crossed suspenders with insignia at the center, and mid-thigh shorts over high-strapped sandals. The sleek fur so displayed was a uniform khaki with gold highlights.

The telepathic information was sketchy at best. Sharon, as Steele had more than expected, received nothing more than the equivalent of vermin stowaways. Wallace was having tremendous difficulty with thought patterns far more alien than Spart's, even though there was no interference from any mental broadcasts in the empty space between the two vessels.

One thing was certain, however; the alien crew were not even close to human, no more in mentality than in feature. And they were for some reason supremely inimical to anything that was.

Their story, even if scrambled, was unanimous. Spart had attempted contact with visual communication; one look, and the felids had recoiled with furious loathing and started blasting. Their fear and hatred were fanatical, and neither Wallace nor Steele, nor Vickie as she listened in, could find any reasonable basis for it. They were determined to follow Spart until he tired, and when they finished with him they would go on until everything smart and hairless was dead.

"Recall the Banshee. The report isn't worth the risk." Tsin flashed a split-second signal and the trainer headed back.

NIL SPART WAS WELL AWARE that he and his crew were about to die. They were running now, but he knew they could expect neither escape nor rescue. He was a courageous man – the fact that he chose to command a single exploration cruiser at his rank was an indication of his character – and soon would come the time when he would turn his ship and go out in a blinding blaze of spectacular nucleonic fury. He intended to leave behind alien debris for his Confederation colleagues to examine, making his sacrifice worth the cost. But death, even a proud one, was far from welcome.

He opened his tired eyes and gazed around the control room of the *Kaltim* from his seat at the aft console. The command team, nine people from six species of the eleven that comprised the Confederation, were stolidly attentive at their stations that faced inward around the circular chamber. They were taking care of business with a dedication that made him release a sigh of admiration.

He stared into the meters-wide three-dimensional hologram elevated in the center of the tall chamber, with the *Kaltim* represented by a pulsing purple dot soaring through the varicolored starfield. Behind her, at the narrow distance of three light-seconds, the vanguard of the largest fleet he had ever seen outside the Confederation stretched off into the distance, each ship represented by a fluorescent green spark.

The pursuing cruisers were somewhat smaller than their Confederation counterparts; their pace was an infinitesimal bit faster than his heavier ship, a difference made significant by the days the chase had lasted.

Within nine hours they would catch him. But long before then, Spart would turn and fight, denying them the technological coup of a capture. And in leading them, then delaying them, he might make it possible for the Confederation to mobilize and stop them before they could cause the havoc they clearly intended. He would use every strength of the *Kaltim* and every iota of his combat experience to...

What was that? He sat up and narrowed his eyes at the edge of the hologram. Far away, on the very fringe of his sensors' range, a bright pink point of light representing an unknown vessel materialized and began to grow. Second by second, the point became a dot and then a disk as it came nearer. Spart marveled at its apparent size and speed.

"Tukhu, focus on that new intruder," he spoke to his Dwatan sensors officer. She swept her prehensile tail up and over her furred shoulder in acknowledgement and flew her four-fingered hands over her board.

On the bulkhead in front of him, the large primary monitor focused a quantum-collected closeup image of the unknown ship, with statistics building in a column to the side. Shape, roughly spherical, but reflecting his sensors as if faceted. Size, thrice his, more than that of the pursuing ships. Motive force, eleven-plus standard gravities per second squared, *decelerating* despite showing no blaze of drive engines. Huge, powerful, mysterious.

The stranger was coming from a direction not quite behind the enemy fleet. Spart sagged. He doubted that the cat-like warriors would leave an enemy so formidable at their backs. It had to be allied with them.

Spart knew their time had come. Eyes burning with resolve, he said, "Prepare to come about."

Swiftly, efficiently, and without hesitation, his bridge crew moved to obey: The Leosan navigator plotted the course for the Fthlonian helmsman; the Sabarian communications officer broadcast the action alert to the rest of his compartmented shipmates; the Hasgondi environmentals officer activated the color-coded warning for closing crash doors; the Kanitak defense engineer extended and strengthened the deflection screens; the gunnery chief, another coarse-pelted Fthlonian, alerted his gunners to stand to.

His Kanitak first officer, halfway through one of its species' voluntary sex changes, circled through the room checking each station, then exited to report to its station at the emergency bridge amidships. The Sabarian analytics chief muttered a jest to the Leosan damage control liaison and got an apprecia-tive burble in response.

Spart watched them with pride, listening to them giving their orders in their mutually understood

254 ♦ Keith Huntsman

native tongues with cool professionalism. They were explorers, courageous entities all, knowing they were about to face their final battle and accepting it with unruffled stoicism.

"Admiral..." The sensors officer waved her blue velvet-furred arm toward the hologram and chittered, "The fleet is turning."

Spart snapped erect and glared into the crowded cluster of ships. The fleet was indeed sheering off. In twos and threes the eighty cruisers curved in unpracticed disorder and headed back toward the stranger. Spart saw a ray of hope.

"Helm! Cut power. Let's see what's up." If the stranger was attacking the fleet, he definitely wanted to watch. If it was here to attack him... well, no extra speed or distance would help. The *Kaltim*'s nucleonic drivers rumbled down to idle and the ship continued toward the edge of the fleet's warp sphere on her hyperlight-speed momentum.

The mighty gem-ship grew to impossible size. She was close enough now, twelve light seconds, that she was quite distinct to their excellent quantum particle sensors. He stared fascinated at the glittering blue spheroid, wondering what the motive power could be. He could see no flare of violent energy; any such would have been detectable since the ship was back-driving to decelerate. The familiar silver-black of solar accumulators was offset by scintillating disks that were probably electronics arrays, and huge reddish-gold rings in each quadrant of each facet that could only be the engines. Spart felt a flash of excitement. Could it be some sort of gravity drive?

The giant globe continued to decelerate until it entered the fleet's warp sphere and assumed the pace of the fleet. Its defensive screens, of a type and intensity the *Kaltim*'s sensors could not identify, shimmering with a misty glow that showed she was ready for trouble.

And she found it.

With no further investigation and without any discernable warning, the leading elements of the massive fleet opened fire!

Thirty-eight powerful bolts of searing energy leaped from nineteen ships, each potent globule followed in less than a second by another, and another. The plasma blasts struck and spread, tearing and punching at the stranger like strobe lights striking a wall. They stopped a full ten diameters from the hull with no effect whatever.

Correction, he could see one effect. Spart snapped a curse of amazement. The nanosteel sides of the spheroid glittered with visible light – light that the photovoltaic accumulators would gobble up with a ravenous appetite. The mighty ship was actually *fueling* from the beams meant to destroy her!

The giant jewel just hung there in space, glowing under the bombardment, as if to tease the fleet with its impotence. Spart wondered if the stranger would even bother to respond. But after a few moments, as more and more ships came into range and joined the assault, dark areas appeared on the faceted hull as hatches two meters across spiraled open. Huge, thick tubes that had to be offensive weapons slid outward, swiveling as they sought and locked onto targets. And then, with no more warning than the sinister fleet, the massive fortress answered the challenge.

From at least twenty dark cylinders, reddish spheres burst outward at tremendous velocity. Less than half a second later, twenty more followed. Second after second, the great cannons spewed out sphere after sphere of solid energy. As if screen and nanosteel alike did not exist, the spheres crashed into the massed ships.

Each shot was a hit. Every hit was a hole almost two meters wide in an enemy hull, many of them going through and through. A dozen torn and riddled hulks spun away, screens flickering in their death throes. Ten more exploded with brief but eye-tearing coruscation as their ruptured power plants vented their energies in one all-consuming blast that devoured the oxygen in the ships, and the massive concussions threw countless shards of debris in all directions. Several other targets were crushed like bugs under a boot as their inertia absorption generators failed and they were brutally compressed under their own mass.

Even as their loose formation became even more chaotic trying to evade the terrible carnage, dozens of other ships opened fire. The stranger changed course at a speed that would have torn any Confederation ship to shreds and bore down on another group of the disorganized fleet. Again the great guns spoke, this time joined by another type that shoved out meter-wide pillars of violent destruction, clubbing and chopping the enemy ships into pieces, each fraction collapsing like crumpled paper. Back and forth, up and down and sideways, the mighty stranger spun in a dizzying dance, dealing incredible perdition with every blow.

Spart came alive. "Well?" His crew jumped, so fascinated by the sight that they forgot where they were. "Are we going to let them do all our work for us? Let's go!"

Howling like savages, the suddenly galvanized Confederation crew leaned into their stations. Under their furious direction, the *Kaltim* retroed end for end and relit her main engines to kill her momentum and drive into the fray.

STEELE, A RASP IN HIS THROAT and a tight, approving smile on his grim face, sat back in satisfaction. Almost two thirds of the enemy ships were crushed metal, drifting derelicts or dissipating clouds of volatile gas, and the rest were fleeing to all points in abject panic. It would be a cold day on Rigel before the ferocious invaders penetrated this region again.

Nwoye Lam had settled into a furious rhythm and was attending to his helm with gusto, using the magnificently efficient superconductive gravity drive under his command to shift the *Angel* in the direction of the largest clumps of enemy. Kalanev's gunners did the rest. The weapons had more than met their expectations, and those who wielded them were trained on simulators to be hard-eyed, expert shots.

Steele had watched with silent respect as the *Kaltim* had charged into the enemy flank, dealing death, if not as abrupt as the *Angel*'s, then every bit as final. Steele had considered cutting the force of a beam projector to push the Admiral out of the way with its pressor effect – it would only take one stray shot from the *Angel* to pulp the little cruiser – but he decided to let Spart have his day. He had led a dauntless chase, and anyway he was entitled to a bit of revenge. Besides, sweet-natured Yukio at her sensors station had wasted no time flagging the *Kaltim* as friendly, directing Angela to abort any gunshot that might endanger her.

"We're running out of easy targets, sir." Lam called. "The blessed remains are scattering to the solar winds."

Steele nodded. "Cobra, cease fire. Revert to amber ready. Scatter, hold position. We'll wait until they're out of sight."

"Here comes the Admiral." Kurino highlighted the frame of a monitor displaying a side view. Tsin switched the scene to the primary screen without being asked, and the *Kaltim* leaped into focus.

"He's signaling, sir. Tight beam tachyon."

"Ignore it." The Confederation cruiser paused in

front of them, then circled, looking over the *Angel* from every possible angle. Steele wished he could see the Admiral's face.

"Mr. Pashkov, do you know where we are yet?"

"Yes, sir. And I know where Gaea is in relation to us."

"We're not heading for Gaea. We don't want either of our playmates to have the slightest clue to our origin. Just see that you do." The navigator grinned sheepishly. "Mr. Lam, come to course twelve-thirteen, nine gravities squared."

Nwoye's fingers and mind flew over his controls and the *Angel* leaped away in the direction between hull panels twelve and thirteen, at right angles to their previous course.

Spart, knowing he was far outclassed even within the lesser pace of his warp sphere, did not try to follow. Within minutes the mystery ship's image on his sensors dwindled to nothing.

CHAPTER 23

Hours later, undetectable, the *Angel* crept back to the scene of battle. The *Kaltim* was still there, searching the wreckage for clues to the fleet's origin. Under Kurino's meticulous direction, the *Angel*'s sensors staff created a three-dimensional hologram of the battle sphere and displayed it on the Bridge in front of Tsin, but for the most part they waited, knowing what was certain to come.

Three days passed before Confederation battle squadrons began to arrive, among them a fuel freighter for the *Kaltim*. For weeks thereafter, behind a heavy screen of warships, the scientists of eleven species plowed through the wreckage collecting reams of data: anatomy, electronics, chemistry, engineering, weapons, environmentals, a thousand and one details of life and science in Sfor society.

And around the derelicts, between the Confederation ships, through and through the battle sphere, the *Angel*'s shielded Sprites watched and listened, picking up every iota of information gleaned by the Confederation inspectors. Unseen and unsuspected, the Corps learned everything the searchers learned and a lot more.

After three Gaean weeks the cruisers and the science ships departed, frustrated in their attempts to find clues to the location of the Sforan homeworld. They left most of the wreckage behind, and something they would have given their collective arm for — a survivor.

It was Alpha herself, aboard a baffle-screened Sprite shuttlecraft, who detected the alien thoughts. A lone crewman was tucked into a compartment for air recyclers that had retained its integrity despite the violent destruction of the rest of the ship. At a moment when the Confederation investigators were looking the other way, Steele threw an airtight mental screen around the injured Sforan's hiding place and broke it down. Vickie penetrated the orphaned piece of ship and secured the survivor with her telekinesis. The Sprite slid back into the *Angel*'s hangar, opened its hatch to receive the quantum pulse designed to eliminate contaminants, and the felid was half-carried, snarling and spitting despite his terror and his broken bones, into the *Angel*'s sickbay.

Vickie, whose telepathy was unsurpassed, nonetheless ran into great difficulty trying to read the alien's disjointed thoughts. Still, she was able to discern that he was a technical assistant attached to his ship's navigation division, which was exactly the kind of crewman the Confederation was seeking.

That got a fist pump from Jander, who saw the great advantage of making first contact and presenting the Confederation with a coup to prove the Corps' value.

But digging the information out of the Sforan's

scattered mind would require forcing him to concentrate.

After hours of challenging work, Terry Kirkland and her team managed to repair the uncooperative captive, and he was healthy enough for questioning. Since Gaean and Sforan vocal structures were so different that neither could speak the other's language, the survivor had an educator meshcap designed for Dwatans crammed onto his head to learn and understand Sabarian.

He was then brought by a pair of telekinetic guards to the spacious gravity gym for interrogation. Its padded walls were lined by several Corpsmen that included a werewolf, two ghosts in spectral form and two more telekinetics suspended in mid-air. To further impress the Sforan the Corpsmen were in full dress uniform: black slacks, matte black boots, and gold-accented crimson turtleneck under a flare-shouldered nanosteel-blue jerkin, cinched by a wide black utility belt and topped by a flat cap also in silvery nanosteel blue.

To ratchet up the tension even more, the Corpsmen waited with their captive in sinister silence. After several minutes of that Jander at last made his entrance, flanked by Vickie and Denny, and stood and glared down at the much smaller alien for several seconds. He turned abruptly, eliciting a flinch and a blink of nictitating eyelids from the cat-man, and went to sit in a thronelike chair installed for the occasion. Vickie, by now well-known to the captive as a high officer, stood at his right with her hand on the high back of the throne. Walter Rosenberg, in wolf form, padded over to stand to his left.

Steele fixed the Sforan with an iron stare. "I am Orion, lord of this ship and the master of your fate. Your fleet attacked a Confederation exploration ship without warning. You chased it hundreds of parsecs intent on destroying it, and when our ship responded to their distress call you dared to attack us. Your fleet instigated an act of war without provocation and without cause. Why?"

The felid stood with Doppelwulf in front of him and Kodiak behind. It was impossible to tell whether the titan or the werewolf frightened him more. Looking into his alien mind, Vickie saw only hatred and dread, with a complete disregard for his damaged first-level nerves that Terry Kirkland's transmutation could not repair. Reasoning with him was not an option. And the Sforan proceeded to prove the fact.

He spat on Orion's boot.

Connors waved a hand, and the felid flew through the air to smash hard into the padded bulkhead. The titan reached the stunned cat-man with one huge stride, lifted him by his cross-belted suspenders and shook him like a rag. Poking a finger the size of a fluorescent bulb and a million times as hard at the Sforan's fuzzy nose, he said, "You oughta be more polite."

"Toss him over here." Denny underhanded the alien to sprawl at Steele's feet. Instantly he scrambled to a crouch and leaped to the attack. Vickie made a dramatic open-handed gesture and caught him in an invisible net of telekinetic energy that squeezed him to a halt in mid-air. Walter tensed his canine haunches and took a lunging pounce forward with a vicious snarl and snapped inch-long fangs right in the Sforan's face. His nictitating eyelids slammed shut as fright became terror.

"Keep in mind," Steele said in an even voice, "that if it weren't for us, you would be dead. But if you continue this level of cooperation we can remedy that easily, by pieces. I want some answers and I intend to hear them."

"You will get no information from me, *skinface*." The word was a curse. "I am a Sforan soldier. I do not fear death and I do not fear you." His thoughts belied his words, as did the wet patch on his shorts, but somehow he held his ground.

"What are the coordinates of your home world?" Steele rapped, and Vickie bored in with an over-whelming telehypnotic demand. But she found something entirely unexpected; the alien's felid instincts sensed the influence and fought it, thinking of anything but his planet. He glared his silent defiance and allowed Vickie only a blur of his written language. Steele realized that this was going to be a lot tougher than he had expected.

"Very well. Kodiak?"

Playing his part to the hilt, Denny assumed a ruthless grin and reached. The Sforan again flew across the room, but this time he did not land. Connors, with the speed that enabled him to run a mile in less than two minutes, darted back and forth across the high-ceilinged room playing a spirited game of volleyball with himself. After a dozen or so brutal slaps and flips, Kodiak caught the half-crushed cat-man with one massive hand in the utility belt holding up his wet shorts and again held him forward.

"Well?" Steele was appalled, but he did not permit it to show. A look into Denny's mind reassured him that the titan was anything but overjoyed with this brutality himself. "Are you ready to cooperate?"

The battered felid spat again. "I am not impressed by your strongman. A real commander would do his own dirty work."

Steele had to admire his guts, but he had a job to do. Fighting his own conscience, he pointed with his first and second fingers. A coruscating nimbus enveloped his hand and lightning flashed, enhanced by a sizzling sonic wave, and one of the alien's high-set pointed ears fell to the floor. "I could do my own dirty work, as you say." Another sizzling flash and the ear split in two. Its previous owner gaped at it. "But my friend Kodiak, here, kind of enjoys it." Flash, and one of the Sforan's twelve fingers bounced at his feet. "Don't you, Kodiak?"

Keeping his almost casual grip on the felid's belt, Connors stooped and picked up the severed finger. With a ferocious smirk, he held up the gruesome relic and turned it slowly, allowing the stunned Sforan to get a very good look at it. Then, with every evidence of enjoyment, he bit off half of it and chewed.

The Sforan's bowels failed and he fainted.

Steele almost did. "Shit, Kodiak!" Vickie looked very sick.

The titan, looking rather green, spat out the piece of finger. The mangled remnant bounced in front of a spectator, who gagged and turned away. Denny spat repeatedly, the unconscious Sforan still dangling from the end of his reach. "Damn. Don't ask me to do that again."

"Don't worry, man." Dazed, Jander strove to gather his thoughts. "That's enough of that. I don't think I can continue this line of interrogation. We'll try a different tack from now on. Peregrine!" A Corpsman stepped forward. "Take this poor bastard down to sick bay and get him cleaned up. When he regains consciousness ask Dr. Kirkland to put him back together. I want him to see the process."

Jack Whitney, a former criminologist and better used to carnage, mentally pulled the alien from Connors' loosened hand, picked up the scattered body parts in a telekinetic net and floated the still form out of the room.

Vickie recovered somewhat, grimaced and rubbed her nose to try to alleviate the stench of carnivore scat. "What are your intentions now?"

"I want him to see that we can be as compassionate as we are implacable. Superior force he understands. Now that he's convinced we'll go to any lengths, maybe he'll be more reasonable. At least he respects our power now."

"I hope so." She was still a little shaken. "I was starting to get into his mind. Denny's... act... impressed him considerably, believe me."

"I did kinda get carried away, there," the titan rumbled, "but it seemed like a good idea at the time." He was still spitting.

"It was, buddy, and it sure worked," Steele assured him. "Go get a drink." Connors almost bowed and strode from the room. Still spitting.

THE NEXT CONFRONTATION took place in sickbay, less Denny and the werewolf. The Sforan sat on a diagnostic stool with his hands free, with Whitney close by. Terry stepped back with a professional glare of disapproval, then slipped into the background. The Sforan held up an intact six-fingered hand and touched his brand new ear. "Why have you done this?"

"Because an intelligent being does not cause damage without reason," Steele responded. "Do you have a name?"

The felid took the implied insult without a quiver, if he noticed it at all. "Habo Esfha, Technician Second Class. Yours?"

"I'll ask the questions," Steele reminded him. "The first one, you've been asked before. Why did you attack the Confederation ship?"

The alien sat stolid. Steele pointed a finger. Esfha recoiled, and decided that further hesitation was unwise.

"A few thousand years ago," he said, "Mother Sfor was attacked by creatures much like you. Millions were murdered without cause, and we were smashed back into a period of barbarism the like of which you could never know. Worse, they wanted nothing from our world. They killed, destroyed, and went away. That was thousands of years ago, and we have lived with the dream of vengeance ever since. Indeed, it was the purpose behind our determination to reach outer space."

He paused, clearly revising his thoughts with what he had learned the past few days. "The ship we pursued, from that Confederation you talk about, was not the first to come into our reach. About fifty years ago another came right to our Sfor. The skinfa – the people landed, and we killed them and studied the ship. A lot of it was beyond our understanding, but we learned enough that we could build a fleet and strike in the direction the ship had come from."

"And it did not occur to you that they may have come to you in peace?"

"Why should it?" The Sforan's bitterness was obvious.

Vickie stepped in over Steele's momentary pause. "We know of several relatively hairless species in this region. We are one; five members of the Confederation are the others. Both the Confederation and we have an unbreakable law of non-intervention that would prohibit such a landing – or an invasion. The landing was probably made by another species, and the invasion by still another."

The Sforan eyed her skeptically. "How am I supposed to believe you?"

"You're alive, aren't you?" Vickie pointed out.

"And so are billions of other Sforans. Will that hold true after you use me to find them?"

Jander had an inspiration. "Harmonia! Direct Cindy to come here."

Sharon Gibson nodded, and her brow creased with effort. "Angela, clear the way for Cinnamon by telebooth."

Steele addressed the Sforan, "A couple of descriptions for creatures in your language correspond to two of ours, 'monkey' and 'cat'. You are descended from the cat line; we are members of the ape family. On your planet the feline type became intelligent and prospered; on ours it was the primates who progressed. I can show you proof that any planet's evolution can be similar to any others'; nature does not believe in taking chances. If one species fails another can succeed."

Right on cue, Steele's cat trotted into the room. She looked around, spotted the unfamiliar Sforan, and tiptoed to sniff at his ankles. Steele went on, "Is it logical to assume that if our two planets could produce similar forms, many more could do the same?"

Esfha stared wide-eyed at the tortie. "We have animals... so much like this..." Gently he reached down to touch her head. Excited by the feline scent of the technician, Cindy leaped into his lap, laid her paws on his furred chest and butted her head on his chin, purring in mad abandon.

Profoundly shocked, totally confused, Esfha curled his broad hands around the cat and lifted his eyes to the Gaean's. "Lord Orion... I must think. May I humbly request a place of solitude?"

Steele smiled and nodded, and gestured to the watchful Whitney. "Show our guest to a room, and see to his needs."

Carrying the cat as if she were the most precious creation of the universe, the Sforan followed the Corpsman out.

CHAPTER 24

The *Angel* drove its warp sphere through normal space at a reduced pace that would allow the battered fleet time to return to Sfor. Jander Steele and Habo Esfha relaxed together in the park, watching Cindy scramble along a branch after a far more nimble squirrel. The Sforan emitted the moist hissing that served his species as a chuckle and leaned back against the tree with a sigh.

"This is the most wonderful feature of your magnificent ship," he said. "I cannot reconcile the fact that such a mighty instrument of war could contain such beauty." He looked at his host. "I do not suppose…"

"That I'll let you see the rest? No," Jander responded, still in Sabarian. English was too unique to Gaea to risk using. "Our superiority in arms and science is our greatest security. Second is the fact that our origins and the location of our homeworld is unknown even to the Confederation. Most of our people have no real desire for outside contact – in fact, we have some who have considerable aversion to it. This ship is crewed by what is a minority of our species, those who are adventurers at heart and have the open-mindedness to see the Confederation as a friend. But not even the Confederation knows what our true power is, much less have they seen it. We're not about to let anyone have free run of the *Angel*."

Esfha swallowed his double-talk whole without the slightest sign on indigestion. He pondered for a moment, then said, "I noticed that during my... interrogation that someone was trying to twist my mind. And I've seen other evidence of great mental power. The gi-giant –" he swallowed reflexively "– is understandable. He had to have been born on a planet of tremendous gravity. But the doctor? And the guard, who binds me without chains. And the lightning from your fingertips. What is the explanation for those?"

Steele thought a moment, working to modify a description of the skills of the Corpsmen to fit the audience. "Every member of this company has at least one ability beyond the first level of intelligence. Most of the talents are mental manifestations of physical phenomena, or a mental extension of the senses. But about twenty percent are telepathic to some degree. One of us can influence the thoughts of others. The fact that the attempt failed with you is a result of the essential difference between the evolution of our minds. Otherwise. you would have babbled until told to stop."

No one could tell if the Sforan turned white under his light brown fur, but his fists clenched. "That is tremendous power, frightening power." He took a deep breath. "Do all your people have such power?"

"Not all, no. Enough."

Esfha did not ask what it was enough for. "With all that power, both of mind and machine, how is it that you are content with such a small role in the galaxy? If my people were so endowed, we would conquer all of space."

"And perhaps that is why you are not so endowed." Jander lay back and closed his eyes, ending the conversation. The Sforan's eyes glazed over in thought. After a while, he slowly rotated a shoulder in his species' equivalent of an introspective nod.

DESPITE VICKIE'S VEHEMENT PROTESTS, Jander decided to accompany Esfha to the surface of his planet.

"Why you?" She was almost steaming with frustration. "Why not Mimic? He can gather information just as well as you can. Why not Pavel? He's not only a telepath, he's a trained spy, for heaven's sake. Why does it have to be you?"

Steele sighed and tried again. "Because the Sforans will shoot on sight, Esfha or no Esfha. Not only can I protect myself, but I'll be undetectable until the last minute. And these people best understand power. They won't listen to just anybody; it has to be the number one big kahuna. And with the ambassador in the first boatload, we won't need telepathic reconnaissance. Why should I send someone down into danger, then haul him back up, wring him out, then go down myself?"

"Then take me! I'm a telepath, I can protect myself, and you can cover us both with your shield."

"Aha. I thought that was what you wanted – and it's still no. I may be down there for hours. You know as well as I do that Habo isn't the brightest bulb in the footlights, and we'll have to go at his pace. I'm not all-powerful; eventually I'll run out of energy, and the less I have to cover the longer I can keep it up."

"But –"

He stepped into arm's reach and put a finger to her lips. "I know how you feel, honey, but please, think. I am the one person best suited for the job. Two could do it no better, and to remove the top command from the ship in one swell foop would be stupid." Her lips twitched into a bitter smile despite herself, and his fingertip traced the curve of her lip. "That's more like it. I need someone I trust completely on the bridge. You are the only one in the universe I trust completely."

She pulled his hand down with both of hers and stroked each of his fingers. "If you're trying to turn my head, it won't work. I'll miss all the fun." She attempted a grin; it wavered and failed. She stepped closer, buried her head in his shoulder and clung to him, dry-eyed and strong, but very, very much in love.

At last, she looked up into his eyes and stepped away. "Be careful, darling."

"I promise, I'll act as if it were *your* life I was protecting." He closed the distance between them and kissed her, then walked away.

HABO ESFHA MATERIALIZED IN a quiet corner of the Fhoa equivalent of Central Park. Fhoa was the administrative capital of Sfor, as well as base for the fleet. Reconnaissance from the *Angel*'s invisible orbit had shown that the remnants had finished straggling in some days before.

Esfha was momentarily dazed by the sudden change of scene. Teleporting by machine was slower than by mind, but it was still almost instantaneous.

The park was a lush island of dense trees, untrimmed undergrowth and mulched paths through wildflowers in great variety. It was surrounded by gleaming towers of glass and steel that soared a minimum of ten stories each into the pale blue sky.

Jander was astonished by the architecture. Since the Sforan people were somewhat smaller than Gaeans, he had expected structures to scale. What he did not expect was the shape. The buildings were cylindrical and quite thin with few interior rooms, and each story of even the highest structures was encircled by an open balcony accessible through clear glass patio doors. He wondered how such a culture of open vistas could stand to operate in the airtight and windowless environment of a spacecraft.

"Where to?" Steele had had his vocal chords altered by Terry so he could converse in the Sforan primary language, which was otherwise impossible for humans to speak. But other than that, he had retained his shaven face and robust human form, clad again in the Corps dress uniform that was currently rendered invisible with the rest of him.

Esfha jumped at the disembodied voice. He had been told very little of what to expect, so that Steele could get unpremeditated responses from him. "I will have to find out. I need someone who knows me, and what ship I was on. They must be convinced that I could not have returned by myself. What makes this difficult is that I have no idea which ships were destroyed."

"Would the fleet publish a list?"

"Yes, sir. There should be one at the spaceport. But that is several thousandspans away."

"Take my hand."

Esfha felt the touch and closed with it. Instantly he could see the tall Gaean. He hunched low and looked around him in alarm.

"Easy," Jander soothed. "I'm not visible, you are invisible. You're inside my shield. Now we can both fly to the spaceport. Which way? I'm turned around."

The Sforan squinted, then decided to ignore the expression and pointed.

"Okay. Close your eyes, Habo. The sight may unnerve you."

The cat-man did so, but when he felt no change, he opened them again. Shrieking in fright, he whirled and wrapped himself around the startled Orion.

Jander cursed and made the screen opaque. "I told you not to look," he chided. "I need an open screen to navigate. If you think you can stand ten thousandspans of nothing, okay. But if you're going to act like a scared rabbit, close your eyes and keep them closed!"

Steele disengaged himself and set the Sforan down on the floor of the sphere. Chastened, Esfha stood trembling, staring in fascination as they continued on their way. His was an odd culture; thanks to the alien landing a mere fifty years before, the Sforans had gained space flight without transitioning through aircraft.

The broad concrete avenues below were filled with four- to six-wheeled rear-engine vehicles emitting gray clouds from tall exhaust stacks into the chill air. Steele noticed several circular farms within the city that had small foundries in the center. The farms seemed to produce a fast-growing hardwood tree harvested in pie slices, with the wood turned into charcoal in the foundries to power the steam-driven economy. That would define the city farms as fuel stations. The entire city appeared to be ever hazed by the coal exhaust as the cool climate tried to combat the pollution of an early industrial age.

Habo eventually got used to the altitude, and was even beginning to enjoy it as they left the city behind. They flew over an endless plain of dark green fern-like vegetation, populated with herds of bison-sized animals that were likely a food source.

Before long, the concrete and gravel expanse of the port came into view ahead and a bit to the right. "Not bad," Steele complimented him. "Only two points off. You sense of direction is excellent. Where would that list be?"

The felid preened a little at the praise. "In that big building, there." He pointed all six of his left fingers at a low, flat complex covering about four city blocks. It was constructed of domed glass columns with silo roofs, honeycombed with open courts to let in the cherished air and light.

"Okay. Remember, you're invisible. When we go in no one will see us."

They glided down and through wide double doors into a high-ceilinged circular lobby. Suspended above the heads of passing soldiers, Esfha grinned despite the gravity of their mission. He was getting to like this.

"Where to now?"

Esfha spun with a startled snarl, and Steele held up his free hand. "Relax! They can't hear us, either, though we can see and hear them perfectly well. Just trust me and follow my lead. Where is that list?"

Preferring to remain mute, the Sforan pointed down a nearby corridor that wound between the glass cortiles. Unnoticed, the pair glided in twists and turns through the building to hover beside a tall and broad announcement board. Esfha pored over the list for several minutes, then turned to Jander and rotated a shoulder.

"Got it?"

"Yes." He was still reluctant to speak aloud. "My childhood friend, Schach, was in a ship that came back. That makes me very happy."

"I know how you feel." Jander thought briefly about Spart, then he pushed it out of his mind. "Let's get out of here." He looked again at that long, long list and shook his head.

Not for the first time, he regretted the terrible object lesson his decisions had wrought. It had been necessary at the time to shock the warrior race into backing off their feral mission. But the sparkling city showed him that the Sforans were capable of peaceful cooperation and great communal splendor. It made the price of their education all the heavier on his conscience.

They lofted upward out of the building from a nearby open court and flew toward rows of ships broken by far too many empty spaces. Beyond them rose several hundred needle-like barracks, to one of which Esfha guided his strange pilot.

Jander landed them just outside the door and turned to the cat-man. "From here on, you're on your own. I can no longer communicate once you become known. But remember, I'll always be right behind you as long as you give me the room to navigate. Don't worry about incarceration and absolutely refuse to tell your story until we reach the top. And I mean, the top!"

With that firm admonishment and a quick look around, Steele released Esfha's hand and stepped back.

With no hint of transition his tall companion was no longer visible, and Esfha knew that he himself was back to normal. He took a deep breath to steady his nerves, then strode to the glass door and pushed his way in, holding it open for a few seconds before letting it close behind him.

"*HABO!*"

Esfha spun at the sound of his personal name. "Schach!"

Schach rushed forward and grabbed his friend by the shoulders. "Habo Esfha! I thought you lost!"

"I was," Esfha replied. "Or rather, I was rescued."

"Rescued – by whom? As cowardly and unworthy as it may sound, we all turned tail and ran from that terrible ship." His eyes watered. "All who could, that is. How were you rescued?"

"By the crew of that ship," Esfha told him, obviously forgetting Orion's instructions. "They treated my wounds and brought me back."

"Back here?" He looked around, his nictitating eyelids sliding to clear his vision. "Where are they? And why did they do it, after crushing us?"

"They crushed us because we were the aggressors, not from any will to cause harm. As to why they brought me back here and left me…" he tried to repair his blunder, "… I may tell only to the Sovereign. Will you help me, my friend?"

Schach recoiled. "The Sovereign! How in the world could I help you?"

"By testifying that my ship was destroyed. By swearing that I could not have returned any other way." He grabbed his friend by the crossed straps at his chest. "You must trust me, Schach, with your life!"

"And that's what I'd be doing." He dropped his own hands to Habo's wrists, his broad six-fingered grip encompassing most of his friend's forearms. "Such a task is too big for me alone. The Captain knows you — you've visited us here often enough." He considered, scratching the fur on his chest under the straps Habo still clutched. "For you, Habo. No one else would I trust so. If one of my own brothers came to me with such a story I would call him a liar." He yanked at Esfha's arm. "Come on. We'll go see the Captain."

They almost ran to the Captain's office. Schach slapped it perfunctorily and burst inside; Esfha, as he had been told to do, hesitated a few seconds before following. A slight breeze ruffled his fur, and he went in.

The Captain looked up with a frown. "What is it, Hoan?" Then he saw the slim figure behind him. He stared, incredulous. "Esfha?" He rose slowly, jaw hanging as if he'd seen a ghost. "Esfha! But your ship was lost!"

Esfha repeated his story, and so it was that three men sped to the squadron commander's office, four emerged and continued. And onward and upward, gathering numbers and momentum as they went. By the time they returned to the city and invaded the etched glass walls of the Residence of the Sovereign, they had grown to quite a squad of noisy, excited felids.

One by one the senior officers were summoned in to be seen by the Sovereign. At last he was convinced enough to interview the technician. The last high official to emerge from the elegant opaque glass office brought his message: "I will see this dead man, alone."

Esfha, by now quivering with stress, stepped between his superior officers and into the curtained room, hesitating three seconds as always before pulling the door closed behind him. He came to a halt before the ornate desk and threw his head back, exposing his neck in submission. "I am at your service, Sovereign."

The Sovereign, his only badge of rank being crossed straps of woven silver, stared at him for long seconds, searching for any sign of mental incapacity. "Tell me your story."

Esfha told him everything, starting with the first sighting of the stranger before the battle; through the fleet firing the first shot and the drubbing they got for it; the shattering of his own ship and his survival within a protected cubicle; then his capture, medical treatment and interrogation; and ending with his transportation to the surface; in precise detail, omitting nothing except for revealing Orion's presence.

He recounted the magical healing of his wounds, his many conversations with Orion and Alpha, his conversion from prejudice, and the powers of the Corpsmen and the *Angel*. The Sovereign sat passive, listening with apparent disinterest, yet hearing and remembering every incredible word. The technician was hoarse by the time he finished.

The Sovereign paused long in icy stillness. At last he said, "You swear this is the truth?"

"Yes, my Sovereign."

'Do you realize that if I choose not to believe you, you will be tried for desertion?"

"I understand, my Sovereign," and he could not resist adding, "although Lord Orion has promised me protection and safety."

The Sovereign stiffened and bared his teeth. "You presume to threaten me? You think your mooted miracle man is more powerful than I?"

Esfha stood silent, unmoving, with jaw clenched in fear but stubbornly determined.

The Sovereign rose to his feet, offended that this mere technician could deliver such an affront. His voice rose to a threatening snarl. "You fear this Orion more than you fear me?"

"Yes, Sovereign." Esfha was terrified, but he held his ground. "I fear him greatly, but I trust him more. If he swears to protect me, I believe him, and I stand firm!"

The Sovereign stalked around his glass desk to confront the impertinent upstart, then stopped himself short. This would not do. He had allowed this madman to agitate him almost to the point of physical contact. That would never do. He glared a moment, then stepped back, a furious glint in his slitted eyes. "Very well," he sneered. "Let us meet this miracle man."

That was the moment Steele had been waiting for. He dropped his shield, stepped forward to tower at Esfha's side, spread his empty hands wide and inclined his head forward in the exact opposite of the submission stance.

The Sovereign stood stone still, in absolute shock, for long seconds. Esfha used the time wisely, scrambling behind the only man in the galaxy who could now save his life. As if galvanized by the technician's movement, the Sovereign backpedaled to the frosted glass back wall and screamed, loud and long.

The door flew open, guns leaped into hands, and the room was filled with pyrotechnic fury!

CHAPTER 25

Orion stood calm, erect and unmoving in his dress uniform. The terrified Esfha cowered behind him, huddled almost lower than his protector's knees as spectacular hellfire blazed around them. The most powerful hand-held energy weapons ever developed or stolen by the planet Sfor clung to his defensive screen in spectacular waves.

He spent a moment being grateful that he had not given in to Vickie. The strain of covering three, as well as absorbing the violent energy into his shield and converting the worst of the wildly spattering fury to harmless flashes of light, would have been too much without taking offensive action. And that, Steele wanted to avoid at all costs.

The firing died down as guns emptied. But the wild expressions of fear and hatred, of all-consuming repugnance, remained far longer than the blasting energy. For of all the people in the room, only Esfha and the Sovereign knew that the man they had all served to bring here was wholly, purely and unequivocally, a big hairless ape.

At last the gunfire ceased. The Sovereign rose from the protection of his scorched desk and glared in fearful defiance at the invader. Steele kept his silence for log seconds, looking around to each of his attackers in turn. Not one of them tried to reload or to attack him physically. When at last he spoke, his voice held a perfect mixture of bland amusement and biting sarcasm. His psychologist wife would have been proud of him.

"Are you done?"

The Sovereign's furred jaw opened and closed repeatedly, gasping like a fish. It was seconds before he worked himself up to a splutter. At last he found his voice. "Out! All of you. Say nothing. Let no one enter or leave the Residence. Out!"

One by one, the frightened and humbled crowd filed out, leaving the Sovereign with his abhorrent guest. The last, a shocked and disillusioned Schach Hoan, closed the door behind him.

Steele reached back and helped Esfha to his feet. Turning to the shaking Sovereign, he said, "I am sure you have noted no offensive action on my part. Rest assured that I have come in peace, for the purpose of discussion only. Please feel free to take your chair."

The Sovereign was recovering from his fear, yet the loathing remained full force. "I shall remain standing, *skinface.*"

"As you wish. Please allow me to sit; I've had a tiring day." With that admission of weakness, he sat down in midair and propped his feet up on absolutely nothing.

The Sovereign found he needed his chair after all. "In one particular, at least, the technician was right. You are a remarkable man."

Steele's smile reflected only a fraction of his inner relief. The Sforan labeling him "man" in his own language was a huge step forward. "With your permission, I would like Technician Esfha to continue with his story. This tale does not end with his setting foot in the park."

At a nod from his leader, Habo started from his landing, this time including Steele's presence in the narration.

The Sovereign listened in scowling silence, then growled, "I see. Some form of mentally produced force-field, stronger and more adaptable than anything we have developed by machine. But I don't see your point, unless you're trying to impress me."

"Well, partly," Steele admitted. "The main point is this: Did your visitors of fifty years ago have such power as I display?"

"Obviously not. They were easily destroyed."

"Murdered, you mean. They came in peace, openly and without fear."

"Are you here to avenge them?"

"The thought never occurred to me. I am here to prevent such wanton acts of violence from happening again. One bad seed thousands of years old doesn't mean the entire simian tree is rotten."

He put his feet on the floor and leaned forward, still sitting on nothing. "Listen, Sovereign, jam this into your brain and sit on it: there is more than one hairless bipedal species. To my knowledge, the largest minority of intelligent species in this part of the galaxy are primate-based. Your fanatical war against anyone hairless or even remotely hairless is far beyond the laws of nature and reason. The least that may happen is that your outnumbered people would be destroyed, root and branch. At worst, you could send the entire galaxy down to the depths of barbarism just as your planet was dealt thousands of years ago.

"If you continue this course of action, you will not only end up destroying yourselves, but you would be mimicking the very atrocity you presume to avenge!"

Steele paused, gauging the effect of that pronouncement. The Sovereign rocked back in his six-wheeled chair, stared at his visitor for a long moment, then his gaze wandered away as the impact of Steele's words took effect.

Satisfied, Jander went on, his voice low and urgent.

"It is quite possible that the invading species attacked you for the same reason you attacked the recent visitors, or the Confederation ship your fleet chased; that is, simple mistaken identity. If that is the case you may be continuing a futile war of innocents that started eons ago, destroying race after race after race since the dawn of starflight. The cycle must stop, *now*, and only you can stop it."

He sat back and waited, watching the play of emotions on the Sforan's face.

Eyes closed, teeth bared behind taut lips, every muscle rigid, the Sovereign wrestled with his thoughts. Scores of centuries of racial prejudice and conditioning battled with the implacable power of logic, boiling and erupting in fervid, incandescent confusion in the mind of one lone, proud and very tired man. Minute after minute dragged in painful procession through the silent room.

At last the Sovereign opened his haunted eyes. "What can I do?"

CHAPTER 26

The penetration to the planet Dephlet, the seat of government for the Stellar Confederation, was a far cry from their casual approach to unsophisticated Sfor. Dephlet was the Gaealike second planet of a six-planet system around a K7 class orange star called Falgum. The cool and dim star and its system had been explored some two centuries earlier by a joint venture sponsored by the growing Confederation, then headquartered on Sabar. Dephlet had been sparsely settled by several genera before the interspecies government chose it as neutral ground for its seat.

In no time its population had grown into the millions as it developed into a major hub for interstellar commerce and business as well as government. The third planet, Gerephlet, a bit larger than Dephlet with a dense carbon dioxide atmosphere, had become the home of the Confederation Fleet and its dependent industries, housed under powerful domes of energy. Its sweltering, rocky crust held the heavy elements needed to manufacture fuel for the nucleonic thrusters, making it ideal for its adopted purpose.

Each member of the Confederation contributed ships to the Fleet on a rotating schedule, so the system's traffic was heavy as the Fleet exercised its constantly changing squadrons between the shipping lanes.

All of which made Dephlet enormously difficult to sneak up on.

Besides the traffic, sensor pickets were established well over two light years from the star in a globe of surveillance where nothing could escape detection. Even with her baffle screen, the *Angel* was enough of a presence that her technology and her crew were taxed to the limit.

Steele was restless in his command chair, as he used his perception of second level thought to try to keep track of everything at once. Most of the Bridge personnel wore I/O meshcaps to communicate directly with Angela in their specialties.

The quantum plasma mechentity that was the brains of the ship was very capable of spotting everything that may be of interest, but the human mind was far more adept at intuiting what was most important. While Angela could locate, classify and prioritize every physical obstacle in the system, it was Kurino Yukio who decided which could be trouble. Her delicate fingers flew over her sensors console as she marked the hazards that warranted their closest attention.

Tsin Li-san was likewise occupied at his communications board. He listened closely as Angela searched for key words and phrases in the myriad intercepted conversations in dozens of languages, and tracked their origins and destinations.

Pavel Kalanev at armaments, again with Angela's help, charted the locations and strengths of every deflector and defensive screen of every ship and station, gauged their threat level and tracked them through their course and speed.

Geraldo Belocci at analytics concentrated on the *Angel*'s own screens to scrutinize any wayward probes they may deflect, to ensure none were redirected enough to betray their presence.

Alexiy Pashkov and Nwoye Lam worked in tandem to absorb the information from their colleagues and navigate a weaving, speed-shifting course through the thick traffic and negotiate a safe and undetected approach to the planet.

Richard Ford exercised his self-appointed function as Jander's adjutant to direct a crew of Corpsmen to ensure that all the stressed and busy Bridge crew lacked for nothing to keep them going. When any of them needed a break, their skilled reliefs watching from the wall stations continued the work without pause.

Nineteen hours after they crossed the picket line, the exhausted crew tucked the *Angel* into a spot near a little used flight lane eighteen thousand kilometers over the capital, within range of mechanical teleportation. Then it was Vickie's turn to go to work, coordinating the efforts of a strong team of linked telepaths who spread their mental nets through the capital complex looking for one familiar mind. They succeeded, and a trio of clairvoyants joined the link to find a safe place to touch down.

VICE ADMIRAL NIL SPART stood brooding by his office window, damning the motions of fate that had taken him from his beloved starship. After so many contented years of avoiding "promotion", he had stumbled upon something that the Director was convinced only he could handle.

He had been given two tasks: find out where that hostile fleet had come from, and discover the origin and ownership of that magnificent stranger. And how in all the hells of all the planets in space was he going to do that behind a desk?

He sighed. Well, let's see. The fleet was relatively simple; he may not know where they had scattered to, but he knew the direction they had come from. He had run smack into them. All he had to do was send a fleet in force along that line and investigate every planet for a thousand parsecs. Relatively simple. He sighed again.

In contrast, finding the stranger was impossible. That ship had come from nowhere, unique and alone, with technology far superior to anything ever before imagined. It crushed eighty to one odds with ridiculous ease, then zipped off at an acute angle from its original line of flight. It had left no clues, not even the slightest hint to its origin. A huge, silent, awesome, invincible galactic paladin.

For the fleet he had a line of flight. For the stranger he had a string of marvels, each more spectacular than the last. The only thing he could do is look for a land of miracles, populated by miraculous people and ruled by a miracle man. Spart knew of only one magic man in the entire galaxy, and he was a savage on a barbarian planet, doomed to struggle his life away on one tiny mudball in space.

"Good morning, Admiral."

Spart yelped and sprang centimeters into the air. He spun in mid-leap and slammed off the wall, then his legs buckled and he smashed hard to his knees. He went to all fours and rolled his eyes wildly until they found their target. Steele was doubled over holding his arms across his belly, helpless with laughter.

Slowly, awkwardly, Spart climbed to his feet and started cursing. He could not stop cursing. All the frustrations of the past weeks came bubbling from his mouth in a steady stream of invective, noun after adjective after noun, until Steele stopped laughing and listened with admiration. Seldom repeating himself, he exhausted language after language as he dragged himself behind his desk and collapsed into the chair. Finally out of breath and probably out of words, he just glared.

Still grinning, Steele sauntered over to a chair and threw himself loosely into it, as befitted his comfortable polo shirt and jeans. "Good to see you again."

Apparently, the Admiral was not out of words. Another fifteen or twenty seconds passed before

Steele was able to speak again.

"Oh, I'm all of that," he grinned, "but I build one hell of a starship."

Spart's mouth fell open like a hangar door, and his face went from flushed to pallid in seconds. All of a sudden he was speechless.

"Yes, that was me in that spherical ship," Steele told him, "and Alpha, and three hundred members of the Omega Corps. Did you think I walked here?"

Spart was now white as a sheet. "How... how did you...?"

Steele smiled. "You may remember our previous meetings, when you tried to discover who and what the Omega Corps consists of?" He could sense that the Admiral was tensing up to go on another cursing spree, and held up a staying hand. "I now feel free to tell you. In my organization we have clairvoyants, telepaths, eidetics, teleporters, computopaths, micro-voyants, telekinetics, transmutators, spectralists... in short, people of any and every second level talent necessary for successful industrial espionage. We studied your ship, Admiral, from keel to bridge, and applied some of its principles to Gaean knowledge and our own variant abilities. We are here thanks to you."

Spart was stunned into silence for seconds as he assimilated the implications. He was successful, and the shock almost knocked him cold. "Oh, my..."

Steele nodded solemnly. "I have told you this so baldly not to shock you, but to let you know immediately and precisely where we stand. I have used you, Nil, and it would seem callous and without conscience. But I had my reasons, good ones I feel, and I want you to know exactly what they are."

He sat up straight in his chair, the better to drive home his sincerity. "The people of Gaea, as I have told you, are a race in transition. We have the potential of being among the greatest planetary powers in the history of this galaxy – but only if we survive.

"In the 'interests' of that survival we have rival sciences and militaries, a deliberately weak international debating society, and a common will to neutralize anyone of any class, country or ideology that appears to be a threat. We are destroying our planet and ourselves in a selfish, mindless, overwhelming conflict of attrition and greed. Such a drive coupled with our level of technology is suicidal; any species that does not recognize the fact is doomed.

"Into the breach steps the Omega Corps. We work subtly, underground, in a desperate battle against hatred and prejudice and avarice, handicapped by the very nobility that makes us effective. We are the greatest hope Gaea could ever have, but to the hundreds of nations, thousands of exploitive industries, and billions of anarchical individuals, we are the greatest threat.

"Yet we persevere. We are not after glory, though there is amazing splendor to be had. We are not in it for the thrills, though we find excitement aplenty. We do not seek riches, though great wealth is ours for the taking. We fight our silent fight and gain our unheralded victories with no expectation of thanks.

"And we are proud of it. We are the unsung heroes, Hercules' shield bearer and the good right arm of Beowulf. We guard those who fight openly for reason and justice, and secretly oppose those who work to compromise the champions we guard.

"We could set ourselves up as superheroes, the ones with greater-than-human gifts, the mighty magnificent Galahads who wage an unending battle for the good of the cheering multitudes. It would be easy.

"But this is reality, and the multitudes are not cheering. They would not, if they knew who we were. They would hunt us down like monsters, burn us and stone us and torture is in vain efforts to learn the secrets of our power. The world needs superheroes, but it cannot stomach them.

"So we stay underground. We continue our impossible and thankless job, in the hope that someday Gaea will be a better place for it. And slowly, painfully, we are winning the fight."

He fell silent and sat back, waiting for Spart to absorb what he was trying to say. At last the Admiral raised his eyes, and for long moments they studied each other, each gauging what he saw. Spart saw sincerity. Steele saw hope. Satisfied, Orion spoke again.

"By means of the telepathic gifts of Lady Alpha, I have studied your mind until I know it like my own

— painless enough, since we are much more alike than you may want to admit. Aside from that, I have seen in your memories every problem I have seen on Gaea, magnified a thousandfold.

"Within the Confederation and without, you and your forces face the same threat to existence that we of Gaea have. Each planet, each species managed somehow to drag itself from the mire of self-centered barbarism and reach the stars. But there they found another kind of barbarism, an all-consuming plethora of self-interest and discontent. And each and every one of them left behind them a cancer, created of crime and greed and all the other injustices that can sometimes be controlled but never eradicated.

"You know this. That is why you agreed to let the Omega Corps remain in existence. You wish you had such a force yourself, so that the Confederation might not only survive, but prosper in an atmosphere of peace and equity."

He leaned forward, hands on knees, and locked the Admiral's stare with his own. "I am here to offer you the services of the Omega Corps."

Spart sagged back and swallowed hard, his widened eyes watering. The chill down his spine was matched by the thrill of excitement that coursed through his brain.

Steele could sense where his thoughts were going and threw in his qualification. "We will not be yours to command, Nil, just as we would never ally ourselves with any nation or agency on Gaea. Look at it this way: just as Gaea is unaware that it is under the protection of the Confederation, or us for that matter, we will do what we can to assist you without interfering.

"But out here the situation is exponentially different. The galaxy is too large for any one group or organization to monitor. Doubtless you will see trouble spots or situations that you cannot handle and we haven't even noticed. For us to help you, you must help us. All we ask in return is that the Confederation continue to protect Gaea under the First Law. No one must know our origin."

He drew a small Confederation-style data disk from his pocket. "On this you will find a set of both quantum and tachyon frequencies you can use to communicate with us. They will be monitored at all times, and with a strong enough transmitter you should be able to reach us pretty much anywhere."

He skimmed the disk in Spart's direction. The Admiral bobbled it twice before he clutched it in both hands.

"Orion..."

Steele held up his hands. "No, Nil. Wait until you pull yourself together lest you say something you'll regret." He smiled soberly. "Whether you choose to call on us or not is your business. Whether we help you or not is our business, as are whatever our armament and motive power may be. You'll find enough on that disk to tell you all we need you to know. Any exchange between us will be strictly on that basis."

He rose to leave. "Oh, by the way, we followed up on your unfriendlies and made first contact. Also on that disk are the coordinates for the Sforan homeworld, and all the information you will need to initiate peaceful communication. The Sforans are, well, reluctantly awaiting their first interstellar ambassador."

He nodded once and tossed the Admiral a mock salute, then strode to the door. Without a backward glance he opened it, stepped through, and pulled it closed behind him.

Nil Spart sat still, staring at the spot Orion had just vacated. A magic man, indeed. He had no doubt that Orion could deliver. Between what he had learned on Gaea and what he had witnessed in battle he had every reason to believe the rest. He had in his hands the answer to every plea the Confederation would ever have. He smiled slowly, shook his head and reached with the disk for the console on his desk.

Suddenly it hit him. With a gleam of triumph in his eyes, Spart leaped to his feet and rushed to the door Orion had just walked through. Jerking it open, he peered within.

The storeroom was unoccupied.

"I don't believe it," he muttered.

Then he started and frowned, cocking his head to the side. For a moment he thought he had heard, deep in the corner of his mind, a soft, ghostly, and incredibly musical laugh.

About the Author

Keith Huntsman moved from Maine to Texas as a teenager and never left. After the University of  Texas and a stint in hotel management, he took a temporary job in government civil service for food money while trying to make it as an author. The temp job became permanent and he's been there ever since, rising from the mailroom to project management and legislative analysis. But *The Omega Corps* was always there, waiting forty years to mature with him and find its way to print.

An inveterate reader, Keith lives in Austin with a tortie named Rita and her two daughters, and an enormous media library touching every subject.